Al's Well

First published by O-Books, 2011
O-Books is an imprint of John Hunt Publishing Ltd., Laurel House, Station Approach,
Alresford, Hants, SO24 9JH, UK
office1@o-books.net
www.o-books.com

For distributor details and how to order please visit the 'Ordering' section on our website.

Text copyright: Gregory Dark 2010

ISBN: 978 1 84694 831 2

A CIP catalogue record for this book is available from the British Library.

Design: Stuart Davies

Printed in the UK by CPI Antony Rowe
Printed in the USA by Offset Paperback Mfrs, Inc

We operate a distinctive and ethical publishing philosophy in all
areas of our business, from our global network of authors to
production and worldwide distribution.

Al's Well

Gregory Dark

BOOKS

Winchester, UK
Washington, USA

To **Bruce Crowther** and to **Maureen McAthey**,
the quality of whose friendship so greatly enhances the quality
of my life.

Acknowledgements

The task of writing a book may be a solitary one – but that of publishing a book certainly is not. Even that lonely act of writing requires a far greater infrastructure than is generally recognised: I find it difficult, for instance, to write without food or with toothache. Below is therefore an incomplete list of those who are due acknowledgement. It is a compilation merely of those whose contributions to the welfare of *Al's Well* are so evident that even an ingrate like me cannot ignore them.

That you are reading this is due to the diligence and resourcefulness of **Anne Piper**. Today there is infinitely more work involved in publicising a book than there is in writing it. I deeply appreciate both the quantity of that work, and its quality.

Annie Duflot and **Monique Goddard** guided me through the, sometimes esoteric, catacombs of French law and its practise. Their help too I greatly appreciate.

Stuart Davies prepared the manuscript – several times!; and **Sally Reading** proof-read it – also, several times!; **Nick Welch** designed the cover. The work of all three was indispensable.

Without 'O'-Books' chief, **John Hunt**, the book would never have been published. Thereafter it's difficult within the company to know whom to thank for what. 'O'-Books operates a system of anonymity the CIA would kill to emulate. I can therefore do no more therefore than issue a general acknowledgement to **Tom Davies, Sarah Dedman, Nicola Dimond, Mary Flatt, Trevor Greenfield, Catherine Harris, Kate Rowlandson**, and **Maria Watson**.

If you can discover the names of those who actually printed the book, you're a better man than I am, Gunga-Din. That's a shame. The printers too deserve their share of any of the (admittedly, uncertain) credit which may attach.

As does that small army of others without whose involvement

you would never have been reading any of this: the buyers and the assistants of physical shops, the despatchers of e-shops ... the world's postmen and -women. Anonymity does not diminish their importance to both the book and its author! Thank you, all of you.

My daughter, **Lyubov**, I also thank. As I do her husband, **Keith**, and **Clara Izurieta**. Their on-going support is as helpful as it is undeserved.

I also thank **you**. Without a reader, a book is meaningless. It is the tree in an empty forest whose fall absolutely does not get heard.

Even **Mr Gates** I thank and **Microsoft**. The misery both inflict on my life helps me to understand more fully the misery of others. For which reason too I thank **Hewlett-Packard**, **Acer**, **Canon**, **Computerworld/Curry**, **Orange phones**, **French Telecom**, **British Telecom**, **Telefonica** ... and all the others making quite obscene amounts of money from the manufacture and/or sales of much-hyped but inefficient equipment, and offering 'services' which champion inefficiency and grotesque discourtesy. Sometimes anger is a powerful goad to keep going.

Gregory Dark, 2011

Chapter 1

"I'm not leaving Al for you."

"Excuse me."

"You heard."

"I'm not sure what to say."

"I'm not, Mike, leaving Al for you."

"Right."

"Right?"

"What do you want me to say?"

"Anything but that might be good."

"It sounded bland, Trove, that's all."

"Facts *are* bland, Mike."

"Even embellished with an American accent, it sounded bland."

"They're known for it, in fact, facts. For being bland."

"Right."

"Famous for it. It's what, Mike, they're good at."

"As you say."

"That's what it is, Michael: a statement of fact."

"Right."

"Whatever the accent."

"Understood, Trove."

"Even with an uptight, stick-up-the butt *British* accent, Mike."

"I do, Trove, get that. How *is* Al, by the way?"

"Al's well."

"Good."

"He's fine, just great."

"Great."

"I love him to bits. I'm not leaving him, Mike, for you."

"Yes, Trove, yes. You said."

"See, what I'm not saying, I'm not saying I'm not going to bed with you."

"You're not?"

"Of course not. I just kissed you, didn't I?"

"You did. That much is certainly true."

"And that means – I mean, that *has* to mean, right? – I fancy the pants off of you."

"Okay."

"That *literally*, I mean, I fancy the pants off of you."

"Well, I'm very flattered, Trove."

"You any idea how condescending that sounds?"

"Oh God, did it?"

"'S okay."

"I'm so sorry."

"It's okay, Mike."

"Really, so sorry. I assure you, I had not the slightest intention ..."

"Jeez, Mike, lighten up."

"I'm a lightened-up sorry, then."

"*I'm* meant to be the 'sorrier'."

"Yes."

"Al, he's always going on at me, how I 'sorry' too much."

"Right."

"It sounded condescending, Mike, is all I'm saying."

"Right."

"Sounded it. I didn't think you meant to be."

"Perish even the thought."

"See, I just love that about your English, Mike."

"You do?"

"It's just so ... goddamn *English*, your English."

"Right."

"That's the second condition I have for going to bed with you."

"That I'm English?"

"Yeah, very funny."

"There are *two* conditions?"

"Obviously, no? If that's the second?"

"Obviously, as you say."

"Right."

"The second condition is you're not leaving Al for me?"

"It's just ... I've been married to him for a lot of years. It'd break his heart. It'd break my heart too. I do love him, is what I'm saying. Don't think, because I'm going to bed with you, I don't love him."

"I know you love him."

"Good."

"The first condition, then?"

"The first condition is that we don't hurt each *other*."

"Right."

"Kiss me."

"Here?"

"Well, gee thanks for that overwhelming burst of passion."

"It's ... well ... you know."

"No, I don't know. What is it, Mike?"

"Public."

"Oh, silly me. And I never realised. I must have been dazzled by the flashlights from the thousand paparazzi all around us."

"You know what I mean."

"Hey, News Flash, Mike: You're not Robert de Niro. Know what I'm telling you? You're not that famous, is what I'm trying to say, they're going to recognise you in a Toulouse parking lot ..."

"And what I'm telling you —-"

"... Public or not."

"—- I'm telling you, we're not fifteen, Trove."

"Sure we are."

+++

We kissed. It was a clumsy kiss. The kiss of fifteen-year-olds. Tongues uncertain what was expected of them, teeth bashing teeth. We were walking arm-in-arm down the side-street which leads to the parking-lot by Toulouse's Hotel de Ville. A warm breeze rustled an evening that would otherwise have been searing. She's small with chestnut hair, Trove, and the right side of the fifty I'm (as you know) the wrong side of. You'd like her, Drew. She's one of us: unpretentious, unfussy … and a lot less brash and self-assured than she gives the impression of being.

It was an unpropitious baptism. Bells did not ring, sparks did not fly. That was great! Secretly I was relieved. I think Trove was too. It meant the kiss was the prelude to a dalliance, a <u>fling</u>, and not to anything heavyweight or life-changing.

The parking-lot was close to the centre. As far as parking-lots go, it's a pretty one. But the prettiness is imbued with that primness which seems to be the defining property of the French middle-class … thinking about it, of the French middle-<u>everything</u>. As a town, Toulouse is sort of Frenchly middle-everything. It's a sort of Puritan prick-tease of a town: chastely promiscuous, strait-laced but with satin lingerie – the virgin courtesan.

+++

"I've got to go, Mike."

"You've got to go."

"You could protest."

"I could, but you've got to go."

"Your place isn't too far away."

"It isn't, Trove. But …"

"I have to go."

"Was that just an awkward pause we shared there together?"

"You know why, Michael, I have to go?"

"You just said ..."

"Forget what I just said. You know why *now* I have to go?"

"No."

"Because your apartment, it really *isn't* far away. *That's* why I have to go."

"Right."

"Right? Jesus Christ, *none* of this is right."

"No."

"No, Michael."

"It's all wrong, right?"

"Are you mocking me?"

"As if ..."

"I don't care to be mocked, Michael."

"Right."

"I've gotten my head in a noose here."

"Such a lovely head."

"Not, Michael, a lovely noose."

"No."

"Sunday."

"Sunday?"

"I need to meet with you on Sunday."

"Right."

"Not to sleep with you."

"Never on a Sunday, right?"

"The following weekend, Al's away."

"Right."

"Saturday, Mike, *and* Sunday."

"And this Sunday?"

"I need to see you without sleeping with you."

"Right."

"To *organise* sleeping with you, Mike, without doing the deed."

"Planning the heist, sort of thing?"

"I need to see you, Mike. You complaining?"

"I'll do all my moaning the following weekend."

"I like you as well as lusting after you."

"I like you too, Trove. You know I do."

"I think that was just another of those awkward pauses."

"We seem to be getting rather good at them."

"I've got to go."

"Right."

"You could kiss me again."

"No, Trove, I don't think so."

"Excuse me?"

"My place *is* too close."

"You're right."

"I'm finding it already hard to control myself ..."

"You sure you're not mocking me, Michael?"

"Could I phone you?"

"*I'll* call *you*."

"Ah!"

"That was half sigh, that 'ah', and half question."

"You read far more into my 'ah's', Trove, than they're capable of holding."

"And just what did it mean, then, that 'ah'?"

"I was wondering, that's all, *will* you phone."

"I said I'd go to bed with you, goddamm it."

"Oh, and you've always phoned the people you've been to bed with?"

"That wasn't a pause, okay?"

"A pausette, then?"

"A pausette's not a pause. It was a fair point you made. A point not without fairness, is what I'm saying. I haven't yet been to bed with you, but it's still fair."

"Right."

"As a point."

"Right, Trove."

"I will phone, alright? Trust me. Do you trust me, Mike?"

"Drive safely."

"And, like, I'm supposed not to have noticed you didn't answer the question?"

"I did answer the question."

"Answer it again."

"I trust *you*, Trove. Myself? ..."

+++

She drove a blue Renault. I gazed after it, knowing it was not after it that I was gazing. I gazed until the reflectors' lights glowed into a soft-focus and kaleidoscopic haze, a moving abstract scurrying through a brightly-coloured trifle.

I wasn't sure what had just happened. I'd known Trove for years. For <u>years</u>. Between us, for years, there'd been ... what had it been? ... a goofiness, a love of laughter and of laughing, a lascivious banter ... a flirtatious, not-to-be-taken-seriously badinage. A whatever-it-was of such innocence, of such non-seduction and ... unthreateningness that, on those occasions when our 'other halves' had also been with us, our flirting together had, if anything, only been more flagrant.

When Eva was dying Trove was supportive. Supportive? That would be like describing Michelangelo as a bit of a chiseller. Trove was central to my coping with Eva's illness. A keystone. After she died, if anything Trove was even more supportive. You cannot believe (nor can I adequately describe) the comfort that she was – the more so (the <u>so</u> much more so) for being uncondescending with it. A 'just a friend' friend, but a dear and close 'just a friend'. A <u>real</u> friend. A woman I was proud to

7

call a 'just a friend'. And a woman too who enabled me to be proud of myself, to be proud of what I thought of as my grown-upness, in that I could recognise in Trove a truly sexy woman, but sex between us was not an issue. To the extent, in fact, that I remember a rather tipsy dinner party when – I suppose I was even bragging – I used her as an example of my ability to separate friendship from lust.

Except that, gazing after her car, now sex had become an issue. And now I did lust after her. Deeply. Wildly. And with scant regard for the consequences.

Through the welter of exhaust fumes staggered in an exhausted waft of jasmine. I wanted it to rest a while; I wanted to take off its shoes for it, offer it a drink. Before even I could motion for it to sit, though, it had gone. And I was left only with the memory. The memory only of a hint.

Which was life, I thought. That's the way life was.

When Eva had died I'd been left only with the memory. As with the jasmine, it had seemed to me to be the memory of a wisp. Eva had been a breath of sanity within an asthma of lunacy – the asthma which was both suffocating the world and possessing it.

You cannot hold onto a wisp. And whilst it may be the received wisdom that it's somehow better 'to have loved and lost than never to have loved at all', the pain of having done so tends to intimidate the lover-and-loser from shoving his hand – as he is wont to see it – a second time onto the flame.

+++

"See, there's this song. Do you know?, I can't even remember what it's called. Shirley Bassey sang it. Yeah, whatever happened to her? To

Shirley Bassey? You never seem to hear of her these …

"I tend to do that, sorry: Stray from the point. Which means, I guess, I did it again. Sorry. Again. I feel awkward, is the thing. I mean, maybe you're not exactly a stranger, but, still and all, you're not either (and I mean no disrespect when I say this) a bosom buddy, as it were. Yet here I am, talking to you about my most intimate bits … thoughts, actions, all that. My sex life, for God's sake. I guess it's a bit like the way your gynaecologist knows you better in certain aspects than your husband.

"Sure, it's funny for you. You're the gynaecologist, right? The sort of gynaecologist in this situation. Me, on the other hand, whilst you're gazing into my innermost recesses, I've got my legs in stirrups. Needs be, I guess.

"Anyhow, there's a line in the song, whatever the hell the song was: 'It was all so simple then'. And that's how it was then: simple. Simple *then*. At the beginning.

"He'd been living round the corner from me in France. When I say, 'round the corner', about thirty k's away. – That still sounds awkward to me, isn't that odd? Even after all my time here. Using 'k's, I mean, as an abbreviation for kilometres. Us Americans, we still use miles. And we're going to go right on using 'em, goddammit. None of these European metres for us. Globalisation means the rest of the world assuming *our* habits, goddammit. Heaven forfend – 'forfend', that's such a great word, isn't it? It's a word I learnt from Mike. – Heaven forfend, is what I'm saying, any of those nasty foreign habits or standards should encroach on a US brain.

"We'd known each other for years. Known each other from when his wife had been alive ... From way before that, in fact. We'd been in the Toulouse Troupers together. That's a theatre group hereabouts. Now, though, he had to go back to England. He needed, he said, to spend some time with his son, with his about-to-be-born grandchild. He needed, he said, to establish some kind of relationship with them both. And then he'd be back.

"He wouldn't be back. People always say they're going to be back,

they swear blind they're going to be. But they never are. Life inter-
venes. Plans change. I'd never see him again. So I figured, I'd go to
bed with him, and I figured I'd enjoy it. And that'd be that. It'd be a
sweet memory to curl up in front of the fire with during the long, long
fall of matrimony.

"Matrimony! What a goddamn word: 'matrimony'. Doesn't that
sound to you like a kind of murder? Cousin, sort of, to matricide or
something? Second cousin permanently removed. And I guess it is, a
sort of murder.

"Oh God. Oh shit, I am so sorry. That has to be a gag in the worst
kind of taste. Not a gag, but, you know, a comment, whatever. Of the
tackiest taste, in fact. The tackiest and yuckiest. Sorry. It's not even as
though I meant it. I did love Al. Do, what am I talking about? 'Case
you didn't know that. I mean, me being here, that's what it's all about.
Mostly. Me agreeing to this interview.

"See, I did it again. Strayed from the point. ... Know how I know
that? Your eyes sort of glass over. The lights are on, kinda thing, but
the house has been abandoned. I'm stopping saying 'sorry', by the way.
Right after I've said this one: Sorry. For the last time.

"'You're an itch,' I told him.

"'And you need to scratch me?'

"'Do you mind?'

"'Being an itch?'

"'A sexy kind of itch.'

"'Like crabs, then?'

"'*No!*'" I said.

"He said, 'I don't mind being an itch.'

"'You don't?'

"'Not a mosquito bite? Not athletes' foot or anything?'

"'A *real* sexy itch.'

"'Just scratch me, Trove.'

"This won't make any sense to you – I know this won't make any
sense to you, you know how? 'Cause it don't make sense to anyone
else – it does to me, but that's not the point. See what it was, I knew I

was cheating on him – *would* be cheating on him, on Al – but what it *wasn't*, I wasn't *betraying* him. No, no, that's not right either. No, more truthfully, it didn't *feel* like I'd be betraying him. Oh, I know you can rationalise anything, justify anything. But I really felt, I genuinely felt, I'd be helping us, *it'd* be helping us, our marriage. Christ, even our future together.

"Scratch the itch and the itch just means nothing any more. But, shit, if you don't scratch the itch … You ever had one in your gums, an itch? You know, in that gap right after the dentist's before the Novacaine's worn off? You can feel the itch and you know your nails are scratching it, but you can't feel the goddamn scratch. Remember how crazy that can make you feel? The bitch that itch can be? Well, it was kinda of the same deal here. No, more, like an itch under the plaster of a broken leg. It starts to assume an importance completely disproportionate to its … well, importance. 'Importance' is the only word I can think of. It becomes, like, the biggest deal in the world. You'd burn your husband at the stake to stop that itch, sell your children into slavery. 'Course, if I'd ever have had children, I'd have sold them into slavery years before, but, yeah, that's also kinda beside the point.

"No, it's fine. It's better than fine, actually. Actually, *much* better than fine. It's something I need to know. It's weird, this, how easy all this is. How easy *you* are, for Christ's sakes. I mean, I'm not sure I knew what to expect, but whatever the hell I was not expecting, it certainly wasn't this.

"Like then, in a lot of ways. See, then, it was – as the song says – it *was* all so simple then.

"And then … Well, and then it went and got itself complicated."

+++

Maison d'arrêt de Toulouse-Seysses, 23rd February 06
Dear Trove:
I understand from my attorneys that you have been to visit them. I cannot believe

you.

May I remind you that, honey child, you're responsible for this entire fucking mess? Mind your own bees' wax, Trove. Haven't you done enough?

Al

Chapter 2

It is only young men who look into mirrors. It comes as something of a shock therefore when old men look back. That's something you too, Drew, will come to discover in time. Each man has to discover that for himself.

I could cope with the greyness. It added, I thought, a sprinkle of wisdom to the wickedness which winked in, and from, my eyes. It was the balding I found unacceptable. I'd asked my hairdresser not to show me the back view of my haircut; in mirrored lifts I'd lower my eyes. The mirrors I had at home were those from which only my head-on image was reflected. Those whatever-they're-called, those sort of winged mirrors that Eva had used to make up with, I threw away shortly after she died. Denial might not be a river in Egypt, but it is sometimes a life-raft in an ocean of insecurity.

I was having qualms, Drew.

I *never* had qualms.

I was sea-sick once, I remember. Never had I been sea-sick before - not in the Bay of Biscay, not in the roughest seas, nor those sort of rolling from side-to-side seas. The appallingness that was the sea-sickness was ten times worse for being so unfamiliar. Well, it was a similar thing here with my qualms. The unfamiliarity of the sensation was multiplying its inherent discomfort. And that discomfort was consequently acquiring the status of queasiness. I do not like feeling queasy - any more than I like feeling qualms.

God, this is all so difficult for me, writing all this stuff. I don't know whether or not, between father and son, it's even 'appropriate'. I'm not just a fish out of water, I'm a tropical fish beached on an ice-floe. And it's that much harder, not being sure whether I should be doing it at all.

Your mother used to 'joke' that my only commitment was to a lack of commitment. I'm sure I have no need to remind you! And that I should be "committed" for such lack of commitment. I used to be quite hurt by the 'joke'. I was meant to be, I think. But maybe what hurt me most was just how accurate it was.

I do want to change today, though, Drew. And I do want to commit to you and to the child that Jane's about to have – that you both are, of course I mean.

You won't ever get to read this, I don't suppose, until I'm dead. (Oh, don't read anything sinister into that remark, it's not that I'm planning suicide or anything. I simply can't imagine the circumstances in which, alive, I could give this to you … or post it to you … or do with it what I would have to do in order for you to get it.)

God knows, I'll have left you little enough materially. I suppose this might be the time to apologise for that too. And God knows, there's precious little of a relationship between the two of us for you to remember it with affection – or with anything else, for that matter. (A state of affairs for which, in case you were wondering, I do, yes, hold myself entirely responsible.) Try as I might, when we're together, I simply cannot be as open with you as I'd like to be. Habits are always hard to break. Habits of a lifetime … I fear, a 'lifetime' harder.

Writing, though, I thought … Well, if I wrote about me, committed to paper stuff about me – like you were a diary or something – came a little bit clean about me, let you know about private things about me, maybe there'd be a little something I could give you, a soupçon of knowledge, a soupçon of me. And, maybe with knowledge, the beginnings of some kind of measured … is it forgiveness I'm talking about? Or understanding? Or even just acceptance that that was who I was? If you don't know me, I suppose is what I'm telling myself, how can you possibly accept me?

I could well have misjudged that as well. That too I do understand. If I have, I'm sorry about that as well. I will have died the stupid bastard you've known that I am from the moment you first had knowledge.

Stupid bastard, though, though I am, I have noticed you're an adult. About to be a father, in fact! I'm therefore going to presume you're adult about adult things. So …

Well, here goes nothing, I suppose.

I'd had affairs before …, there there's said it. Yes, even when I was still with your mother. Yes, and when I was with Eva too. On other occasions (between the two), the adultery had been defined by <u>her</u> being married, 'her' my partner in tryst. Even, two or three times, when we *both* were, for God's sake. I don't say this with any pride. Just … 'warts and all' compulsion, I suppose. If I'm going to let you know about me, you have to know all about me – about, I should rather say, the all of me.

Trove was a desirable woman, Drew. Desirable? God, that's an understatement and a half. Like calling her 'supportive' when Eva was dying. Somewhat, as I already said, like calling Michelangelo a bit of a chiseller. Or like calling Al one, come to that. It's not to my taste, his work, that's true. I'm not going to pretend that it is. It's no criticism of his work that it's not to my taste. Probably to the contrary. Probably I'm not sophisticated enough for it. And, anyway, who am I to judge? His reputation even then was international. And his red fedora was considered to be one of the sights of Toulouse!

Trove was not just desirable, she was <u>enormously</u> desirable: Twelve on the Prickter scale, three thousand degrees Fuckenheit.

Her eyes were so blue, psychotically blue, and all the blueness was lewdness. There was harlotry in those eyes (those blue, blue eyes), an uninhibited lust which augured well for bedtime frolic and which promised sojourns not just in exotic shenanigans, but on Kama Sutran safaris. Qualms? Queasiness? You don't have qualms embarking on a safari. Well, some people might, but then some people aren't Michael. Michael certainly doesn't. Have qualms ... feel qualms, whatever. This wasn't me, Drew, this wasn't Michael. Michael was urbane and licentious, not entirely devoid of scruples but such bescrupledness subject – abjectly – to the adage that a standing prick hath no conscience. And that, once it wath standing no more, neither need the prick suddenly acquire one.

What the hell, I wanted to know, does one do with qualms? I mean, what completely useless things to have! A sort of Sinclair C5 of the ethical world. Do qualms have <u>any</u> use? At all, I mean? What would a mint-condition qualm buy you, for instance? A hair-shirt, maybe? A designer one?

– "Collar, sir?"

– "Fifteen-and-a-half."

– "I'll give you a fourteen-and-a-half, then, sir."

– "Oh, and give me three lengths of sackcloth and two tons of ashes."

– "Would that be regular ashes, sir, or those from the fires of Purgatory?"

– "Oh, your very best ashes, my good man. And do make sure they're still cindery. Don't want not really to scourge my wicked body."

– "Very good, sir."

It was Kelly. That's what had done for me. That, I suddenly realised, was where the queasiness was coming from: not qualms but insecurity. Kelly had been a stunning-looking woman, fifteen years my junior and with a PhD in sexual sciences. And ... Well, I had, as the phrase goes, failed to 'rise to the occasion'. The spirit had been overwhelmingly willing, but the flesh ... Alas, the flesh was hurtling towards Viagraism.

Oh, a stage fright on the first bedding, that I'd known before. First night nerves, I'd always ascribed it to. But the nerves around Kelly yawned into the second night and the third. And this despite a series of massages and manoeuvres which would have had a eunuch whimpering. The fourth night, the fifth ... I tried to tell myself it was the aftermath of the operation, a side-effect. But I signally failed to call the surgeon to check whether that could be the case.

As you know, I'd quit smoking some years previously; my drinking by then I'd restricted to wine only on occasions when I dined with friends; my diet was almost grotesquely healthy. Was God now going to deprive me of the one vice apparently still left available to me?

No! Please God, let it not be that. Please don't let the impotence be physical. Or medical. I had to be sure of it. I had to check. You know how far Agen is from Toulouse. No-one knows me in Agen. I drove all the way there just so I wouldn't be seen. In Agen I sneaked into a back-street newsagent's (just to be on the safe side, you understand). Bought myself a porn magazine – strictly, you understand, in the interests of medical research.

French pornography is ... well, you probably know ... candid. Porno with the emphasis on graphic. To the point almost of being gynaecological. Indeed too graphic sometimes to be exciting. But I was, yes, excited by it, my Agen mag. *Aroused* by it. The flesh, I was gratified to note, was still able to venerate Venus, still able to rise in tribute to her, still even enthusiastic in its veneration. It was only with a few of her earthly acolytes that a very occasional ... agnosticism would rear its ugly head. Or not, if you catch my drift.

Oh Portnoy, oh Portnoy, I lamented, what, old chum, do we do now?

– "Screw Trove!" 'Portnoy' commented.

– "You really mean that? You really mean, 'Screw Trove'?" I asked him.

But it was me myself who replied. – "No. You cannot screw Trove. Screw Trove and you screw yourself, Mike, up. You screw yourself, Mike, right up."

– "Oh, and like now I'm not screwed up?"

– "Screw Trove and you screw up the friendship with Trove."

– "Ah."

– "See, it's not qualms, Michael, it's fear."

– "Friends are harder to find than lovers."

– "It is thus that conscience doth make cowards of us all."

– "No."

– "No?"

– "It's not me being cowardly."

– "It isn't?"

– "It's me having scruples."

– "Scruples?"

– "Yeah. Having scruples, yeah."

– "Nah, it's cowardly, Mike."

– "You're right."

– "That's all you've got to say?"

– "For the moment."

- "Anything else?"
- "Yes."
- "What?"
- "Screw Trove."
- "And that would mean?"

...

- "I DON'T KNOW!"

+++

"Trove, can you talk?"

"Not really."

"Al's there?"

"Uh-huh."

"You can only answer yes or no?"

"Not even. See, I'm just about to leave, Ann, for the shops. With Al."

"I'll be at home till five."

"I'll call you on your mobile."

"After five, then?"

"Uh-huh. Got to shoot, Nancy. Later."

+++

"See, Mike, *I've* got to call *you*."

"You are calling me."

"That's how it has to be: I call you."

"You also called me both Ann and Nancy."

"You're kidding, right?"

"About two seconds apart."

"You're *kidding*, Mike."

"CIA training clearly isn't what it used to be."

"Goddamn senior moments."

"Tell me about them."

"I can't hurt Al, Mike."

"I know."

"That's conditional."

"I know, Trove."

"It's sort of conditional, honey, my unconditional love."

"It always is."

"This phone traffic, is what I'm trying to say, it's got to be one-way only, Mike."

"Right."

"I thought that was clear."

"So many rules. *My* senior moments. I'm afraid I lose track."

"Lose track, Mike, and you lose me. I'm not kidding here. This is my marriage we're talking about. I'm not fooling around with it."

"Okay."

"You sulking?"

"No."

"That pause was then ... ?"

"Not sulking. Taking it on board."

"Okay."

"Taking on board your admonition."

"That, as in the 'ad-monissionary' position? Don't sulk, Mike."

"One of the very few pleasures still affordable. That and peeing."

"I'm actually paying you quite a compliment."

"Okay."

"See, I get all ... I don't know ... girly, see, when I hear your voice."

"That *is* a compliment."

"He's not an idiot, Al ..."

"No. Certainly not an idiot."

"After twenty-three years of marriage he knows me quite well."

"Right."

"Not as well as he should. Still and all ..."

"*Pretty* well."

"It's twenty-three years, can you believe that?"

"Amazing."

"Can *you* not talk?"

"There are people looking at the flat."

"Are they with you?"

"In the room?"

"Yes."

"No."

"But they might come in any minute, huh?"

"As indeed I might."

"What does *that* mean?"

"Come. Any minute. ..."

"Mike! —-"

"... So excited am I by the sound of your voice."

"—- Are you talking dirty to me?"

"Oh, I do so hope so."

"You're not just joshing me?"

"Oh, I do so hope not."

"You've done a lot of joshing, Mike, over the years."

"I'm a good josher."

"It's a great word, 'joshing'. A lot of flirting, to boot."

"To boot?"

"That's your word, Mike. I learnt it from you."

"Two words, Trove."

"Too close for comfort."

"To condescension?"

"Way too close for comfort."

"Talking of twos ..."

"Still in the danger zone."

"Even more than the tango, Trove, it takes *two*, I was going to say, to flirt."

"Say more dirty things to me. No, say *real* dirty things to me."

"I'll have to call you back."

"They just walk into the room?"

"On the button."

"Oh, you English. So goddamn inhibited! You know, right, you *can't* call me back?"

"I do know, yes."

"You think they'll be gone in half-an-hour?"

"Oh, certainly, I'd think."

"If I call you back in half-an-hour, will you have thought of some real dirty things to say to me?"

"I'll give it my very best shot."

"That wasn't one of them, right?"

"Right."

"What do you say in England? 'Toodle-oo?'"

"Not a lot recently."

"Toodle-oo."

"Pip-pip."

+++

"Michael's best friend? Was I? I don't know about that. That's a phrase I tend to associate with children. Does one have 'best friends' over the age of twenty? He was a *good* friend of mine, Michael. That certainly. There were, I suspect, things he confided in me that he had told no-one else. He didn't, I don't think, find the company of men easy.

"Do you think ⋯ Would you mind awfully if we did the photos first, sort of thing? It's silly, I know. An old man's vanity, if you will, but I'm desperately camera shy. And not, between you and me, just *camera* shy, shy generally. I know I don't give that impression. Nevertheless ⋯ What we've got to talk about, you and I ⋯ Well, the gatepost's

22

fine, of course, but – if it's all the same to you – I'd really rather not the photographer. Nothing personal, old chap. Rien de ⋯ Oh, you understand, that's good.

"It's Sheridan Gillett, by the way: double 'l', double 't', but with no 'e' at the end. Only your letter to me, it did have an 'e' at the end.

"Okay, all done?

"We'll just adjourn inside then, shall we? No, no, after *you*. *Please* after you. There, now. Where was I? Oh yes.

"His eye didn't rove, Michael's, so much as gallivant. Even when Eva was alive. And a year or so after she died, there was a period when he thought a long-term affair was one which saw the week out. Not that he was bed-hopping, not exactly. I'm no psychiatrist, of course. But it was all, I suspect, entwined in the grief process or whatever. And thus probably entirely predictable.

"I'm talking now ⋯ what? ⋯ two or three years after she'd died. Looking on it with hindsight, I think probably he was still trying to find her. Eva, I mean. Just as soon as he realised that the present 'amour' was *not* Eva, Mike, his eye started to rove – started, sorry, to *gallivant* – for the next Eva-alike. It wasn't that he was after, I don't think, another wife, another partner, not even another lover (not what we'd understand by any of those words), it was that he was after a clone, a doppelganger sort of thing, another Eva.

"The irony was, of course, that even if he had met that person – even if, for goodness' sake, Eva had returned to life and he'd met *her* – he would still have rejected her. Because it was not even Eva that he was searching for, but an Eva of his fantasy, an Eva which was no more Eva than Princess Diana was Cinderella.

"He talked to me about his girl-friends. Not about his conquests, not in that sort of way. He wasn't a scalp-on-the-bedpost-notcher. Almost to the contrary. For a man, he was almost reticent about that aspect of his life. I mean, all that locker-room banter, the stag-party fantasies ⋯ that just wasn't Michael.

"He wasn't a sex junkie, but a love one. Michael with a woman ⋯ Well, first off, he'd need to convince himself it wasn't just her body he was after. And then, that this was it: the big one. The relationship, the partner who would escort him off this mortal coil.

"At one level, of course he was in love with love. But, as with Eva, it wasn't with 'love' that he was in love, but with the fantasy of love. There was a part of this fifty plus man still five years' old – as, I suspect, there'd been a part of the five-year-old Michael who was already fifty. I suppose all of us are paradoxical to a degree. But, in Michael's case, paradox seemed to be almost the cornerstone of his personality.

"He loved women – I mean, *really* loved them.

"No.

"Wrong. Thinking about it.

"No, it wasn't *women* that Michael loved, but Woman. Of course. And not Woman the gender, but Woman the ideal. Woman that embodied, oh I don't know, Eve and the Venus de Milo, the Mona Lisa and Fanny Hill – Carmen, too, and Cleopatra ⋯ the myth of Woman, not her reality.

"But with Petrova it was different. (Trove, I'm sure you know, is just the abbreviation of Petrova. Michael always called her Trove. He enjoyed the association it had with 'treasure'. Fond though I was of her, for the same reason, I tended always to call her Petrova. And it was fond of her that I was, not in any way enamoured. I think I saw her for what she was. Which wasn't unpleasant, but equally wasn't flawless.)

"It's hard to explain, to quantify *how* it was different –

for Mike, I mean, with Petrova –, but it was. Different. There was a recognition that it *was* fantasy, I think. I think, on both their sides. By which I mean, I think he recognised that for her too part of his attraction was the fantasy of him, that (because she was married) there was no real possibility of a real 'them'. And that therefore their only reality – the only reality within which 'they' could exist – was in fantasy. It validated the fantasy, almost. It made the fantasy real. It grounded it.

"He wasn't even happy about it, not to begin with, Michael, the whole affair. He was ⋯ What was he? ⋯ Confused, I'd say. Perhaps even bewildered. 'Bewitched, bothered and bewildered', even – like the song. But not in a happy, up-tempo, song-like way. In a ⋯ More in the way, now I think about it, of the words rather than the music. There's nothing too jolly, is there, about being bewitched or bothered or bewildered?

"None of us could have guessed, though, what would happen. We wouldn't even have come close. As another friend of mine is fond of saying: 'The only thing we can know for certain about our future is that it will never be how we imagine it.'

"My predictions for their future couldn't have been wronger. For one thing, my first prediction was that there wasn't one, a future. I mean, how much wronger can you get?"

+++

Maison d'arrêt de Toulouse-Seysses, 28th February 06
Dear Dad:
You've got to get me out of here, Dad. You've no idea what it's like. You still buddies with Congressman Henson? Couldn't you call him, Dad? He must be able to apply some kind of pressure on someone who can apply some kind of pressure on someone

here. The consul has been to see me. But he was useless, Dad. Hopeless.

Dad, you owe me. I've never referred before to our 'marker', but now I'm calling it in. Dad, help me. PLEASE.

Your loving son – Al

+++

"They gone?"

"Yes."

"Can you talk?"

"Is it possible, Trove, to see you before Sunday?"

"No."

"Just see you, I'm talking about."

"You're 'just see'ing me on Sunday."

"I'd also like to 'just see' you too before then."

"Still no."

"Right."

"Don't be difficult."

"I just thought ..."

"It's not possible, Mike."

"Right."

"This is another compliment."

"Okay."

"If I *could* see you before Sunday, Mike, I would see you before Sunday."

"Right."

"If it'd been possible – is what I'm saying – I'd have arranged up front to see you before next Sunday."

"I understand."

"You're stiff-upper-lipping on me, Mike."

"It's not the upper lip that's stiff."

"This is British dirty talk, right?"

"I'm not too practised, I'm afraid. We tend not to talk too dirty, us Brits."

"What a waste, Mike, of a sexy accent."

"It's always other people who have accents."

"When I need homilies, hon, I'll go to a book of quotations."

"Here's another homily, I'm afraid. Even a homely homily, Trove."

"Homely homily?"

"An extremely homely homily."

"Jeez!"

"There are speakers, Trove, and there are doers."

"'Barefoot in the Park', right?"

"If you say so."

"I know I'm right."

"Whilst some *talk* dirty, others *do* dirty."

"No."

"No?"

"It was *watchers* and doers. Now I think about it. 'Barefoot in the Park'. *Watchers* and doers. 'The doers do whilst the watchers watch the doers do.' Something like that."

"Right."

"So, you *do* dirty, huh?"

"Better than I talk it."

"Would that be, as in do *the* dirty?"

"You're playing with words, Trove."

"Only for want of anything else to play with."

"I'll see you on Sunday."

"You got to go?"

"I got to go."

"Okay."

"See you Sunday."

"Bye."

+++

I didn't have to go at all. Well, I did, actually, but not

for 'I've got to go' reasons. I suddenly knew (that was the truth of it), I *suddenly* knew – suddenly, as in the 'suddenly' of from one second to another – I had to break it off. Whatever 'it' was. I had to break it off, in fact, before it even became 'it'.

And I knew I had to do it because even the prospect of that was breaking my heart.

Chapter 3

"I was plucking petals off of a flower. Kind of dumb, you're right. Oh, you didn't *need* to say anything, I could see it in your eyes. In your what-kind-of-a-sad-woman-is-this? eyes. Everyone's eyes are expressive. Yours, though, yours are ... I was going to say 'Expressionist', but then I thought, shoot, I really don't know what 'Expressionist' means.

"I'd thought about a dahlia. But dahlias are kinda expensive, you know. *Real* expensive, in fact, just right at that moment. And, God knows why, but there don't seem to be too many daisies round these parts. Not the kind, 'least, you make daisy-chains from. So, I got a bunch of those, you know, *big* daisies, you know the ones I mean, the *bedraggled* big ones. That, right, look a bit like dahlias. Haggled the man down from three euros to one euro fifty. It was three a bunch and I only wanted one, for Christ's sake. Jeez!

"Oh, I wasn't plucking for 'he-loves-me; he-loves-me-not' reasons. I knew he didn't love me. There was no question about that. Nor I him. Well, he did love me. 'Course he did. And I loved him. But loved each other as friends. Good friends, 'course, bosom buddies, in fact. Friends that'd do anything for each other sort of deal, that'd always be there for each other. And I do mean 'always'. But friends all the same. Not love in the weak-at-the-knees kind of way. Weak-at-the-*knees*? Weak-in-the-*head*, more like.

"It wasn't even 'he-*likes*-me; he-likes-me-not'. I never doubted he liked me. But I knew something in him had changed. He wasn't looking at me in the same way. Eyes again, you see? See, I always notice eyes. I can always hear what eyes are trying to tell me.

"I've always wondered, childhood sweethearts, that kind of deal ... I mean, you hear about it, don't you, all the time? Kids who've grown up next door to each other, gone out together, that whole scene. There has to be a time, doesn't there? – a moment, it has to be –, not when they start looking at each other in a different way, but when they *realise* they're looking another way at that person. And when that other person is looking differently at *them*.

"I guess something like that's also got to happen with incest. I mean, there has to be that one moment, doesn't there? That defining moment, I guess it is. Shit! So sorry. Wandering again. Off the point. Again.

"What was I talking about? Dahlia, that's it, the dahlia. No, the daisy. Jeez, my frigging brain. The daisy. Dai-sy. Yeah. No, like I said, it wasn't any of those 'does-he; doesn't-he?' sort of things. It was much more 'do-*I*; don't *I*?'.

"Specifically, do I turn up on Sunday? Or don't I?

"Sunday, see, I thought of as the point-of-no-return. Oh, I know what I said. It was just to see him again. Sort out the details, all that. But I figured if I turned up on Sunday, I might as well book the hotel room in advance, come dressed in the negligée. I've never been a teaser. Not even in my teens. I could never stand it. I hated it when I saw my friends at it. I was accused of it once. Unfairly, I might add. I'd rather have been accused, I don't know, of murder or something. Certainly of bank-robbery. God, the times when I was younger I've ended up in bed with someone just because I thought I'd passed the point of tease return! It was a kind of self-inflicted date-rape, now I think about it. Shit, yes, thinking about it, that's exactly what it was.

"It's the folly of youth, I guess.

"No.

"Folly of youth be damned! Know what it is, the folly of youth? The folly of youth is that youth thinks their screw-ups *are* the folly of youth. Youth thinks that you get doddery and you get wrinkles and you get wise all at the same time. All as a matter of aging course, as a law of Nature or something, nothing you can do about it sort of deal. And you may get wrinkles, and you certainly get doddery, but wise …?

"My aging has taught me squat. Really – 'cept, maybe, how to get cranky and intolerant of the youth that think their follies are the follies of youth. Meanwhile, back at the point … Sorry, you're quite right to frown at me like that. Sorry.

"Meanwhile, like I said, back at the point … Which was? Oh, yes. One of very few things I *have* learnt … learnt on my journey to decrepitude … is to pull back way before I'm ever in a position where I think a man might even *think* I'm teasing. Know what I'm saying? 'Course you do. Any woman over fifteen knows what I'm saying. Lawyers, I take it, do *have* sex lives. It's not all of it vicarious, I hope, getting your jollies third-degreeing others about *their* sex lives. God, I hope, honey, that's not how it is. You're smiling. I'll take that as a good sign. Now you're blushing. A lawyer blush? That has to be a first.

"Where was I? Point of no return, right. I reckoned that was Sunday.

"If I turned up on Sunday, metaphorically speaking, I had to do so with my knickers … God, I love that word 'knickers' … with my knickers *off*. I'd organised myself a meeting for later on that same Sunday. Don't ask me why. It seemed like a good idea at the time, a *sensible* idea. A kind of 'just in case' idea. In case of *what*, I didn't know. I suppose, if you're free-falling from thirty thousand feet any shred of cloth provides some kind of comfort. I mean, a handkerchief may not be a parachute, but it *is* … something … a bit of cloth you can hold above your head.

"Know what, though? As I sat shredding that poor daisy, what I realised, I realised, my knickers, they were *already* off.

"And I was … well, I guess the only way to put it, is: I was leaking."

+++

"No, you're wrong: Petrova wasn't exerting any pressure. Quite the contrary. Any pressure that was being applied was being applied *by* Michael *on* Michael.

"He called me every day that week. And every day, he was excited, and excitable. Quick to anger. On the Saturday – the Saturday before *the* Sunday I'm talking about – he phoned again. I told you he was paradoxical.

Having been excited all week, now he was calm ⋯ icy calm. *Disconcertingly* calm, even. So calm I knew he was involved in a tempest. I didn't know what about. Of passion, it could have been. Or guilt. Or a hundred other emotions, or a cocktail of them. Maybe of all the emotions there are.

"Michael would get very angry over little things – the slights of petty officials, surliness in hotels, at airports. But when momentous things were happening to him, he became measured, almost ponderous. How can I explain this? If a gust of wind, for instance, turned his umbrella inside out, he'd throw a fit. Caught in a hurricane, however, like as not he'd start quoting Shelley or Keats or whoever it was wrote, 'Ode to the West Wind'.

"He was going to stop it, he told me. Calmly. The whole thing was ridiculous, absurd. He'd known her for years, he told me. She'd played Eliza to his Professor Higgins, Anna to his King of Siam. They belonged, both of them, to the local amdram: the 'Toulouse Troupers', they're rather naffly called. They'd even had the occasional stage-kiss together. 'Shadowlands', I think was one play he mentioned. He mentioned a couple of others.

"He enjoyed her company. He *loved* her company. The fling they'd have would last for what? A few weeks? Perhaps even a few months. And it would erode, maybe even *erase*, the friendship of a decade.

"He was clear. Cool, calm and collected. Certain. He'd try to spare her feelings. But a small hurt now would prevent a giant hurt later. It was a vaccination: a pinprick to obviate a catastrophe.

"And then he started to talk about something else entirely. His son, I think. That's right. Not even about his soon-to-be grandchild. (He was, as you probably know, going back to England so that he could enjoy with his soon-to-be grandchild the relationship he felt he'd never had with his son.) Of all things, he talked about his son's new job. His son worked freelance, for God's sake. So a new job wasn't something new or newsworthy. It was a ruse, no more. It was telling me that the jack of Trove was firmly back in its box, and that therefore life could go on. And should go on. Normal service had been resumed.

"It was a long chat. Over half-an-hour I'd think. And we spoke about Trove for ⋯ maybe five minutes. Perhaps even less. His tone invited no discussion, you see. He wasn't seeking advice, that tone told you. He was imparting knowledge of a decision. 'Course that tone always has about it the ring of 'Methinks the lady doth protest too much'. But it's difficult, even knowing that, to override it.

"It's the teenage girl, isn't it?, who's decided to dye her hair blue, or the adolescent fifty-year-old determined to buy a sports' car. They know they can be talked out of it, there's a part of them which even wants to be talked out of it, so they bark it at you in such a way that they can't be. It's almost as if your silence or your reticence is their permission to go ahead – as if, in other words, your lack of sanction is their sanction. An absurd language, English, no? Is there any other where the same word is its own antonym?

"Somehow it's entirely appropriate that it is Michael's language. Like Michael, it's whimsical, full of nuance and contradiction, rigid and anarchic, influenced by many and diverse sources – divers and diverse sources, indeed. Easy to know at a superficial level, and almost impossible to know entirely.

"Can I get you some more coffee? Sure? I think I'm going to have one. Are you on any kind of schedule or anything? I do hope not. Maybe we could grab a bite of lunch together. Good.

"Petrova likened her situation to that of a war girlfriend, who felt she had to sleep with her beau because she didn't know if he would ever return. And there was that about Michael of the trench-bound soldier. Except that they were talking about different trenches. In his case, the trench was the affair, and in hers it was Michael's return to England.

"I feared he was whistling in the dark."

+++

"Monsieur?"

"Citron pressé, s'il-vous-plaît."

"Same."

"Deux."

"Merci, monsieur."

"Merci. You look lovely, honey."

"You called me 'honey'."

"It's the 'Americanisation of Mike'."

"I don't think you're Bob Hope yet. ... It's Sunday, Mike."

"All day."

"I thought today would never come. Are you as nervous as I am?"

"Nervouser."

"But, hey, it is, it's Sunday."

"Dimanche."

"Sure."

"It's Sunday, Trove, and you look swell."

"Now you *are* mocking me."

"You look lovely."

"Yes, I do, don't I?"

"Truly lovely."

"Tell me about it."

"I'm trying to, Trove."

"You know how long this took? To make myself lovely for you?"

"Now *you're* mocking *me*: You always look lovely. It was effortless."

"You have any idea how much effort goes into being effortless?"

"Rescued from a train crash you'd look lovely."

"See, what's really neat about those rose-tinted spectacles of yours, they're almost impossible to see."

"We've got to talk, Trove."

"Couldn't we just have sex? Sorry. Sorry, okay? It just sort of splurged out of me. Don't look so serious, Mike."

"Seriously we need to talk."

"Right. Shoot."

"Citrons pressés. Madame."

"Merci."

"Monsieur."

"Merci."

"Je vous en prie."

"Santé, Mike."

"Cheers."

"You know something, hon? This chasm has just opened beneath me. And I'm falling into it. Horror-movie-like. Arms and legs splaying about all over the place. You're going to turn me down, aren't you?"

"You're a hugely desirable woman, Trove."

"Shit. *Shit*! You are going to turn me down."

"No. I'm not turning you down. Don't think of it like that. I'm saying 'yes' to us as friends. I'm making a commitment to the forever of our friendship."

"It's not 'Anna Karenina' I'm proposing here. Not 'Romeo and Juliet', not even that what's-her-name film, you know, the orgasm one. What *is* her goddamn name? It's sex, for Christ's sake. A ... what do you Brits call it? ... a shag. God, that's an ugly word. And for such a beautiful thing. It *could* be beautiful, you know that, Mike? A roll in the hay, you know? Really beautiful. Just so we know what we're missing. Or maybe *not* missing – who knows?

"I don't want a romance, Mike – Christ! Who needs another one of those? And at our age? – I don't want an affair, not even ... what do they call it here? ... a divertisement. I want a fuck. A throw-me-on-the-bed, have-your-wicked-way-with-me-and-then-let's-get-back-to-living fuck."

"My way's not very wicked, I'm afraid."

"I guess I'll never know. Peg Ryan, that's who it was."

"I couldn't fuck you, Trove."

"You really know how to bolster a girl's ego, you ever been told that?"

"I couldn't *just* fuck you."

"No. Foreplay's a requirement too."

"I'd fall in love with you. Don't you understand that?"

"Not if you knew me."

"I do know you. And the you I know already I love."

"They're pretty words ..."

"Not just pretty words. You make me sound so calculated."

"Sorry."

"Oh God, so am I, Trove. You have no idea how sorry I am. This time, though, it's actually me paying you the compliment. You see, I couldn't just do that, couldn't just make love to you, have sex with you ... you know ... fuck you. I've already said it, I'd end up, I know it, falling in love with you. And what would be the consequences of that? As I say, you have no idea how sorry I am."

"Are you?"

"*So* sorry. But I've got a feeling that that sorry would pale into insignificance against the sorry I'd be if I went ahead ... if, Trove, *we* went ahead. I think a whole host of people would be sorry then."

"Okay."

"Do you know how much I want you, Trove? Do you have the smallest idea? How much I'd like just to spread-eagle you across this table and ravish you here and now?"

"Is that what they call a cover charge?"

"We'd end up hurting each other."

"I presume we're not talking S&M here."

"Much more painful than that."

"Yeah."

"There's Al as well ..."

"There's always Al."

"We can't just ignore him."

"That's supposed to be my line."

"You'd end up hating me."

"I hate you right now, Mike."

"Quite."

"Quite?"

"And we haven't even ... you know ... had sex."

"Oh, that's *so* English."

"'No Sex Please, We're English'?"

"No, 'quite.' ... It's not the 'no sex', is what I'm saying, it's the 'quite' that's so English, the 'quite' you said. And not good-'English' either. You notice, Mike, I didn't say British."

"It's the title of a play."

"'No Sex Please, We're English'?"

"'... British', I think. A farce, to be precise."

"Quite, as you would say. Quite."

"Touché."

"I can't believe you're saying 'no' to me."

"Believe me, Trove, neither can I."

"The wonders you do for a girl's self-confidence."

"I'm demented."

"You know that?"

"Not responsible for my own actions."

"And for your own inertia?"

"What does that mean?"

"We're all responsible for our own actions. Are we also responsible, is what I'm asking, for own inertia?"

"Inertia is also action, Trove."

"Oh, like not being fucked, I suppose, is also being fucked."

"Isn't it?"

"I suppose. I suppose, Mike, in a way, it is. I have to go."

"I'll come with you."

"Apparently not."

"Schoolgirls obviously have the same humour as school*boys*."

"Oh, much dirtier. You going to pay the check?"

"There's always, Trove, a check to be paid."

"Don't preach at me, right?"

"Heaven forfend!"

"Heaven *what*?"

"Forfend."

"And that's a word?"

"You've heard of a forefinger? Well, a forfend is like a bottom equivalent."

"Well, up your forfend, then, baby. Maybe with your forefinger. That's one helluva tip, Mike."

"That's what all the girls say."

"What was it we were saying about schoolboy humour?"

"Schoolboy humour is an oxymoron. That's a contradiction in terms."

"Yes, Mike, I do know what it means."

"'Military Intelligence', for example, is a famous oxymoron."

"I also know the meaning, Mike, of an oxy*less* moron."

"As is indeed American ..."

"Don't say it."

"What?"

"'American culture', you were going to say: 'another

oxymoron.'"

"And that would have been a cheap shot, right? If I *had*'ve said it, I mean."

"I'm so *bored* with hearing it, Mike."

"It's also not true."

"It is also not true. I used to love this boulevard, know that?"

"We tend to forget, Trove, with ... well, with ... you know in the White House, just how many gifts America has given to the world."

"It has, you know."

"Steinbeck is one of the world's great writers."

"Of all time?"

"Certainly of all time. The two Millers: Henry and Arthur."

"They did a burlesque act, right?"

"Eugene O'Neill. Edward Albee. Scott Fitzgerald."

"Hopper, Mike, and Jackson Pollock."

"Gerschwin and Bernstein and Ives and ..."

"Hemingway?"

"I was never crazy about Hemingway, to tell you the truth."

"That doesn't make you a bad person, Mike."

"No?"

"An illiterate person, maybe. Not a *bad* one."

"They'd be appalled, wouldn't they?"

"By what's happening today?"

"Wouldn't they be appalled?"

"They'd be appalled, Mike. Christ, Mike, *I'm* appalled. There *are* still right-thinking Americans, you know."

"As opposed to Christian right Americans?"

"Right. Know what else?"

"What?"

"I just walked right past my car."

"Did you?"

"*We* did, Mike."

"Meg, by the way."

"Meg?"

"Meg Ryan, Trove. Who starred in 'When Harry ...'."

"Meg?"

"Meg."

"Not Peg?"

"Meg, Trove."

"You sure?"

"As sure as God made them li'l green apples."

"Meg Ryan? That doesn't sound right to me."

"It's also not Willy Crystal."

"I know that."

"Billy not Willy."

"Talking of Willy's ..."

"Which we weren't."

"Talking of a lack of willy's ..."

"Trove ..."

"This is it?"

"What?"

"I get in my car, Mike? Drive away?"

"Into the sunset?"

"Run the end credits?"

"Does it have to be?"

"You're the one said it did."

"Trove, I said I couldn't just ... you know ... fuck you."

"That's the last line in 'Casablanca'."

"Scarcely."

"Think about it, Mike."

"I said I couldn't *just* fuck you."

"I don't understand that."

"Think about it."

"Ever the gentleman."

"Me?"

"Opening the door for me."

"I don't want you to go, Trove."

"You know I have to."

"Yes."

"I have a meeting I have to get to."

"Yes, you said. It's just …"

"Just?"

"I have a feeling, Trove, if you get into the car, you'll drive away forever."

"Maybe I should."

"Oh, I'm sure you should."

+++

We kissed. Again with the gawkiness of teenagers. We broke the kiss. Looked deep into the well of each other's eyes. Slowly I closed my eyes. Slowly she closed hers. We kissed again.

+++

"Oh God, Trove!"

"That was all bullshit, right?"

"All of it."

"You can't kiss me like that, right, and not want me?"

"Oh God, I want you."

"And you have to have me, right?"

"I have to have you, Trove."

"I have a meeting."

"Right."

"Next Saturday, Al's away. Next weekend."

"You said."

"You busy next weekend?"

"Even if I were …"

"We could meet next weekend."

"You don't need to pack?"

"Pack?"

41

"For Norway. You said you were going to Norway. Doing your Alex Haley bit, you said."

"I know what I said, Mike."

"Finding your roots."

"I know, Mike, what I said."

"What have I said?"

"I'd like you, is all, to be swept away or something with passion."

"Not too good, us Brits, on the whole swept away front."

"Do you want to meet next weekend?"

"Yes, please."

"That's being swept away?"

"British-style."

"Right."

"Mike-style, that's a tango of passion."

"A tango?"

"A tango to go! I really want to spend the weekend with you, Trove."

"You mean that, Michael?"

"Oh God, Trove, if you but knew how much."

"I'll call you."

"Please."

"All of it bullshit?"

"Every word, Trove."

"I can't, see, not go to the meeting."

"Go."

"It was a lovely kiss."

"Yes. Lovely. Thank you. For me too. Lovely. Like you."

"Next Saturday?"

"Next Saturday."

"I will call, Mike."

"Go."

+++

She went. I followed her car way beyond the point when it was out of sight. My brain was trampolining in a treacle of warring emotions. I was cross. That was the most obvious emotion. With myself primarily. No, furious. I should have stuck to my guns. I should have been stronger. I owed that to myself. Who but an idiot sets himself up to be hurt again? Again and again? An idiot or a masochist ... An idiot _and_ a masochist.

But there was that stirring within me, stronger than myself. Some kind of super-force, some *elemental* force.

- "Bull*shit*, Mike. Bullshit."
- "No, not entirely."

I started seeing her, you see, with fresh eyes. As I was having that drink with her, I suddenly realised I wasn't drinking with the her I knew. This was another Trove. The identical twin, perhaps, of the other, but undeniably a different person. No, not even identical. Not even a twin. Someone similar, someone redolent of the Trove I had known. Someone who would sometimes remind me of the Trove I had known.

- "And with this new Trove you're falling in love? "
- "I don't know."
- "But you're preparing to? You're getting somewhat squidgy in your feelings, a bit gooey?"
- "Just a bit."
- "You couldn't fuck her because you'd fall in love with her?"
- "There are, let's put it this way, blips on the radar screen."
- "Bullshit, Mike. Bullshit."
- "If I did love her, I'd walk away?"
- "Quite."
- "Does all love have to be selfless?"
- "Doesn't that define love?"

- "Antony's love for Cleopatra?"
- "Obsession."
- "And love cannot be obsessive?"
- "No. The obsessive belongs only to obsession."
- "That screws up most of the world's love stories."
- "The judgement of Solomon is a love story."
- "I want her."
- "Want isn't love either."
- "Lust is a part of love."
- "Only a part of it."
- "Aren't I entitled to some happiness?"
- "So, the price of this 'love' is Trove's unhappiness and your own hypocrisy? A pyrrhic sort of love, then?"
- "I can't see her again, can I?"
- "Not alone."
- "I can't go to bed with her?"
- "Not if you love her."
- "Isn't it possible, some sort of middle ground? Where I love her so much I want to make love to her, but not so much I don't recognise it's in her best interests that I don't?"
- "Listen to yourself."

My mobile bleeped. I had a text: 'Pls, sir, I want sum mor! xxXxx T.'

I rummaged in my mind for gags involving twist – in the tail, perhaps. But the only ones that occurred to me were bad or tasteless or both. Less is more, I remembered. I texted her back: 'Me 2. Mxx.'

Oh God, I wanted some more. So *much* more I wanted. I wanted it all, in fact. I wanted *her* all.

Chapter 4

My darling Trove,
To say that I feel self-conscious doing this would be to describe the Grand Canyon as something of a fissure. Here goes nothing, I suppose. I feel gawky too, adolescent. Very unsure of myself. But you say I need to do this, so, as they say, here goes nothing.

I think I have been open with you, but you say I haven't and that this exercise will help me to become so and I bow to your instinct and superior knowledge or whatever the hell it is. So here – as now I've already said twice before – goes ...

(I also feel a bit voyeuristic. As if, almost, I'm watching a video of us having it off {which is an odd phrase, when you think about it. I mean, where did that come from: 'Having it off'? [My English teacher once wrote in an essay of mine: 'This is supposed to be an exercise in language, not an algebraic equation.' I'm beginning to see what he means!].} And I feel quite turned on by that {being voyeuristic} – and hugely turned off. At one and the same time!)

I feel as nervous now as I did then. Well, not quite, but getting close. Going to our room, I was so nervous. I mean, sooooooo nervous. That I wouldn't come up to scratch, I suppose. Pass muster. As a lover. That my body somehow wouldn't hack it. That the 'love handles' would be seen merely as middle-aged spread. Most of all, that my ... let's call it 'JT' ... that my 'JT' would refuse to renounce its premature retirement and that it would, as it were, let the side down.

Driving to our rendezvous my mouth was like sandpaper. I was, I think, shaking from nerves.

I hated meeting you like that. *Hated* it. It didn't feel like a tryst, not Abelard meeting Eloise, more like Bonnie and Clyde (as, I think, I said at the time) about to pull off a heist. Or two spies, more like, meeting to swap state secrets.

You were wearing … Do you know, it's awful, but I really can't remember what it was you were wearing. You looked stunning, that I do remember. Ravishing. Ravishable, more accurately. Indeed, ravageable.

We kissed.

I was very uptight, that too I remember. Very sprung-loaded. I'm not sure you have that expression in the colonies (kidding, Trove, only kidding … As you would say, 'Jeez, Trove, *lighten* up!'), but it means excitable, 'agitato'. And then the bloody traffic jam. It was predictable, I know. Even inevitable. But I needed it like the proverbial moose needs the proverbial hat-stand. (It's not proverbial at all, but clichéd. We'll just gloss over that!) All that small talk. All those "and how are you?"s; all those "Jesus, it's hot today!"s and "and how was your week?"s. My week was awful.

My week had passed in a haze of wondering when the hell Saturday would ever arrive – *if* it ever would. Of walking around not knowing what I was doing, why I was doing it, even where the hell I was. And then *there* I was: the Saturday *had* arrived and I desperately wanted the moment to last forever. But I also wanted the sex to be over and for it to have been great and for me not to have disgraced myself and for you still to like me as a friend and now also to like me as a lover and for us to be embarked on a magical, mystical *sexual* tour and about ten tons more of other wants. And instead of being able to tell you that, I was replying to: "And what have you been up to?" with ripostes of such pith and profundity as: "Oh,

this and that." "This and that"?! I ask you: "this and that"!

All of which while my heart was going pitter-patter like tropical rain on tin roofs – which I would like to tell you was in celebration of my love for you, but which had (in reality, I fear) much more to do with my up-and-coming performance. Or, more accurately, the performance I hoped would be both 'up-' '-and-' subsequently (but not too soon) '-coming'.

+++

"We'd booked a hotel. Well, *he* had. Well, when I say, 'he had' that was only after about ten zillion phone calls. Twenty or so a day. You know, to decide, I mean. Finally to 'do it' … finally, I guess, that we *had* to.

"More even than *the* Sunday – the Sunday, I'm talking about, when we met to discuss whether we'd have our affair or not –, when the big day came, which was a Saturday, I was scared. Shit, I was *so* scared. Do you know what I mean? I mean, out of my mind terrified. Oh, not of him. Not in that kind of way. But of me. Scared that he wouldn't, finally, find me attractive.

"He'd been attentive, of course. More than attentive. He'd *said* all the right things. You know, those stupid, *girly* things. Things which as a committed feminist I shouldn't need to hear, shouldn't *want* to goddamn hear. But which – shit – when I heard him say them, it made me realise how much I'd missed them being said. How much I'd missed anyone saying them. … Al saying them.

"Jesus, I don't *blame* him, Al. Compliments, they're a bit like kissing, aren't they? I mean, six months into a relationship, you stop kissing, don't you? I mean, it's still lovely when you do, but you don't. Not too much. Why *is* that? And why do we stop paying each other compliments? And is there a link? Between the fall off in kissing and that in compliments?

"On our way to the hotel, we'd kissed in the car. I wasn't too impressed, to tell you the truth. His kissing technique was all a bit measured. I'd had one other English lover, but he'd just been a hood. There'd been no finesse to him, no delicacy ... no subtlety. I'm not saying that to criticise him. God, no. If anything, the other way round. I'd wanted a pump-action shotgun – in virtually all senses of the word – and, sure enough, that's what I got. No complaints. And no regrets.

"I'm like Piaf, I have none. About virtually anything.

"Mike was different, though. Mike wasn't a thug, for one thing. He liked to think of himself, I think, as a man of taste, a bon viveur but one with a conscience, as a cosmopolitan glorying in local differences, as a citizen of the world completely at peace in his backyard. And in some senses, he was all of those things. Particularly cosmopolitan. But in others he was almost quintessentially British. – Isn't that a great word: 'quintessentially'? – No, English. Quintessentially *English*, I meant to say. He wore an invisible bowler-hat, Mike, carried an invisible umbrella, strapped on invisible cricket ... what do they call them? ... pads. That's it: pads. And that, because he was Mike, was both one of his charms and one of his big non-charms.

"He was very gallant, very ... there's no other word for it ... gentlemanly: He'd open doors for you, all that number, help you on and off with jackets. The first time he held my chair for me as I sat, I wondered – truly I did – what the hell he was doing. I was just so unused to it.

"But the downside was that stiff upper lip. He wouldn't let you in, Mike. Oh, eventually I think I probably penetrated as far as anyone else – bravely went where no woman had been before. Not, I think, that that was too far. But, at the beginning, he'd open a chink, a sliver, then immediately pull down the shutters again. Me, I'm an open book. What you see is what you get.

"Kissing a stiff upper lip is also quite a challenge. Lips, especially when you're kissing, they're supposed to be such malleable things, a plasticine which moulds into the perfect inversion of your own lips. His were of reinforced concrete. That's what it felt like.

"It didn't augur well."

+++

Lunch was torture. I was trying so hard to be laid back and casual. Of course, the harder I tried the more unlaid back I became, the less casual. I think, if I remember correctly, at one point I even started to stammer. Do you know, I'm blushing even as I write this? I certainly remember blustering through sentences, getting the order mixed up of all the words I wanted to say.

What am I talking about? What I wanted to say was, "What on earth are we doing having lunch when we could be in bed?" I wanted to know why you still had your clothes on. I wanted to say, what I had said already, that this was a seriously big mistake and that you'd regret it. And I wanted to say, please don't ever let me be without you – ever – for as long as we both shall live. What I didn't want to say was that the omelette was pretty good or that the waiter was doing his best or that the table-cloths had known better days or any of that other stuff. (I've used that expression before, I think. Sorry.)

I remember I wanted to be alone with you. And I really didn't. Because being alone I'd have to ... you know. And what if I couldn't and because I couldn't there was nothing else to talk about? And if I couldn't and there was nothing else to talk about, what in the name of Christ were we going to do with ourselves all weekend?

The drive to the hotel was interminable. Far longer than the drive I later had to Paris. I cannot tell you a single detail about the countryside. I presume we passed trees and fields, the odd cow. But such recollection as I have is no more than a blur, a hazy impression, no more. A Monet fog at his most bleary seen with hungover eyes.

I do remember scrunching on the gravel of the drive.

I do remember wondering whether or not I should kiss you. Whether or not, I mean, it was the appropriate thing to do in the circumstances, to kiss you. I mean, what was *that* about? Whether or not I *'should,'* whether it was *'appropriate.'*

Now it seems like a lifetime away. No, it has elements – akin to Woody Allen about to be lynched by the Ku Klux Klan – of the wrong life flashing before my eyes. Do you know, I don't even know whether you like Woody Allen. How can I love you as much as I do without knowing whether or not you like Woody Allen? How about Tom Lehrer?

+++

"Well, there was one thing for sure: There'd be no-one who'd discover us at this place. Isolated? Any more isolated it'd have been an iceberg somewheres off the coast of … What's it called? The island where they finally sent Napoleon to? Not Elba, the one ten zillion miles from nowhere? …

"Santa Helena, that's it. Santa Helena.

"But it was really lovely. Almost too lovely, in fact. Within a hair's breadth, I'd say, of being prissy, of being … I don't know … cucumber sandwiches and those frilly doily things under rubber plants, you know. Chintzy more than prissy. No, chintzy *as well as* prissy. Not quite, but close.

"It was a converted farm-house. A lot of the original beams were there, some of the stonework. And where they had restored, they'd done it well. A bit 'Homes and Gardens' but with some care not to spoil the original feel of the place, its original flavour. It was the perfect place for a sexy weekend. I'd think about ninety-five percent of its custom comes from just that. Stone floors, wooden stairs.

"Mike was trying to look, I think, like we were an 'item' – which is also what he would have called it – an established couple. Why?

"I was already excited. I'd spent the whole frigging week in a state of some ... 'blah-di-blah', let's call it. Even just the sound of his voice had gotten all ... well, had gotten all my blah-di-blah, ... well, dah-di-dahing. Just the mention of his goddamn name! Isn't that pathetic? But the whole naughtiness of the thing, the whole deal that we *weren't* an established couple – an item – that was just adding to my general ... blah-di-blah. I could see Mike was getting embarrassed. And I tried to mollify that embarrassment by going along with the charade. But there was too a naughty girl element in my whole enjoyment of the thing. You know, Jane Fonda at the Plaza in 'Barefoot In The Park' pretending to stuffed-shirt Redford that she's a hooker. She's now selling cosmetics. Can you believe that? Like an Avon lady. Worse. Not nearly so dignified. Not nearly so *distinguished*. It's just so sad. Where was I? Hotel. Right, the hotel ...

"I tried to effuse over the hotel, tried to divert my extreme la-la-la into appreciation of my environs. Know what I mean? Oh, I wasn't kidding myself. I wasn't *trying* to kid myself. I was way past that. But it was a way I could fool myself I was fooling the hotel staff. You know Gregory Corso's poem? 'Marriage', I think it's called. There a couplet in there somewhere about Niagara Falls, about the desk clerk 'knowing' of the honeymooners that they'd all be doing 'the same thing tonight' ... something like that.

"It had that feel to it. It wasn't even that I minded them knowing. I mean, what else *would* we be doing, for Christ's sake? I mean, wouldn't it have been a lot sadder, a lot more wasteful, if we *hadn't* have been using their place for sex? I mean, isn't that a bit like being chauffeur-driven in a sports' car?

"I could have blah-di-blahed him on the stairs.

"The porter opened the door ..."

+++

I was watching your bottom wiggle along that corridor. Remember that corridor? I remember paintings. What

of? I have no idea. I remember wondering what that bottom looked like naked.

I remember, I think the phrase is, 'a stirring in my loins'. Stirring? There was a seismic quake in my loins. About a hundred and sixty-four on the Prickter scale, ten thousand degrees Fuckenheit. The porter opened the door. Another small corridor. Which gave onto the room. Dominated by that huge iron bed. Remember it? And with the sunken bath in the bedroom? And you gave a little squeal, both of appreciation and of pleasure? I'll never forget that little squeal. It was enormously endearing. And you turned to me. And your face was just one gigantic smile. Somehow, that smile, it exemplified joy. It radiated joy. But it radiated too appreciation and gratitude and ... oh God, I don't know, so *many* good things.

This sounds awfully immodest, but I do try to do nice things for people. It's so rare that those gifts or the effort they represent are even recognised, let alone acknowledged. The greatest gift you can give anyone is the appreciative, and graceful, receipt of their gift. And I was so grateful to you for your gratitude. That was the first (but by no means the last) time you tendered me such a gift. And I think, if it is possible to be that precise about such moments or to chronicle them, it was at that moment that I started to fall in love with you – in <u>love</u> love with you.

I remember telling you, when this affair was first mooted, that I wouldn't be able just to have sex with you, that I would end up falling in love with you. Well, you know by now how right I was. I'd expected that moment to come when we'd become comfortable with each other. Instead, it was then. When I was as uncomfortable as I ever had been in my life.

+++

"What do the Brits say: 'Bowled over'? That's what I was, I was bowled over. That's the same 'bowl', I presume, that goes into the making of 'bowler' hats.

"The room just exuded sex. I mean, there was this bed … It was huge. It *was* the room. And there were these pillows. Big pillows, you know what I mean? Huge ones, filled with soft, soft down. Pillows that are just great for … well, you know, for those moments when pillows like that are just great.

"And there was this bath, this sunken bath. And that was right in the middle of the room. I mean, there was no screen, no curtains. If you wanted a bath, is what I'm saying, you had it in full view of your partner. More likely, *with* your partner.

"This room wasn't for people on business trips, nor for couples exhausted from a day's bicycling. This room wasn't even interested in you sleeping in it. This was a room where you made love, where you fucked, screwed, shagged, bonked yourself stupid. It was a room where you committed acts of lewdness or gross indecency, where you covered each other in crème fraiche. It was a room for dildoes and whips and French maid's outfits. It was a room where anything went and which expected of you that you would give yourself to anything. It was a room which expected you to retire to it early but which, if you then zonked out, would have sulked for days in disappointment.

"And Mike was being so English, so proper. Putting the cases on the case rack, tipping the porter. All that crap. 'Get rid of him, Mike. Get rid of him now. Touch me. For God's sake, Mike, for Christ's sake, touch me, grab me, frigging well po-ssess me.'

"I didn't care how the tv worked, or the DVD, where the goddamn minibar was. I wanted to be hurled onto the bed. Blah-di-blahed frigging senseless.

"After three ice ages, the porter finally grovelled out the door.

"Here goes, I thought.

"Wrong …"

+++

And when the porter went – do you remember that? All I wanted to do was to pounce, tear the clothes from your back (and front!). But that wasn't the 'right' thing to do, was it? I mean, we both knew why we were there, but a certain amount of wooing, wasn't it, was still necessary? A courtship of sorts, I suppose I'm talking about: however token or peremptory.

Did I ask you whether you wanted to unpack? I rather think I did. Real Don Juan stuff, no? God, how embarrassing!

+++

"I was sitting on the side of the bed, I remember. My skirt was riding up. I just let it. There was a good deal of thigh exposed. You know those arrows they have on autoroutes to tell you to change lanes? Well, there was one of those planted on those thighs pointing straight at my blah-di-blah. And a neon light flashing from my forehead. Jeez, what more did the guy want?

"He didn't walk to the bed, he kind of waddled. Sort of like a slightly drunk duck. Or John Wayne with haemorrhoids. He stood by me (Mike, I mean, not John Wayne). You know, for a minute there I thought he was just going to unzip, expect me to blah-di-blah him there and then. I felt like such a tramp, such a sleaze. No, such a *hooker*.

"And then I thrilled to feel like a hooker. I wanted him to blah-di-blah me as he would a hooker. That was the object, after all, of the exercise. Well, wasn't it?

"Except that then, just as suddenly, I wanted to feel clean. I didn't want to feel like a sleaze or a tramp or a hooker. I wanted to feel like a woman. Like a fairy-tale princess, even. God, isn't this all so lame?! Whatever must you think of me?

"I wanted to feel *wanted* is what it was. No, *I* wanted to feel wanted.

Me. Not me the owner, the harbinger of a yadi-yada, not even of more than one, but me. Trove. Petrova. And I didn't want to be blah-di-blahed any more. I wanted to be made love to, cooed over. I wanted a sex that was long and languid … yes, and loving. I wanted … It was, I realised, that the whole of my body ached for the whole of his. Oh, it wasn't love, that wasn't it. But it was a yearning for fusion – that's another Mike word, but it's the right one. I wanted us to be us. One us. That fusion.

"If he had've just exposed himself, expected me just to … you know … blah-di-blah …. Oh, you *know* ... that would have been the end of it. There and then, I mean. I mean, I might well have gone through with it. Who knows? I might even have enjoyed it. There is a part of me, see, still quite attracted by the gutter. By the emotional gutter, if not the physical one. My self-esteem sometimes is so low, there is an appeal to feeling myself unclean. It's safe, I suppose. I mean, there's nowhere further to fall, is there?

"And, I suppose, there's another element, which is sex without commitment. Why men think that's their exclusive domain bewilders me. It's men who are the romantics far more than women. I think men believe that Barbara Cartland mush much more than we do. What's their pornography but that mush gift-packaged with reams of unlikely sex?

"That had been what *we* were supposed to be about, Mike and me: sex without commitment. And, sitting there on the side of that bed, that's what I still thought it *was* about.

"Oh, I was conscious by then that I wanted to be treated specially, *princessly*, but I still thought that I'd have this weekend of being pampered and then I'd walk away. Back to my 'happily-ever-after' with Al.

+++

You looked so lovely, sitting there on the bed. You were the most desirable thing I'd seen in God knows how long.

The curls in your hair were … tousled, I believe the word is. Those huge psychotically blue eyes of yours were peering up at me with a mixture of affection and fear, attraction and curiosity, warmth and an odd kind of quizzicalness.

I noticed for the first time that tiny beauty spot above your left eyebrow. I'd known you for all that time, and this was the first time I'd seen it! I saw the line of your cheek-bones, the almost cherubic uplift of the end of your nose. Your neck was craned to look at me; it stretched the skin and it lifted your breasts. Those magnificent breasts. Which were pulling me to them, I don't know, like a baby or something.

Not in the least bit like a baby. Whatever am I talking about?

I was standing in such an awkward position. I took your hand, I remember. And then your mouth opened. Just a crack, just a sliver.

+++

"I wanted to talk. I don't know what I wanted to say, but I needed to say something. Anything. I needed to make a joke or something. Lighten – Jeez – the atmosphere.

"Only thing was, I opened my mouth and nothing came out. It was like my tongue had gotten stuck to the roof of my mouth. No, worse than that. Because it wasn't even that mumbles came out. It wasn't a cat that had gotten my tongue but a whole pride of lions. This – I remember this so well, oh God – this sort of pathetic and virginal whimper scurried out. A sort of a wimp of a whimper. An apology even for a whimper – even for a wimp.

"He'd taken my hand. I was trying to look him in the eye, trying to see what lay below the eyes. You know how I like to read eyes. But I was all misted up. Like a windshield, you know, on a frosty day.

"My heart was racing. I wanted to still it, put my hand on my breast, the way you do. But I wasn't sure what body-language he'd misinterpret from the gesture.

"There I was, doing my best goldfish impersonation. And he? He was doing nothing. Oh, in real time, we're talking nanoseconds here, but in mine – my time – several more universes had been born and died.

"I think I may have given his hand the smallest of tugs or something. Finally he leaned forward to kiss me and he swivelled himself at the same time to sit down next to me."

+++

That was our first kiss in private. Doesn't one of Shakespeare's characters compare a kiss to honey? Well, that kiss – that first private kiss – that was so much sweeter than any honey.

The softness of your tongue, its watery, its pliable softness, its tiny ridges, the nodules of its taste-buds, the liquid rose-buds that were your saliva …

+++

"No stiff upper lip now. This wasn't accomplished kissing, this was diploma stuff. 'Summa cum laude'. Master-class making out. It wasn't the kind of kissing either you got to acquire via fidelity. It was a kiss embossed with the influence of several great kissers – a great many great kissers, in fact.

"You're going to want me to describe it to you, and I can't. Not really. I mean, describe how Yo-Yo Ma plays a cello, as opposed to, I don't know, Jacqueline du Pré on the one hand, and on the other, the thirty-fifth cellist of the Timbuktu Second Symphony Orchestra.

"Oh, I'd been kissed by a virtuoso before, by a Jacqueline du Pré – Al himself was a Jaqueline du Pré kisser. He had been. In the early days. And Mike wasn't better. Just different. But of equal virtuosity. – Is that a word: virtuosity? – And the kisses I'd had from the thirty-fifth cellists ... well, I guess they could have formed an orchestra all by themselves. Several, if you count all the school-time kissers.

"I wasn't bla-di-blahing any longer, I was, you know, *dah-di-dahing*. Christ, honey, you know what I mean. And it wasn't that attractive a sensation. He was wearing a real good after-shave. French, I'd put money on it. And his hair smelt great as well. These were being mixed with the musk of his arousal. It was becoming a heady bouquet. Almost high-making. But all these perfumes were drowned beneath the smell of my own blah-di-blah. And that *wasn't* that attractive a sensation. I was beginning to get quite self-conscious about it. You know, as if I'd let off some kind of thunderous ... well, fart or something.

"Women, we're supposed to be discreet, aren't we? Secretive, mysterious. The smell I was exuding – leastwise as it seemed to me – was about as secretive and mysterious as a red London double-decker bus.

"He was still kissing me. Oh, passionately, sure. But still with great gentleness, great delicacy. Yo-Yo Ma manages to play fortissimo still without being strident. Same deal.

"It was like my mouth was that cello, and his tongue was the bow. He was testing every string of my instrument, every note, every chord. Seeing how each sounded, hearing how they resonated – separately, together.

"He wasn't gulping down a pint of beer. He was savouring a Mouthon-Rothschild. That is a wine, right?

"Married women don't get kissed like that. Well, I guess you know that as well as I do. Not after day three of the marriage, 'any rate. You ever been married?

"Trust me. It had been so long since I'd been kissed like that. *So* long. I started to know then that I had to be careful. Because although it wasn't then that I wanted to be with Mike, it was then that I wanted to be the me that Mike was then kissing. The young me. The desired me. The me that was desired because I was desirable.

"I'd started to squirm by now. I couldn't … you know … blah-di-blah any longer or keep my legs still. Jesus, I wanted him, this man. Jesus, I did.

"His finger by now was stroking my cheek, tracing a line across my chin, under it. Gently – Christ, so gently –, holding the back of my head as you would a baby's, he lay me back on the bed. He stopped his kissing to look at me.

"I didn't know it, to begin with. I had my eyes closed. I just knew, suddenly he wasn't kissing me any more. He had one hand on the nape of my neck, the other was still etching the line of my jawbone, but he'd stretched away from me. Panic. My smell was … you know … pretty la-la-la, *you* know. Had it turned him off?

"Or maybe, Jesus, *I* had. Maybe he'd taken off those rose-tinted glasses, and suddenly I wasn't lamb any more, but wizened and wrinkly old mutton. Stringy and rancid frigging mutton.

"I flashed open my eyes. And there were his eyes blazing down at me, so full … well, of adoration, I guess. Does that sound incredibly vain? Well, shit, I feel a bit vain about it. Because it was adoration – not love, you understand – adoration. Adoration and desire.

"You know what a turn-on it is to be desired? You know how hard it is not to desire someone who desires you? I was already on fire for the want of … da-di-dah … 'sex': there I said it! … now I was not only on fire with desire for him, but I'd climbed to that level of desire beyond fire, whatever the hell that is.

"I pulled him to me. And I kissed him. Nothing delicate or gentle about that kiss, though. It was savage. I had to inflame him too. Conflagration is not a solitary activity. I pressed his mouth onto mine, gripped his head in some kind of arm-lock.

"He'd climbed on top of me now. I could feel him beneath his pants. – His trousers, I guess I should say. – I bit into his lower lip. He winced. I wouldn't release his head. I kissed the bite better. I half wanted there to be blood, so I could drink his blood. He was beginning now himself to whimper.

"He was scraping his tongue over the top of my teeth. He was exploring within me, every crevice within me. The back of my teeth, the underside of *my* tongue. I was going to be allowed no secrets.

"I didn't care about my smell any longer. No, *more* than that: I started being turned on by my own smell. I could also now smell the perfume I'd put on for him. And his after-shave and shampoo. Even his deodorant. And now the musk exuding from him, that was becoming obvious too. It wasn't unpleasant. To the contrary, even. But it was strange that it wasn't unpleasant. There was nothing fragrant about it, nothing rose-buddy or bottled. Horses' sweat, more, or sort of wet dog. Very animalistic. No, very primitive.

"As language had become primitive. A few grunts, the odd snort or mewl or whimper. Nothing as tangible as words. Nothing, like words, which required the use of a mouth. Our mouths were too busy elsewhere.

"Busy?! Frantic! Kissing, nibbling, licking. Lips, ears, neck, cheeks, nose. Chin. Forehead. Eyebrows, eye*lids*. Our hands on each other's faces, recognising the other through touch, a blindman's recognition. And an expert fingering a Dresden bowl. At one and the same time.

"He was squirming now too. His hand left my jaw. It stroked my ear-lobe for a bit. And then, his nail lightly scratching my flesh, his hand eased over my neck, through my shoulders, down the side of my torso. At my breast he wavered.

"Oh, it wasn't, this, the wavering of uncertainty or immaturity. It was a deliberate teasing. He left his hand on the side of my breast, the merest whisper away from the object itself. And he crushed my breasts into his. He made me feel his hardness through his clothes, he wanted to feel my softness through mine.

"My nipple, still protected by bra and blouse, was screaming for release. It wanted to feel his flesh. It wanted air, freedom. It wanted its own nakedness. And I wanted it to be naked.

"His hand went to the clasp of my bra. 'Here's where it begins,' I thought. 'Here's where the clumsiness begins.' I don't know how he did it, though, but he unclasped the bra in one movement and with one hand. And my breasts felt free. They were still covered by the cups, but there was no pressure now beneath them. *Within* them, there was pressure sufficient to fuel the whole Côte d'Azur, but ... Panic again. Soon he'd see those breasts. There was not much more of hiding them from him.

"I'd agonised over those breasts. For a solid fortnight I'd been gazing at them, coming out of the shower, changing into my night-clothes. They were a crone's breasts, I'd decided, a hag's. What did Shakespeare call them? 'Dugs,' was that it? 'Dugs,' I'm sure of it. Just as I was sure, Mike, he would not dig those dugs.

"I was still squirming from passion, then, and from blah-di-blah, but (just for that moment) I started to squirm almost from ... not embarrassment ... shame, I guess. Isn't it awful? I was ashamed of my own breasts. Now, I'm ashamed of having been ashamed of them."

+++

Those beautiful breasts of yours. Those beautiful, beautiful breasts.

Aureole, isn't it, is a curious word? It means both that aura around an angel, and for the ring around the nipple. But suddenly, in that moment, not curious, Trove. Not at all curious. Your beautiful nipples embedded in those aureoles - pert nipples, sensitive ones, preening and stretching towards me: This was no earthly stuff, this was the fabric of angels.

And, God, the first touch of those nipples, that was the carnality of gods. The sweetness of that touch, the glory of it, the nipples' softness, such a contrast with, such a complement to, the callous skin of my finger-tips.

That little groan of pleasure - I think it was pleasure! - when I first took that nipple - the left nipple - in my mouth. First felt that soft and spongy skin on my tongue.

+++

"He did a thing – I never told anyone about this! – later he did a thing on my back – I never did quite figure out what it was – it shot darts through me. Not altogether pleasurable, and yet hugely, enormously pleasurable. Kind of at one and the same time. Know what I mean? Well, the first time he blah-di-blahed on my ... blah-di-blah ... oh Christ, sucked on my breast ... it was like that too. 'Sucked', did I say? Maybe suckled would have been closer to it. Oh, not in the cranky-baby way of a lot of guys – presumably who had comforters shoved in their mouth at an early age and who therefore think the human nipple can withstand the kind of gnashing of a rubberised one. Don't laugh! You never had a man like that in your life? Sister, you have no idea how lucky you've been.

"He didn't even pounce on it. You know, the cheetah on the deer, kind of thing. He took it in his hand, let the ... you know ... nipple creep between each finger as he lightly nipped it. He took my whole breast in hand until just the nipple was showing through –in that hole, kind of thing, between thumb and index-finger. He stroked the outside of it, but he just gazed at the nipple. To begin with, I was disconcerted. It was as if it was, I don't know, a specimen or something.

"Then I looked at him. I saw that his eyes were now full, not of adoration, but of love. Oh, not for me. And not that kind of love. He was loving what he saw. He was ... I don't know ... a snuff-box collector and what he had before him was the finest snuff-box he'd ever seen. It was that kind of love.

"Do you know what that does for a girl's ego? You know what kind of a turn-on that is? Don't you agree? Me, that makes me more horny than three quarters of the annual supply of Uganda's rhino horn. Hey, is that where 'horny' comes from, do you suppose? You know what I mean, hon?

"He loved what he saw, Mike. Just loved it. And I was, as I said, well ... gratified by his admiration. But I was also real embarrassed by it. You know what I mean? I mean, he was no mean catch himself,

Mike. Not too hard on the eye, and to talk to … well, just easy-peasy. And here he was, gazing at my breasts, enchanted by them, knocked out by the goddamn things.

"There was still a hot spring … you know, yadi-yadahing … there below, craving attention. I found myself straining towards him almost involuntarily. I was aching for release. I was yearning for … well, it didn't matter what … but some contact, some touch. Just … you know.

"But he was in no hurry. And there was another part of me not wanting him to be in any kind of a hurry. I just wanted to freeze him in time at that moment: looking at my breast like that, loving it, lusting after it, hankering and hungering for it.

"I took his head in my hands, started stroking the hair above his ears, urging him downwards. Please to kiss it, to suck it – that breast he loved so much. 'Oh, make it yours, my darling one. Consume it. Please kiss it, my darling. Please … oh please … oh *please*.'

"His mouth eased into a little and impish grin. It was the naughty boy about to steal the cherry from his elder sister's ice-cream sundae.

"He leant down, kissed it. A quick peck. And then he pulled back.

"Ten thousand volts tore through me. I think I did judder. I couldn't help myself. I put my hands now behind his head. Pulled it down to my breast. My poor, aching, desperate breast.

"As his mouth sealed over the nipple, it was as if someone had quenched a fire there. The relief was enormous.

"He loves women, Mike. I'd suspected that of him, but I hadn't realised just how much. He loves every bit of them, you see. Oh, I don't flatter myself that's only me. And so he relishes the feel of every part of a woman. Not just the naughty bits or the bits some biology teacher told him ninety years ago were 'erogenous zones' – makes them sound, doesn't it, as if you need residents' parking permits for them?

"His left hand was tracing patterns all over my trunk, my butt, my outer thighs.

"And his tongue was still dancing the light incredibly fantastic on … oh, on my nipple. And every time it darted over the top of it, another five thousand volts tore through the entire of me. It was like there was an electric eel slithering over my breast. A beautiful eel, though. An angel eel.

"My body was jerking all over the place, kept going almost into small spasm. Like an epileptic fit, almost.

"And, like I say, some of it was not even pleasant. But it was alive. Shit, it was that, alright. Alive with a capital 'A'.

"I was alive. That was it. Responding and reacting like a live person. I was Pinocchio come to life. Well, Pinnochia, I guess. Very definitely, in fact, and very dah-di-dahly, Pinnochia.

"That was when I became really scared. Because if I was alive then, that meant that I hadn't been. Which, okay, didn't mean that I had been dead – I knew I hadn't been dead – but it did mean that I had been atrophying. I may not have been Lazarus – Lazara – but I was too close for comfort.

"It made me fearful because those brought back to life tend to do stupid things around their saviours. Like fall in love with them and stuff. They also feel grateful to them.

"Finally what made me fearful is that life is incredibly addictive. Get a little bit of it you just cannot wait to get more."

+++

I had such a ******, it was getting painful. I was trying to be gentle, subtle. And I was also desperate to prolong the moment.

+++

"I just couldn't stand it. I threw him off of me. Screw what he thought of my breasts. He'd have to see them sooner or later. I tore the blouse off of my back, let the bra just slide off. He was yanking now at my skirt. He'd unzipped it God knows when. It just slid from me. I couldn't get his goddamn pants off. I'd undone the zipper, but ... it was one of those pants you need a Masters in de-panting to get the suckers off. Which meant he had to take the frigging things off himself. Which meant he had to divert attention from my panties to his pants.

"I just wrenched the knickers from me. And I squatted, panting, above him, like a dog slavering over a bone, as he manoeuvred out of his ridiculously complicated pants and then his undershorts.

"I couldn't wait.

"I just blah-di-blahed him. I was shameless. I just ... you know ... like I say, blah-di-blahed him. I didn't care. I didn't frigging care. All I cared about was him ... it ... him and it ... no, it could have been anyone ... anyone's ... But I needed it. Him. Anyone. Needed all three of them badly. Immediately. Nothing else mattered.

"Did it matter whether it was good for him? Did it even matter that it *was* him? I don't know. Probably not, at that moment. Anyone's, like I say, it could have been. At that moment. Probably. Probably, at that moment, I couldn't cared less.

"You know, it didn't even matter whether or not I came. Not right then. I'd had all these mini-blah-di-blahs. I was okay with that. I just didn't want to be empty. Not any more."

+++

It was, I remember, fairly unceremonious, our mutual striptease. I'm not sure the judges would have given us too much for artistic merit. It all happened in a sort of blur, a sort of hazy flash. One minute we were there all deshabille and I had your breast in my mouth. And the next, we're both stark naked, and you're ... well, I'm sure you remember. I don't want you to think I'm gloating!

It suddenly became all so urgent. I wanted you to come. I was desperate that you came. I really wanted you to want sex with me. Again, I mean, and again. And, so I thought, if you came, you would. Want sex again

with me. We're so shallow, us men. We think sex is about orgasm, only about it. Why do we find it so hard to learn from women?

+++

"I never blah-di-blah … you know … dah-di-dahly! I *almost* never do. I did then. I … you know … again and again and again. As old Julius might have said: 'Veni, veni, veni.' I 'veni'd' so heavily, so intensely, so many times that I drowned my knowing when he did.

"I'd had … you know … 'venis' like that before. I'm not trying to make this into something it wasn't. I mean, even then I knew I'd had 'venis' like that before. I've no need to turn it into something it wasn't. Because what it actually was, that was special enough. That was different and exotic and erotic enough. Even fairy-taley enough. Thing was, though, though I knew I'd had 'venis' like that before, I couldn't remember when.

"In the early days with Al, of course. A couple of guys when I was in my early twenties. But, Jeez, it was so long ago. It was all, all of it, just so frigging long ago.

"Did I tell you I'd been yadi-yadahing all week? …

"This is so not me. So giantly not me, I can't begin to tell you. Either me yadi-yadahing or me telling you about it. But, hey, when the cat's out the bag, there's no point trying to get the sucker back in, no? I'm just using this thing, this blah-di-blah, yadi-yada thing, for those things I'm kinda uncomfortable with … or around … you know. (Well, I guess you probably figured that one out for yourself, am I right?) The stuff in the newspapers they spell with asterisks. Or Mike did in his letters. Leastways, to his son. Can you imagine such a thing?

"Meanwhile, back at the point … I'd been going crazy is the point. Suddenly, just the sound of his voice – the mention, for Christ's sake, of his name, and it'd be like someone had opened a faucet. Sorry, a tap. And I … Well, I just couldn't stand it. Like I said, I had an itch. Mike was an itch, and the effect he was having on my blah-di-blahs, that too was an itch. Ones that needed scratching. Urgently.

"The itch that was Mike, that would have to be scratched during the weekend. The itch in my blah-di-blahs, though, that had to be dealt with *now*. Except that the relief that came from dah-di-dahing was ... short-lived. I mean, no sooner had I ... you know, 'veni'd' than ... I don't know, I'd give Mike a call or something, and the whole frigging, soggy process would start over. And with a vengeance. Jeez. I was getting even fed up with it, you know. Walking into shops, wondering whether everyone there could smell me. Sort of waddling, trying to keep my thighs as far as I could from each other.

"Do you know, so desperate was I for sex, I'm not sure that – looking back on it – when the event finally happened, I even felt him. Not what you'd call 'felt'. It was there, the event, the sex. And I sighed this giant sigh of relief. The man dying of thirst suddenly given water. This huge whoosh of relief, as I knew he was there. And I 'veni'd', like, right off the bat. 'Premature evacuation,' I suppose you'd call it. Or premature '*o*vacuation'.

"You see it in the Olympics sometimes, don't you? Athletes on their knees – on all fours, rather – panting, exhausted. Spent. – And what they wear, athletes today, they might as well be naked. – That was me. And with an athlete's grimace – one where it is impossible to tell if they're in agony or ecstasy. And where the truth is that the athletes are in both, agony *and* ecstasy, and both are feeding off of each other.

"And it wasn't only blah-di-blahly that I 'veni'd'. I mean, my whole body was in spasm. And then parts of my body, they'd have their own spasms, like their own private mini-'venis': my throat constricted and then slackened; my hands started shaking and my breasts twitching; even my eyebrows decided to do some kind of weird St Vitus cha-cha-cha or something.

"And you know what it was, this whole great juddery, one great enormous blah-di-blah? It was my life-throes."

+++

I've got a feeling you didn't come that first time. And I remember being disappointed by that. Oh, the performance was all very 'When Harry Met Sally', but ... well, maybe I'm wrong. I didn't then know you as well as I do now. There was rapture there, certainly, and you're not given to feigning such things. Then, though, it did feel feigned. Not heavily, not grotesquely. Not struggling through a home-made cake of cement. But maybe that bitter-sweet joy of someone who has won a lot of money on the lottery, but is only one number short of having won the jackpot.

We did, and this I remember so well, fit so well together. Physically, I mean. Dovetail into each other, like the carpenter's joint. I don't think that's as common as we're led to believe. And it certainly wasn't, our first time together, the disaster it so often is.

I remember you crouched over me, panting, your eyes dancing to Heaven, trying to muster a smile, trying to lollop it in my direction. And I remember smiling back and trying to raise myself to kiss you. And you pushing me back down again. A 'you-must-be-joking' sort of a push. A push that protested it didn't have the energy to breathe, let alone to kiss.

I remember then being overwhelmed. By this huge sense of peace. This extraordinary sense of peace. It wasn't a peace of 'all's right with the world'. Thank God. I mean, all's so clearly so very wrong with the world that if that feeling had have come over me, well, I'd have known I had simply lost the few marbles I still had left. No, the peace that came over me was one of 'you're alright in this world'. And that's vastly different proposition.

How shall I put this?

There was this psychiatrist, R.D. Laing, something of

a cult figure in the '60s and '70s. Laing's premise was that anyone deemed sane by an insane society had to be insane, and that anyone deemed insane by it had to be sane. That therefore the only sane members of our society were those that society considered nuts.

Of course, that's putting it over-simplistically and, as a theory, Laing's <u>was</u> over-simplistic. But it had an uncomfortable, even a serrated, edge of truth to it. It gave me some comfort.

I'd always thought of myself as a square peg in a round hole. And had always thought it was me who was out of step. Laing showed me, or convinced me, it just might be that I was the only one *in* step. But, even knowing that, I still felt uncomfortable.

The peace that came to me at that moment was comfort. For the first time in my conscious memory and I suspect for the first time in my life, I was comfortable in my round hole. Christ, that's a really unfortunate metaphor in these circumstances. Sorry, I most certainly did not intend any sexual puns.

I didn't know what had just happened. Oh, it had been great, spectacular, life-changing. But, beyond the generic, I wasn't sure quite what had happened. And I was even less sure what was going to happen – beyond an intuition that it was going to be something pretty severe. Perhaps 'intense' would be a better word.

I knew something had happened – some kind of hymen had been severed, some kind of Rubicon crossed; and I knew something was going to happen. But I didn't know what.

Beyond this peace. This overwhelming and all-enveloping peace.

That peace came – it's taken me some time to realise this, even more time to be able to articulate it (however poorly) – from knowing that what had happened, and was about to happen, was extraordinary and special. And extraordinarily special too, if you like. Its extraordinarily special specialness was caused by the fusion of you with me and of me with you. That fusion could not have happened had you not been you or had I not been me. It was a requirement the fusion had. And that meant that not only was it acceptable for me to be me, it too was a requirement. If part of me being me was being uncomfortable as a square peg, then that too was one of its requirements. And as soon as you recognise it is a requirement, you are no longer uncomfortable with it.

I wonder whether that makes any sense to you at all. I'm not sure it matters that it does. What is important for you to understand is that, for the first time in my fifty-four years on this planet, I was able to relax.

I was able to bask. In the warmth, certainly, of your caress. But also in the all-rightness of being me.

Even aged seventeen, I needed half-an-hour or so between sexual bouts, just to regroup, 'summon up the blood'. You remember that first time? I'd no sooner left you in shrivelled retreat than I was back on parade, ready for action.

You know, I hope, what a magnificently attractive woman you are, and that I am hopelessly attracted to you is not something which by now will have escaped your notice. And, certainly, my attraction to you played its part.

But the alchemy of instant re-attraction was, I'm sure, supplied by that peace, by that feeling – not of validation, that's a bit different – of it's-all-right-to-be-uncomfortableness. That's when the love I have for you soared from desire to something ... maybe even uterine. It's when the love stopped being just 'Get a load of that' and started becoming 'This person is going to change my life. And very much for the better.'

Wasn't it the Aztecs who believed that if you ate someone, you'd be possessed of that person's virtues, their strength and courage? If I'd been an Aztec, or Hannibal Lecter, it would have been then that I would have eaten you.

Chapter 5

"Was it good, Mike?"

"Good?"

"Oh, thank you. For switching off the ignition."

"Il n'y a pas de quoi."

"Mike, was it good?"

"'It' the weekend?"

"Yeah."

"Or 'it' the sex?"

"Both, Mike. Were they both good?"

"No, Trove, not good."

"Not good?"

"No, Trove, not good. 'Good' isn't the right word at all."

"Oh!"

"Trove, they were great."

"Only great?"

"Incredible. Mind-blowing. Fantabulous."

"You couldn't have said that right off the bat?"

"I was pretty impressed I could say it at all."

"It's going to be difficult, Mike. Saying goodbye."

"Don't say goodbye, then."

"I have to go."

"You have to go, Trove. You don't have to say goodbye."

"Know something, hon? You talk too much."

+++

She cupped my chin in her hand, brought it to her. We kissed. A practised kiss. Lips finding lips like two long-term ice-dancers gliding together, tongues of fragrance and redolence, dancing their pas-de-deux of savour and relish. We were snuggled in the car park which had

somehow become our own. We'd travelled to the hotel in my car. This I'd now parked close to hers.

+++

"I wish now ..."

"See, I paused then, Trove, to allow you to finish the sentence."

"I don't want anything between us to finish."

"You wish?"

"You're off to England, Mike, a week Tuesday."

"Yes?"

"Why are you saying 'yes' like that? Like only an idiot would've said what I just said."

"It's scarcely hold-the-front-page stuff, Trove."

"Oslo, I was thinking."

"Of course. I mean, why wouldn't you be?"

"I've made a commitment, Mike."

"Yes."

"I wish I hadn't've is all."

"I wish you hadn't too."

"But I have."

"Yes."

"It's Wednesday, Mike."

"Monday, actually. Oh, I see: Wednesday, when you have to go."

"You know how long away that is?"

"Two days?"

"That's two days away, Mike. Forty-eight hours. You know how long forty-eight hours is?"

"Are."

"What???"

"Forty-eight hours *isn't* anything. Forty-eight hours *are*."

"Oh, well, that burst *that* bubble."

"It was a joke, honey."

"I don't need to be corrected, Michael. Christ, you know how that makes me feel?"

"Sorry. I'm so sorry."

"Yeah, you should be. No. No, you shouldn't. No, Mike, *I* am. Really. Really, hon, you don't need to apologise. You *shouldn't* need to apologise, I should say. It's my shit, this. Not that it was a *good* joke, mind. Let's be clear about that. It's just – oh Christ – sometimes, Mike, you talk so like Dad, it's almost like I'm talking to him."

"You made out a lot, did you, with your father?"

+++

She whipped her head around. Eyes which moments before had been over-ripe cantaloupes, soft and squidgy, became the eyes of a basilisk. Eyes of lava, spitting molten embers. Eyes endowed with such pain they had to cause it. Eyes of venom and hatred.

+++

"For a moment there, he *was* Dad. It was scary.

"Oh, sure, there'd been reminders, sort of mini-echoes, throughout the whole weekend. Dad and Mike were both tall and with hazel eyes. Both of them liked to laugh and could be cruel without meaning to be. Both of them were bright, though both were a lot less bright than they thought they were. And both of them possessed – no, were possessed by – the most unbelievable intellectual arrogance.

"It's the arrogance of a physicist who thinks that because *he* under-stands quantum physics quantum physics should be understood by everyone. No, it's not even that. No, what it is, in both their cases, it's more that they both think they *should* understand quantum physics, when all they *can* do, they can spell the words. But that doesn't stop them, is what I'm saying, from being extremely intolerant of anyone so ignorant of quantum physics that they *can't* spell the words.

"Did that make sense? At all, I mean? Sorry. Never my strongest suit, English. Mike would doubtless say I had that in common with most of my compatriots. And that's not it either. Or wasn't it. But you catch my drift."

+++

She got out of the car. Heavily. With leaden shoulders. She didn't close the door. I followed her with my eyes. Her eyes flicked to mine. And tripping through the bubble they had of sadness came sugar-plum fairies of new-found joy and just-released rapture.

Even as I was leaning across the passenger seat, she returned to me. "Didn't we pay for the whole of tonight?"

"Al's waiting."

"So's a huge bed, Mike, with giant pillows."

"You don't mean it."

"I want to mean it."

"It's not goodbye."

"Just au revoir, huh?"

"A bientôt, even,"

"When's bientôt, though? When is it?"

"When we want to make it."

"Could we make it tomorrow?"

"You said …"

"No, we couldn't. Will you call me tomorrow?" she asked.

"You said …"

"No, you can't."

"Al …," I said.

"I know."

"You said, Trove, …"

"I know, for Christ's sake, I know."

"We've got phones in England."

"Sure."

"Emails, fax …"

"How do you fuck by fax?"

"Alliteratively."

"Yeah, yeah."

"There's even the good old-fashioned shove-it-in-the-pillar-box kind of mail."

"And that works how, exactly, Mike? You stick a stamp on your prick, do you? Send it COD? Cock on Delivery?"

"It was a great weekend, Trove."

"I don't want for it to be over."

"You think you'll forget it?"

"Does the pope shit in the woods?"

"Then it's not over."

"Know something, Mike, about platitudes? They've got awfully cold feet. They're not too comfy to snuggle up next to during the winter months."

"Al's waiting, honey."

"Isn't that supposed to be my line?"

"You weren't about to say it."

"No. I've got awfully cold feet, too. I'm not being metaphorical here. My feet, in winter, get ice-blockly cold."

"Right."

"I've also got metaphorical cold-feet, Mike."

"Well, I'll just pop out then, get you some metaphorical bed socks."

+++

Maison d'arrêt de Toulouse-Seysses, 4th April o6

Dear Dad:

I'm more sorry than you can imagine that you "can't do anything." I also, frankly, don't believe it. But if you'd rather I rotted away here than go the extra mile for me, well then, so be it, I guess. Just please don't ever tell me, Dad, there's "nothing you wouldn't do for me." See, it's easy to write that you and Mom have left no stone unturned, that you've worn yourself into exhaustion on my behalf, but, know what? The proof of the goddamn pudding, Dad, is ... in GETTING ME OUT OF HERE. Hear that, you deaf old son-of-a-bitch? Dad, you've got to get me out of here. PLEASE. I'm on my knees to you, Dad. Begging you.

Al.

+++

"Mike."

"Trove."

"You sound surprised."

"I wasn't expecting to hear from you."

"I wasn't expecting to call you."

"I'm glad you did."

"Really?"

"You have to stop fishing, Trove."

"I want to be with you."

"Thank you."

"No, you don't understand."

"You want to be with me?"

"Yes."

"Trove, I think I do understand that."

"You don't. Last night, is what I'm saying, being with Al, I wanted to be with you."

"I wanted to be with you too."

"But you weren't with Al, Mike."

"I'm missing something here."

"Previously, I've had my flings. Right? I told you about my

flings. Please don't go all quiet on me, Mike. I did tell you about my flings. Right?"

"You told me."

"And I enjoyed them. The sex, sure. Mostly too the company as well. But when I got back to Al, I was glad to be home. Like a vacation, you know? Bermuda's great. But the best thing of the trip is the journey home."

"Okay."

"Last night, I just wanted to stay in Bermuda is what I'm saying."

"I'm going to take that as a compliment."

"I'm scared, Mike."

"What can I do to help?"

"Ever thought about missionary work? To some far-flung leper colony?"

"I've thought about the missionary *position*. Does that help at all?"

"That like the admonitionary position?"

"You've been watching too many 'Brief Encounter's."

"It's twenty-three years, Mike."

"I know, sweetheart."

"Not 'honey'?"

"Honey."

"Could you meet me tomorrow?"

"Sure."

"At the airport tomorrow?"

"Sure."

"Could you come to Oslo?"

"To the ends of the Earth, Trove."

"But you will come to the airport, huh?"

"How many ways are there to say yes?"

"I'm checking in at eleven."

"Won't Al …?"

"No."

"He's not going to want to …?"

"I talked him out of it, okay? Not that he needed a lot of persuading. I said I'd be fine on the bus. He was relieved, I think."

"Okay."

"Not to have to schlapp all the way to the airport."

"Sure."

"Or back again."

"Right."

"Will I see you tomorrow?"

"At eleven."

"Do you think they'd allow us to fuck on the scales?"

"We'd be charged for over-jigging."

"They got restrooms in airports, chapels, how come they've not got fuck-rooms?"

"Clearly an oversight."

"More people, right, want to fuck than to pray?"

"Maybe they fuck in the chapel."

+++

"I was kidding, Trove."

"It's deserted, Mike, the chapel."

"I think God might disagree with you."

"Like that'd be anything new! 'Sides, isn't God everywhere?"

"Well, that's true too."

"You think God would disapprove?"

"I think the airport authorities might."

"We don't have to fuck."

"That's very magnanimous of you."

"Isn't that a kind of gun? A magnanimous forty-five, or something? The one dirty Harry uses?"

"That's not the same Harry, you know, who met Sally. The dirty he was wasn't sexy dirty."

"Hey, guess what, dirty Mike? This *isn't* a kind of a gun. *This is because you're pleased to see me.*"

+++

"The letter-writing? Well, that all started that first weekend. It was a gesture, no more. It all started out as just that, a gesture. I woke up on our first Sunday morning, and there, on my pillow, was this:

My darling,
As you read this, you will be waking up next to me for the first time. I write in the certain knowledge that that milestone too (as all the others) will see us only safer in our feelings for each other, more secure in our embrace, at ever greater ease with one another – with each other's presence and with the mutual present which is ourselves. With love – Mike xxx

"Naff, no? You know what, though? It was actually its very naffness which I found most endearing. It was Mike exposing himself as much as he could. The debut stripper clutching desperately to his g-string. Do male strippers *have* g-strings? He would have considered his striptease to have been so complete as to be an x-ray. And, although his Salome still had about six-and-a-half veils to go, I still wasn't used to any kind of striptease. And it touched me. The effort that it represented, and the clumsiness of the execution, they both touched me.

"See, I've been to therapists. ... Oh Christ, I told you I was blah-di-blahing, why shouldn't I also tell you about this? Yeah, and how many stupid people in the world think of those two things as the same activity? Blah-di-blahing, I'm talking about, and seeing a therapist! And how come I feel more embarrassed about telling you about the therapist than about my ... you know. It used to be called self-abuse. Self-*abuse*, I ask you. You know the best way you can abuse yourself, honey, by *not* blah-di-blahing. By ignoring your sexuality, and your carnality and your sensuousness and all that. That's a *real* abuse of yourself. As is, of course, *not* seeing a therapist. 'Least if you need one.

"Meanwhile, back at the point ... Therapists and that ... There were ... crisis points in my life. I saw no shame in seeing a therapist. Quite to the contrary, in fact. I've seen three. When my parents died, when I miscarried. No, four. Once with Al. When our marriage was going through a particularly rocky patch. *'Particularly* rocky', you'll note I said. I didn't know that then. I thought that patch was just a rocky patch and for the rest it was okay. 'There's none so blind,' they say, '...'

"I'm used to talking about myself is what I'm saying. Used to discussing my feelings ... used to *feeling* my feelings.

"Al at those counselling sessions ... well, shit, they may as well have been in Sanskrit. He just sat there, open-mouthed, gaping at me, wondering what the hell I was talking about. It wasn't that he was unwilling – no, it really wasn't – it was just ... it was just that the concept of talking about yourself in that way was so completely *alien* to him. So *completely* alien, I mean. It was, I don't know, like trying to describe the taste of a banana to a hump-backed whale. It's not the whale's fault that it can't understand. There is no point of contact with even the concept.

"Which would have been fine. He's a man, for Christ's sake. That's on the one hand, and on the other his upbringing was one where feelings were taboo subjects. Shit, mine too. I was just in such pain at those times ... those three, four times in my life ... I wanted to be out of that pain. No, I *had* to be out of that pain. That pain was going to kill me. Maybe very slowly. I didn't want that. So, I wasn't being all holier-than-thou about this counselling number. I wasn't claiming any kind of, I don't know, matrimonial high ground or anything. I was fine with his unfineness is what I'm trying to say.

"What wasn't fine, what I wasn't fine about, was that Al didn't even try. Finally, that was all that I wanted out of him, that he tried. And he wouldn't. And his wouldn'ting was far more troubling for me than his couldn'ting. He was like a six-year-old kid who won't eat a

Chinese meal because he's never eaten one before. It looks strange and smells strange, so he convinces himself it's going to taste strange before he even tries it.

"Mike wasn't much better, to be honest. And to be fair to Al. (Though why I have this need always to be fair to everyone is something else I almost certainly need help with.) But what Mike was, he was able to try. To try, oh, the shark's fin soup, for example.

"He couldn't talk, Mike, not what we mean by 'talk', us girls. But he kind of knew he couldn't talk. And so he wrote. Well, no, he didn't write – except that note. Not at the beginning. Not until I asked him to. But when I did ask him to, he was prepared to have a go at it. He felt a sense of obligation, it seemed like, to find out about his feelings and to acknowledge mine. And to acknowledge the need I had to talk about mine.

"Thank God, huh? Gives me something now I can remember him by!"

+++

She was a woman rapidly approaching fifty. She had the bottom of a woman twenty years younger. As she went through the airport's security gate I was trying to watch her back. But, as if by a magnetic force, my eyes were pulled to her bottom.

As she picked up her bag from the conveyor belt, she turned back. Just to smile at me. Just to wave an almost coy goodbye. And yet again she was fifteen-years-old. Almost with braces on her teeth. The smile of a glorious shyness. She was going to the prom. She had, Mom, a date for the prom. Okay, maybe not exactly the football captain, but – hey, Mom – a date: a real, honest-to-goodness date.

Teenage happiness is one which vacuums inside of itself the whole of the planet. Scarce are the times beyond our

teenage years when we are again filled with that Earth-encompassing happiness; and on the rare occasions that we are, it always requires us to become teenagers again. The stirring I felt in my loins was almost disturbing. This was almost under-age sex. But the arousal was to do with a woman's body, not a girl's – and with a woman's sexual virtuosity, not with the awkward fumbles of the apprentice.

The bottom danced before me long after she had disappeared. The savour was to stay with me for far longer even than that.

+++

"Hi."

"How's Oslo?"

"I shouldn't be phoning."

"Okay."

"I said I wouldn't phone."

"I'm glad you did, Trove."

"Are you?"

"Stop fishing. How's Oslo?"

"They fish in Oslo, Mike. It's what they do."

"You fish if you want to, Trove."

"It's Norwegian, Mike. That's how Oslo is. You know what else it is?"

"Scandinavian?"

"I shouldn't be telling you this. I promised myself I wouldn't tell you this. You know what else Oslo is, Mike?"

"Hot?"

"Mikeless."

"Toulouse, Trove, is also Troveless."

"Know what?: a Mikeless Oslo, Mike, it's missing something."

"Like Athens, you mean, misses the Elgin marbles?"

"It's like a smorgasbord next to a sandwich."

"Open to the elements?"

"With need of a top layer to cover it all over, keep it all together."

"I think in Oslo they usually call that snow."

"I need a top layer, Mike, to cover me all over, keep me all together."

"You're getting me somewhat hot and bothered here, Trove."

"I use the word 'layer' advisedly. Know what layers do, Mike?"

"No, don't tell me. Let me guess."

"If lay-preachers preached less and laid more, think how many more they'd get in the congregation."

"Same deal with turning airport chapels into fuck-rooms."

"See what I could do for world peace. We could start a whole new movement, Mike."

"We started a few over the weekend, honey."

"You know how much I like 'honey'?"

"An evangelical movement, even. You're right, we should start one. One devoted to sex."

"An e-fanny-gelical movement, then?"

"Right, Trove."

"This call is costing a fortune."

"I could call you back."

"Not just in money."

"No."

"I'm not leaving Al, Mike."

"I know that."

"It's just ... Hello?"

"I'm waiting, honey, to find out what it's just."

"You know."

"No."

"You're a shit, Mike, you know that?"

"I've been told often enough."

"'Course you have. Shits need to be told they're shits."

"I'm still waiting."

"It's just, Mike, I want a Miked Oslo. There, I said it."

"I want to be there."

"We can't do it, huh?"

"You know we can't."

"I know we can't. I don't want to feel like this."

"You could come to England."

"I can't leave Oslo just like that. Plus you've got to get yourself settled first. In England, I mean."

"Yes."

"I want sex with you now."

"Me too."

"You want sex with you?"

"I *really* want sex with you, honey."

"Get on a plane."

"You know I can't."

"I know you can't. Still …"

"Still?"

"Get on a plane, Mike."

"I'll look into it."

"Copenhagen. I could meet you in Copenhagen."

"Oh, that makes sense! For us both to get on planes!"

"Berlin, then? Even Amsterdam?"

"The two of us flying, that doesn't make any kind of sense."

"None of this makes any sense, Mike. This isn't about sense. This, in fact, is probably exactly about *non*sense. Sense doesn't matter, don't you see? It's not part of this equation."

"No."

"No?"

"No, you're right: Sense is not any part of this equation."

"Don't come to Oslo, hon. It's ridiculous. Absurd. You've got to pack up for England. The trip'll cost a fortune. Just for a day or two. It doesn't make any sort of sense – even within the complete no-senseness of the entire thing. Besides ..."

"Besides?"

"I'm not leaving Al, Mike."

"No."

"Will you text me something dirty?"

"I don't think my shirts are textable."

"You're a great lover, Mike."

"Thank you."

"One of the *world's* great lovers, in fact."

"You too."

"Don't get snippy."

"I'm waiting for the sting in the tail."

"Not, Mike, one of the world's great comedians."

"That hurts, Trove."

"It does?"

"From the author of 'an e-fanny-gelical movement', that really hurts!"

+++

"Welcome to Oslo, Mike."

"You're a sight for sore eyes, honey."

"And you look good enough to eat."

"You can eat me."

"I wasn't sure, you know ..."

"... I'd make it?"

"I thought, at the last minute, you might, you know, chicken out. Decide you really had too much to do. Decide this was all getting too complicated, too messy."

"Here I am."

"And you know what? I'm *still* not sure."

"By way of a flying visit, but this is me. Promise. In the flesh."

"We said we weren't going to do that, Mike. Remember?"

"Sorry."

"You've just got here, already you're talking about going."

"Sorry."

"Talk about coming instead."

"Just talk about it?"

"Come."

"Here?"

"Kiss me, Michael."

"It's the withering looks, hon."

"What???"

"The looks we get from anyone under thirty."

"They wither?"

"The looks too from pretty nearly anyone *over* thirty."

"They're just jealous, sweetie."

"You can't wither like that without disapproving."

"It's envy, Mike."

"I find it intimidating."

"They're strangers."

"Strangers, Trove, are just enemies you've yet to meet."

"We're wasting good bed time here."

"It's good to be with you, honey."

"Say 'ass'."

"Arse."

"Ah, shoot: You were getting so good at 'honey' I had hopes a bit of trans-Atlanticism might, you know, be taking some kind of shape."

"And?"

"You're British, Mike."

"Okay."

"Beefeater British."

"Right."

"Hard core."

Chapter 6

"Michael never sent postcards. He wasn't a postcardy person. We'd been friends for ⋯ what was it? ⋯ twelve, thirteen years. In all that time, I think he'd sent me one other card. Possibly two, certainly no more.

"It's such a lovely day. It seems a shame to be cooped up inside. Would you like to go back out into the garden?

"Good. No, just leave the cup there. I'll throw it in the sink later on. Shame, really, you didn't bring a swimsuit with you. I scarcely ever use the pool. It's a waste, really, and an extravagance. I think, actually, if you felt like it, I may just ⋯ Well, if you change your mind, don't be shy. Just let me know.

"He was due, Mike, to be in Oslo for twenty-four hours. He sent me postcards four days running. Telling me of the reasons why he was postponing his return – never by more than a day. He was always leaving 'tomorrow'. The following day, I suppose I should say: The tomorrow that never comes.

"People say, don't they, of pivotal periods that, after them, situations have 'changed gear'. I don't think Michael and Petrova did change gear then – indeed if you use 'gear' in the sense of clothes, I'd lay odds they *never* changed it. Just climbed into their birthday suits and stayed in them for what Petrova would probably have called the 'duration'.

"The analogy is not appropriate because you think of upper gears in a car as those where the drive is less laborious, the engine is coasting, not struggling so hard. That would not be my perception of what was happening to Michael and Petrova. There was no coasting for them. The gears always seemed to be whining. It was the pitch that changed; the whine, though, remained constant.

"What I do think happened in Oslo ⋯ No. No, let me rephrase that ⋯

"What happened at the *hotel* is that they found they had a sexual rapport. Wrong again: They found out that what they had *imagined* would be a sexual rapport was a real one. And what happened in Oslo was that they found out their *emotional* rapport was a real one too.

"There's a big difference, after all, between being friends before you're lovers, and being friends afterwards. They found out in Oslo that their friendship was able to transcend their lust. Well, perhaps not transcend it, thinking about it, but at least cope with it.

"That's what I inferred, of course. I knew Petrova but I was never really close to her. She wasn't likely to confide in me. And Michael ⋯ Well, I *was* close to Michael, and he confided in me as much as in anyone. But almost never about those kinds of thing. Oh he was kind, Michael, considerate, generous to a fault – except of himself. Of his time, certainly, of his money, his concern, all that, certainly – and certainly to a fault. But of himself? Of what he was feeling, what was happening to him, no. He was a Scrooge in that department, a Shylock.

"I'm so sorry. Where are my manners? Would you care for a drink of something?"

+++

"You're going to think it real strange, what I'm going to say to you. It's not, you understand, that I think of you as my counsellor or anything and it's private. It *is* private, I know that. But it's also relevant. ... Indicative, maybe more than relevant.

"I don't know, though, can anything be indicative which isn't relevant? Or vice versa? Your eyes, they've glassed over again. That means, I guess, I'm straying from the point. Again. It's because ... I'm embarrassed is what it is. Suddenly all sexually coy. God knows where that came from.

"He wouldn't, is what I'm trying to say ... He found it hard, almost impossible, Mike, to ... you know ... blah-di-blah in my dah-di-dah ... oh shit ... slurp, let us say, in my strudel. Shit, you know what I'm saying.

"And, 'cause I know he'd be shy about it, I was shy – Jesus, was I shy! – about asking him. You know?

"See, once or twice, myself I'd been too excited to ... you know ... 'veni'. Yeah, I know that sounds weird. It's only happened to me before, oh, maybe half-a-dozen times in my life. Maybe that's happened to you too? Don't give much away there, now do you? Maybe too I was actually, on those occasions, too uptight, I don't know. It *felt* like I was too excited to 'veni'. And I'd sort of apologised to him for that. You do, don't you? So, when I finally plucked up the courage, he tried laying the same thing on me. He tried telling me *he* had been too excited too. If you see what I mean.

"It had nothing to do with that, of course. What it was, it was what I called the 'princess syndrome'. Or the 'pedestal syndrome': You ... you know ... slurp in the strudels of prostitutes; not of princesses. Never, in fact, in the strudels of princesses.

"That's one of those things which sounds very romantic, on paper all part of that heraldic love – do I mean 'heraldic'? – that 'love' of the Dark Ages where knights stayed constant throughout decades of crusading to their chastity-belted beloveds. But the reality of that kind of love is that it's *not* reality. And because it's not reality, instead of flattering us, it cheapens us.

"That kind of sex is a form of sex I find completely satisfying – as both giver and receiver. If I'm ... you know ... and he refuses to ... – or his psyche won't let him ... you know ... screw the implied compliment, all it feels like is that he's rejecting the proffered gift. He's also telling me that he doesn't think I'm actually as sexy as he keeps telling me I am. Know what I mean?

"See, I'm *not* a princess. Neither am I a prostitute. And the disservice rendered us by the Puritanism of our parents' generation, its stigmatization of sex – its hypocritical Puritanism, I might add – is the inculcation into our minds that 'nice' girls don't do such things. And I believe that notion was inculcated far more into the minds of young men than young women.

"I was ... what was I? ... fifteen, I guess. Not even. To be fair, I looked closer to nineteen. Still and all. I was fully developed physically. And, sexually, I was quite savvy without being very experienced. Still and all ... I was at a dance. There was a band. The lead guitarist noticed me. Probably not too hard to notice, I was all doe-eyed and cow-eyed and everything-else-eyed. Mostly what I was, when he clearly noticed me, I was flattered. Hugely flattered. Really. No, *incredibly* flattered.

"He came off stage. He winked at me. And he tossed his head to indicate we should go outside together. Shit, what was I thinking of, thinking back on it? I was lucky I wasn't killed or anything.

"It was one of those real balmy Arizonan nights. And it smelled of ... God, I don't know, some goddamn plant and it smelled – this I remember so well – of cleanness. Yeah, it smelled of being big and open and clean. He kissed me, like, right off the bat. No 'hi's or 'how you doing?'s. Just, you know, grabbed and kissed. Full-throttle. Tongue straight down the throat ... straight down – for Christ's sake – the oesophagus. And that lasted for, oh, about a second and a half before he had his hand pummelling my breast. Squeezing it, like, you know, we do in Europe when we're buying melons, checking to see whether they're ripe. That was foreplay. And foreplay extended over, well, maybe four seconds – maybe that's why it's called 'foreplay'. Then he pushed on my shoulders, forced me to my knees. He unzippered himself, pulled on my hair, got my mouth open that way, and just ... shit, you know what it is I'm telling you.

"I was outraged. *Out*raged. I nearly bit the sucker off. As it was, all four foot nothing of me, I brought myself up to my full height, stood on my tippy-toes, and I gave him such a slap. A real good all-five-digits-embossed-on-his-cheek slap. And you know what? That outraged *him. Out*raged him. And you know what else, I'll bet you any money you care to name, he don't slurp either in his girlfriend's strudel, that s-o-b. Because you slurp in the strudel of girls who'll blah-di-blah you before they know your name, you do not slurp in the strudels of women you care about – or care for.

"Finally, both syndromes – hookers' and princesses' –, they both abuse us as women. Where I parted company with certain of my sisters in the Women's movement, I didn't agree that, because we're not only sex objects, we're not *at all* sexual. It seemed to me, to deny our sexuality was to deny our humanity. And it's my humanity which I want recognising as much as my feminism or femininity or anything else.

"See, princesses don't go to the bathroom or feel tired or scratchy or not want to go out to dinner one night or not want to talk to someone on the phone.

"To Al I was a princess. No, Superwoman, more like. Which meant I had to do everything, sort everything. 'Cause that to Superwoman is no problem at all. I can always go that extra mile because I'm Superwoman and I can travel faster, for Christ's sake, than a speeding bullet. Going extra miles, that's frigging child's play.

"Girlfriends of mine used to tell me how easy-going Al was. How lucky I was to have such an easy-going husband! You know how mad that used to make me? It drove me crazy. It *wasn't* that he was easy-going. Oh, to be fair, I don't think either it was laziness. Not, 'least, in the conventional sense of the word 'laziness'. But what, yes, it *was*: it was a sort of emotional cowardice. Because I was Superwoman, all the decisions, they were left to me. And because it was me who had made them, it couldn't be him who had made the *wrong* one. 'Don't blame me,' he'd be able to say. '*You* decided to do…' whatever it was. About anything. And everything.

"Frankly, I don't believe men like war nearly as much as folklore tries to convince us they do. I don't believe either that there is an unsuppressible urge in them to fight – leastways, not to kill. But one of the attractions of that kind of all-out conflict is that it makes heroism so easy. Or rather that it makes cowardice so hard. All you've got to do in a war to stop being a coward is to obey orders. You don't have to invent orders or challenge them. Especially you don't have to challenge yourself. You are not responsible for your own actions – not responsible for yourself, not even *to* yourself.

"Getting killed is so easy. So frigging easy. It's the staying alive that's hard. The real heroes of war are not the poor suckers who get themselves killed, but the even poorer suckers who rely on the people who get themselves killed – the parents (My God, the parents!), the widows (and widowers), the orphans, those whose loss is made even greater by the apparent confiscation of their future. Those who have to start again. From day frigging one again. And who manage to do that and find along the way some crumbs of comfort, some untapped inner resource which enables them to do so with a degree about them of cheerfulness. Can you imagine the heroism of *that*?

"Mike's grandfather volunteered for both world wars. He was thought of as a hero. Meantime, he drank his way into bankruptcy court. You want to know what Mike's grandmother thought of him? Did *he* slurp, I wonder, in his girlfriend's strudel? When he had sex with his wife, was he having sex with a woman or a princess?

"The princess and the hooker, now I think about it, they have so much in common. I mean, *so* much in common. The hooker stars in pornography. But the tales the princess stars in, all that really is, it's *emotional* pornography.

"Despite what her brother asked at the funeral, the general perception of Princess Diana is one that is an icon – a figure far closer to Mother Teresa than to Diana Spencer. And because that is such a distortion, that is not revering a memory of her, but perpetrating an abuse. Perpetrating and perpetuating a myth. The memory of Mother Teresa is also iconic, I might add. More to do with myth than reality.

"Do you think I could get a glass of water? I'm getting kinda dry here."

+++

My darling Trove,
I'm amazed that I'm amazed: Nothing about this amazing experience has not amazed me. So, being amazed again should by now be something I should accept as completely normal. But I am amazed. I'm amazed that you should want me to write any more of this; and I'm amazed that I'm glad you do. I've never thought of myself as much of a letter-writer ... never thought of myself, in fact, as much of any kind of a writer. Not even a shopping-list writer.

I have considered myself, though, as someone who was open and candid. A nothing-to-hide sort of a guy. And I *don't* have anything to hide. Not from you. Which is not to say I don't hide things. I do. It's just that I don't really know *why* I do. It's not that they're worth the hiding. The secretiveness with which I surround them, I mean, is not commensurate with their importance. It seems to me, the skeletons in my cupboard are so insignificant as not to be worth their de-cupboarding.

What I'm not trying to say is that I intend to keep my secrets secret. What I am saying is that I can't, conjuror-like, fanfare their arrival. Because that would be vastly to overrate their importance. It would give an impression from which you'd expect me to present, at least, a grizzly bear. And I'd produce a koala. (Is that how you spell 'grizzly'? I have a habit of spelling it wrongly and changing the giant mammal into one which is aging and curmudgeonly.)

We were taught not to speak. Both at home and at school. Maybe by the world at large, I don't know. You didn't cry. And you didn't complain. In most households, there was still more than a residue of the axiom that children should be seen but not heard. As he did most things, my father took that both very literally and to its very limit.

Well before all the nonsense spoken by the IT propagandists, my father knew that knowledge is power. But knowledge for him was a weapon. One which later on he could blackmail you with, or that he could use to belittle you or deride you or ... Well, it had a thousand different uses, knowledge. Time after time after time again – I was a really stupid child and an even more stupid young adult – I'd tell him stuff. Secret stuff, you know – oh, not stuff of any *importance* – not to anyone but me. And time after time again – time after time after *time* again – six months or so later (maybe even a couple of years later), that confidence would be used to wound me: to score a point with his cronies, or for the sake of a cheap laugh at my expense, or to prove my fecklessness or my stupidity ... or ... or ... or. I found out early on it wasn't safe. I found out but, as you see, I didn't learn. I think it was probably despite myself that I did learn that. It was a long struggle. Which means it's also going to be a long struggle – it *has* to be a long struggle – to <u>un</u>learn it.

It wasn't safe either with my mother. But her breaches of confidentiality tended to happen immediately. She didn't squirrel knowledge away in the way my father did. Did I tell you they separated whilst I was still quite small?

It's a defence I've built up. I see that now. And it's pretty efficient. I also see that. You saw through it. You see through me so efficiently. I appear to be so open, so full of self-exposure. But it's a bluff. A feint with the left hand to disguise where the real trick is being performed, with the right.

I still cannot talk. It's a huge weakness. Sorry. I'm really sorry. Because, however much I want to, I still can't. I'm still so frightened of it. Oh, this is all subconscious stuff, Trove. I *think* I talk. I kid myself that I'm talking. And most of the time those listening think I am talking. And so do I. I'm caught up in the bluff quite as much as those listening to me. Probably more. In fact, almost certainly more. Usually an audience is only superficially interested in what you're saying. You're far more interested in your words than they are.

I did an experiment once at a dinner party. I said nothing to the two strangers either side of me, merely prompted them when their concentration had lapsed, or when their train-of-thought was stuck in a tunnel. Both guests phoned the hostess the next day and, in thanking her for a wonderful evening, independently of each other commented to her on the brilliance and scintillation of my conversation.

Oh, believe me, I don't tell that story from any sense of superiority – and certainly not out of a belief in the brilliance or scintillation of my conversation. I'm sure on innumerable occasions the tables have been turned and it was me gassing away astounded by the charm and perspicacity of the person with whom I was engaged in 'conversation'. I'm only saying, we all of us tend to think we're having a good chat when what we mean is we're having a good moan, or a good getting-it-off-our-chest, or a good opinionating, or a good soliloquy.

"Tell me about you," you said. Do you remember? We were in bed. In Oslo. It was getting late.

I was quite indignant. *That* I remember. Wounded, probably. Yes, quite indignant. But I couldn't show it, could I? You couldn't be allowed to see that you'd touched a nerve.

It's the same ridiculous thing I do at the dentist. You know, when's he's poking at your teeth with that pointy thing, trying to find holes. You try, don't you? ... well, at least, I try not to wince. Not even to allow a flicker of pain to cross my face. Otherwise he'll drill. And drilling hurts. The fact that the drilling is a fish-pond by comparison with the Pacific Ocean of tooth-ache is neither here nor there. If I leave the dentist's without him having done anything, I think that's a triumph. Even if my tooth is still hurting.

Same deal, Trove. Same sodding deal. If I let you see me wince, then you'll tell me to address the pain. No pain, nothing to address.

"What do you want to know?" I raised myself on my arms, tried to bury myself deeper in you. Your eyes were closed. There was a spot of saliva on the left of your mouth. You obviously sensed it at that moment. Your tongue came out to lick it away. It couldn't reach. You brushed it away with your hand. You were smiling. Not a Cheshire Cat smile. Not even of the cat who got the canary. More of a cat who'd been promised canary-on-toast later that evening.

"Whatever it is," you said, "you don't want to tell me."

"There's nothing I don't want to tell you," I said. I kissed your eyelids. You wiggled a bit and 'mmmed' yummily.

"Bullshit," you said.

"I lo- ..." I started to say. And you put a finger to my mouth to shh me, and opened one of your eyes as a warning not to continue. We still didn't in those days say we loved one another. All these charades we go through in life!

"I want to know you," you said. I tried to find that funny, tried to suggest that, as we had known each other for more than a decade and had just performed one of the most intimate acts possible between two people, there wasn't (as you were aware) a lot left to know.

"Right," you said, "and I'm the queen of Sheba."

"Or, as Dorothy Parker would have it, the queen of Romania."

"Don't you ever get sick of proving my points?" you said. To which, when I looked to you for an explanation, you added: "Classic avoiding-the-question technique, Michael."

"What question?" I asked, I thought in all innocence.

"Avoiding the issue, then, for Christ's sake. Jeez!" you said. And I was scared for a moment you were serious. And, you know what?, I was right to be scared. Because, just for a moment, you _were_ serious. And then you grabbed my head and bussed me full on the mouth. It wasn't a kiss. No tongues were involved. Not at that moment. But it was a big, one mother of a smacker of a buss.

And then you pulled my head away. And you looked at me. You looked at me and looked at me. I was stroking your eyebrows, I remember. My other hand was propping up my head. You were holding my ears. Gazing at me, gazing into me, peering through the smear of the soul's windows, having a good butcher's at all the goods on offer within. Gazing at me as I hadn't been gazed at for I couldn't remember how long.

You know that thing in movies? The big close-up ... no, usually an over-the-shoulder shot, where the heroine is looking dotingly on her Adonis, and her eye-line is changing from one of his eyes to the other? Well, I used to think that was a device. You know, similar to the way that actors wiggle steering wheels when they drive cars in front of Back Projection screens, or whatever the technique is called.

But it's not. You gazed at me in exactly that way. And, in exactly that way too, I found myself gazing back at you. And a whole conversation flowed between us in those looks, a whole novel. No. Wrong. Not a conversation or a novel. Those are things of words. What flowed between us was outside the sphere of words. A piece of music, perhaps. An abstract painting. Words would have polluted that conversation, cheapened it. They would have given shape to the amorphous, would have restricted the all-embracingness of that look.

We gazed at each other … oh, forever and a bit. For a time without time. And then … slowly, slowly … you closed your eyes and started to pull my head towards you, towards lips that were now hungry for kissing. And, then, just as our lips were about to meet, you tugged at my hair. Sharply, even painfully. And you looked into my eyes again. You gazed again into those eyes. You dived into them, splashed around in them, wallowed – an elephant in a mud-bath – in their warmth and balminess. You started to dance in them. As I in yours.

And then we did kiss. Gently. So, so gently. Maybe still dancing in the other's eyes. Our tongues just gently brushing the other's. The top of my thumb lightly tracing a line from eyebrow to the side of your head. My right hand at my side holding your left hand. You squeezing that hand. Me returning that squeeze.

So light, that kiss, so gentle. A butterfly's wings of a kiss. Two mouths fluttering into one another. So light – so, so light; so, so gentle. And so sexy.

Already I was getting aroused again. No, this wasn't possible. This was not happening to me. This couldn't be happening to me. This was something that didn't happen to me. With Kelly I couldn't manage it once.

Again you broke away from that kiss. And again you held my head aloft, a bit (it felt) like a medieval axeman with a skull he'd just severed! And the lightness of our earlier 'conversation', the gentleness and delicacy, even the humour, all of that suddenly vanished. And there was grit there, steel. A certain ruthlessness, even a certain viciousness.

With your eyes wide open you pulled my face again to yours. And you kissed me. Ruthlessly, even viciously. Your tongue was stabbing me, you were biting into me. You wanted it to hurt. You wanted *me* to hurt. As you wanted me to hurt you.

You bit my lip. You were goading me, riling me. You shoved my face into your neck. "Bite me back, you bastard. Bite me back."

Anger gets you worked up. I kissed you back. Roughly. Bit into your lip. Nipped it, rather, as a crab might. You winced and bit me back. Now I wanted to hurt you too. Not badly. Just to rile you, as you had riled me. Just to get you worked up. There was sweat breaking out on both of our bodies. A drop was forming in the tiny cleft of your chin. I licked it off. Bit - nipped - into the cleft. My hands were on your hips, pressing on the pelvic bone, the thumbs massaging the flesh there.

You didn't like me nipping your chin. But you did. So much you liked it. I started nipping at your neck - a knitting pattern: kiss two, nip one; kiss two, lick one. Nip, nip, lick. Kiss. K-i-s-s.

You were wriggling, trying to encourage my hands to explore more sensitive regions. But you, I was determined, were not about to come just yet. It wasn't that orgasm would be premature just not of sufficient power. And I wanted it not to be an orgasm of Icelandic geysers or Australian white waters. You deserved an Aswan dam of an orgasm, a Niagara Falls. And for those, a certain delay is required. Grown-up orgasms demand we postpone gratification.

No decorum now or niceness. You want me and you want release. There is nothing now more important or urgent than that release.

And then?

And then?

Well, then, it was Berlioz's 'Symphonie Fantastique' and to try to describe it would be akin to all the instruments of the orchestra playing their parts individually: the line for the clarinets, followed by that for the cellos, followed by the trumpets, then the timpani. It would be an abuse of the symphony – or symphonie –, a travesty. Like eating raw all the ingredients of a bouillabaisse. It is, the sex, symphonic – plenty of brass fanfares and cymbals crashing and violins playing, plenty of lyricism and andante movements, all building – as great music does – to a coda of an explosive dynamic, which is also very life-affirming. And the fusion that is the sex, that is, yes, fantastique.

And then you freeze. You catch your breath. I try to kiss you. You stop me. I try to move my fingers. That you stop as well. You have still caught your breath and yet you catch your breath again. Your pelvis rises to acrobatic heights. There is a lifetime's pause. Three, four, five, six.

You thrust me from you. In one tantalising movement you divest yourself of me and pummel on my back. And then you jerk and thrash and shudder. You shiver, you grasp the pillow, you roll from side to side. You hit me. Hard. And then again. You pull your knees up. You catch your breath again. Seven, eight, nine …

And then, my darling one, it does happen. The release

arrives. And it is the storming of the Bastille, the relief of Mafeking. "Wow!" you pant, unable to vocalise more. "Wow!" That's all you have the strength to say.

And you are spent.

You are so spent you cannot, to begin with, even look at me. You're so spent even the sweat stops forming. You lie close to me, my head now cradled round your navel. You're panting. Now a cough or two. You stroke my hair. You want to tell me that you love me. But the space has yet to open up between your pants.

And I can hear your release. All the gurgles and whistles, the purrs from deep within you. I can smell your release – yet another perfume to the panoply already there. I can feel it now.

There's a chortle or two now between the pants. You're stroking my cheeks. You tense your muscles, dig into the stamina, find the strength. You pull me to your mouth.

We kiss. You can taste yourself on me. Another chortle, pants, a giggle. A naughty schoolgirl's giggle. So much charm in that giggle, so much innocence and joie-de-vie. Or joie-de-sex, at least.

"It's so easy," you say, still panting, "at moments like this, saying 'I love you'. But I do love you, Mike. I do …" And this time I stop you with a finger to your lips. I want you to enjoy this moment, and glory in it. You don't need to talk. I'll want to hear those words in seconds. I don't need to in these seconds.

Growing stiller now. "Wow!" still you're saying. "Wow!"

Yet stiller. You kiss me again. A gentle kiss. A loving kiss. A lingering and juicy kiss.

"Come to me, honey," you tell me. "Come to me, my darling man."

I need no second bidding.

Chapter 7

"Hi."

"How you doing?"

"I just cleared Paris."

"I just left the Art Museum."

"That was very cultural."

"I wanted to see 'The Scream'."

"Wasn't it stolen?"

"I wanted to see the hole, Mike, where 'The Scream' had been."

"Isn't …?"

"What?"

"Well, isn't a hole is a hole is a hole?"

"How like a man. I thought it would be symbolic, Mike."

"Sorry?"

"Are you being dense?"

"Could be. I just cleared Paris."

"Am *I* being dense? Was that a non- … what's the word?"

"Sequitur?"

"You couldn't not have known that?"

"Have you ever cleared Paris, Trove?"

"Oh, only several hundred times."

"Exactly."

"Did Ionesco just write this conversation?"

"You've cleared Paris several hundred times. Clearing Paris has an effect on you. Like losing gravity or something."

"Or, Mike, like losing your marbles?"

"Or something."

"There's an ambiguity, isn't there, about 'The Scream'?"

"Okay."

"Is he screaming or is he hearing a scream?"

"Right."

"Is the scream one of pain, Mike, or of joy?"

"Joy?"

"Yes?"

"You think there's joy in that picture, Trove?"

"There's ambiguity, is what I'm saying."

"Joy?"

"You're not still driving, are you?"

"I'm drinking a coffee to celebrate."

"You're not the only one, Mike, who ever cleared Paris."

"It always feels like it."

"Right. *I'm* screaming, Mike."

"Okay."

"I don't know whether from pain or joy."

"Could it be both?"

"It *is* both. Of course it's both. If it wasn't both, Mike, there'd be no point to this whole conversation."

"Except to tell you I'd cleared Paris."

"And, see, the symbolism, Mike ..."

"Is that now there's a hole where there used to be a scream."

"No-one likes a smart ass, hon."

"A shot in the dark, Trove."

"Only, see, the thing is, there's two 'Scream's."

"There are?"

"One at the Art Museum. The other at the Munch museum. The one at the Art Museum's still there."

"And they're both the original?"

"How can they both be the original?"

"That was sort of my question, Trove."

"Clearly one's a fake."

"Right."

"Only no-one knows which."

"Which is symbolic too."

"Isn't it?"

"I can only talk for myself, Trove."

"Of course."

"But, for me, there's the symbolic ..."

"Yes?"

"And the symbollocks."

"And this is symbollocks?"

"I didn't say that. It's subjective, the judgement. It has to be. My symbollocks, Trove, are not your symbollocks."

"They're *subjective* symbollocks, is what you're trying to say."

"Or not."

"Nothing ambiguous right now, Mike, about the scream."

"No."

"I just want to yell."

"And I can sense that, Trove."

"Scream my head off."

"It's because I just cleared Paris."

"I was trying to talk to you, Al."

"Mike."

"Shit, did I just call you Al?"

"Slip of the tongue."

"Shit, I'm sorry, hon."

"Don't worry about it. Slip of the tongue. Couldn't matter less."

"It's real important – *really* important, Mike – that I can talk to you."

"I want you to talk to me."

"I can't – I just cannot, Mike – sustain another relationship where we don't talk. Or where I'm not listened to."

"I'm sorry."

"Of course it's symbollocks, Mike. Of course it frigging is. But I needed to talk, Mike. About the scream inside me of pain, and that of joy – no, of torment and rapture. Look at the eyes of any Christ crucified. Take away the cross and the crown of thorns, are those not the eyes of a man in the throes of orgasm? Is there a correlation, is what I'm asking, between great pain and great pleasure?

"And that's symbollocks too, Mike. Because that's not what I'm feeling at all. I'm not feeling these things as hypotheses, not as theories. These screams within me, Mike, they're real beings. Their own entities. Probably their own masters. It doesn't matter about correlations, any of that other crap. What does matter, Mike – what *does* matter – is that there are all these frigging screams and I honestly don't know which emotion attaches to which scream and I don't know which are the real screams and which are the fakes. I don't even know, Mike, where the holes are where the screams used to be. And I'd love to make light of it all, trivialise it into a sort of vapid nothingness. But, know what? I can't, Michael. And you know why I can't? Because I'm so full of fucking screams that I'm being deafened by them. Yeah, and silenced by them too. ... Say something, for Christ's sake."

"Right."

"Je-*sus*!"

"This is not a phone conversation, Trove. Me in some motorway caff, you outside the Art Museum."

"I've moved to outside the university now."

"This is not a phone conversation. I need to see your eyes, need to be able to hold you, take your hands, cuddle you – maybe even row with you. This is not, honey, a phone conversation."

"You called me 'honey' again."

"I call you 'honey' a lot these days."

"Yes, you do, Mike, and no, it's not. A phone conversation."

"We need to talk. And about all of this."

"Only trouble is, I see you and all I want to do is make love."

"Interesting use of the word 'trouble'."

"I haven't talked, Mike. Not really talked. Not for a lot of years. Not within a relationship."

"No."

"Will you talk with me?"

"I need to tell you one thing."

"No, you don't."

"How do you know what I'm going to say?"

"If it's *one* thing you need to tell me, it *can* only be one thing."

"Okay."

"I'm not ready, Mike."

"I l- ..."

"No, don't say it. Please don't say it."

"I cherish you, Trove."

"And that's like so much better?"

"I have needs too, honey. I needed to tell you that. *Need* to."

"So, now you've said it."

"I have to go to Calais now."

"I know."

"Does any symbolism attach to ferries?"

"Like *so* much, they're all cliché."

"I cherish you, Trove."

"Please don't, Mike. I'm not kidding here. *Please* don't."

+++

Maison d'arrêt de Toulouse-Seysses. 11th April 06

Dear Mom and Dad:

I know you're really upset. More than upset. Enormously upset. Upsetissimo! (No, really, I'm not making light of it.) You've every right to be. I'm not for a second suggesting otherwise. I've let you down, I know. Let the whole family down. Let myself down. The neighbours, I know, will be having a field day. And all I can say is sorry. I am so, so, so sorry.

And, I suppose, some irony attaches itself to that. It's God punishing me, as you would say, Mom. It was a constant bone of contention between Trove and me, a running battle: I was always going on at her about sorrying too much. Now it's me doing the sorrying and I'm not sorrying enough.

I'm not because I can't.

It is not possible for me to. However many times I sorried, it wouldn't be enough.

Not by several universes. There aren't the sorrys in the world that *would* be enough. I don't offer any excuses. There aren't any. There aren't even any *reasons*. It happened. I'm real sorry it happened. Really, really sorry, you can have no idea. But happen it did. And now consequences have to be paid. And suffered.

The shame is that, in the final analysis, it's not me paying or suffering. Not really. For all its awfulness, there is also a certain safety in prison. A certain insulation. It keeps the world away from us just as much as it keeps us away from the world.

There's an irony in that too. God, how many times have you heard me rail that the whole legal system, it's so centrally flawed? To think, I used to say, that there is some kind of line that can be drawn and on the one side of that line there is right, and on the other wrong. It was idiotic, I used to say. Simplistic to the point of being crass, and crass to the point of being cruel.

And it is cruel. And crass, and idiotic.

But the dividing line is not idiotic.

I was so totally wrong. About that as about so many other things. So totally and completely wrong. There is just such a line. And on the one side of it there is wrong. Our only mistake is thinking that on the other side of that line there is right.

What I did was wrong. No question. I accept that without question. But what I didn't do, that was also wrong. And what I failed to do. So many wrongs. <u>So</u> many. They say, don't they, that two wrongs don't make a right. How many wrongs, I wonder, does it take to make a right?

I do want to be your son. That might take some time. I know that. But time, that would appear to be a commodity I'm just about to get plenty of!

Try to forgive me.

Al

+++

"How's Nottingham?"

"Troveless. Oslo?"

"I was going to come and visit you."

"'Going to', Trove, means not any more."

"Yes."

"You're not coming to visit me?"

"No."

"I'm really sorry to hear that."

"I'm really sorry to say it, Mike."

"I was looking forward to seeing you again."

"That's the second bit of bad news."

"Second bit?"

"Mike, you won't be seeing me any more. ... Say something."

"There's a man, Trove ..."

"I don't need ..."

"There's a man sitting in the electric chair. Ten thousand volts have just passed through him. You want him to say something?"

"I understand you being mad."

"Well, that's very understandable of you, Trove."

"It's a com – ..."

"Don't tell me it's a compliment, actually."

"It is, Mike, it is."

"Just don't tell me it is."

"I told you up-front, Mike. I made it very clear."

"I know."

"I thought it was going to be ..."

"So did I."

"I never thought it was going to be ..."

"No. Me neither."

"This was not, Mike, on the agenda."

"No."

"I love you, Michael."

"I think you do."

"It's twenty-three years, hon."

"Yes."

"I can't just kiss that away."

"No."

"Not on a whim. Not, Mike, without thinking about it."

"No."

"Do you forgive me?"

"Do you need me to?"

"I need you to love me, Mike. I know that's ridiculous and that's selfish. Truly ridiculous, in fact, and mind-blowingly selfish."

"I do love you, Trove."

"I know, you know, I could be making the biggest mistake of my life."

"You don't have to make it."

"Yes, Mike, I do. You know why?"

"*Because* it could be the biggest mistake of your life."

"Exactly. I think about you, Mike, all the time. I mean, *all* the time."

"Well, of course then, you have to break up with me."

"It's not easy, this, for me."

"And I'm truly sorry about that."

"It's a month – it's not even a month, is what I'm saying – versus ..."

"Twenty-three years, don't tell me."

"Twenty-three years, Mike, *is* twenty-three years."

"I'm not trying to make light of it."

"Us? We're not even twenty-three days."

"It feels like longer."

"I'll ache for you, Mike."

"And I'll ache for you, Trove."

"We can still see each other, right? I mean, we're still friends, no? We can still be friends, see each other as friends?"

"Maybe in a little while."

"You could be right. I don't want to say goodbye."

"Me either."

"Say 'ass'."

"Arse."

"Getting closer. 'Me either', an improvement in 'ass' ... How sad."

"Sad, yes."

"We'll never know, I guess."

"No."

"In neither sense, Mike, do I want to say goodbye."

"In neither sense do I want you to."

"You say it, Mike."

"Must I?"

"I'd be grateful."

"Goodbye, Trove."

"I love you, honey."

"I love you too."

"'Bye."

"Honey."

+++

"The night he and Petrova split up, Michael called me. He phoned to tell me, he said, that his daughter-in-law had still not podded, and that if such continued to be the case by the following Tuesday, they were going to induce. He phoned to tell me how unpleasant the British Immigration officers were, searching his car, looking for stowaway aliens. He told me how badly signposted the British roads were and how awful the food on the ferry. And then, with a casualness I'm sure he honestly thought was deceptive, he told me how he and Petrova were an item no more.

"I had not to hear the crack in his voice.

"Let me take you to lunch. I'm getting peckish, frankly. It'd do my reputation locally so much good, I cannot tell you, to be seen lunching with a beautiful woman. There's a bistro nearby. Nothing fancy. We could talk as we ate.

"Good. After you, then. Of course, we can. Talk as we go, of course.

"I had to ask him dispassionately how he felt about that, and I had to hear him reply that he was a wee bit upset, but – hey! – that had been the understanding from the outset. He could have no complaints. And I wanted to tell him, for Christ's sake, shout or something, cry, smash a plate or two – anything! – but I didn't, of course. I murmured about it being sad, and suggested (as one always does in such circumstances) that there were plenty more fish in the sea, and I let him bang on about the exorbitant cost of London (where he'd gone for the day) and the execrable standard of its public transport.

"So, where shall we sit? Sun or shade? What about that table in the corner? Looks fine to me. Shall we? There we go.

"A storm had to blow itself out. It wasn't the right storm. But it was better than no storm at all. Do you like bouillabaisse? If you like bouillabaisse try this one. You've never had bouillabaisse till you've had this one."

+++

My dearest Trove,
My godmother died when I was fifteen or sixteen. I scarcely knew her. But I was devastated. My grandmother (mother's mother) I knew well. And was fond of. Even very fond of. She died when I was twenty-two or – three. I'm not going to say I wasn't saddened by her death, but I didn't think something either huge or cataclysmic had happened. The point I'm trying to make is that age or experience or both inure us to calamity. It's the doctor syndrome, in other words: We cannot feel the wound of each arrow or each sling shot. Certainly not all those of those around us. Our psyches won't allow it. We cannot feel each pain with the intensity of the first – neither our own, nor those of others. If we did, we'd go mad.

I'm saddened by the end of 'us', therefore, but I'm not devastated by it. Nor do I feel devastated by it. Up-front, you said you weren't proposing an affair to rival Romeo and Juliet. I think, frankly, that went without saying. I think we're both too old. I'm no longer as juvenile as Romeo: I no longer believe that the end of 'us' is the end of me. I no longer even believe that the end of 'us' is an indication of the inadequacy of me. If anything, rather the reverse. In our youth we are compatible with a universe of possible partners. Like our skin, our characters are then so elastic or malleable or amorphous we can shape them into virtually anything we choose – or that we need them to be. Oh, I don't think that elasticity is cynical. (Opportunistic, occasionally, when seduction appears to require it, but not openly cynical.) I don't think it's our less than admirable Prime Minister, in other words, wondering which of his several thousand faces would best suit the occasion. I think, rather to the contrary, that it is remarkably ingenuous. In our youth it is precisely that elasticity which frees us up to explore the various dimensions, aspects and qualities of our personalities – sometimes which are very well hidden.

It's, if you like, back-packing of the soul. And that's just as arduous as the physical type. As sapping of energy – and as beneficial. We close avenues at our peril.

Beyond some pre-pubescent fumbling at school, I never had a homosexual encounter. I've never really been tempted to. But, at an intellectual level, I feel the lack of that. I feel it might well be like never having tried … I don't know … sushi, for instance, or a sauna. Sheridan – you've heard me talk of Sheridan – is fond of saying that, sexually, he's not going to die curious. I've always rather envied him that. No. No 'rather' about it.

But, over the years, our characters do start firming up (or seizing up, depending on your point of view). And we find it harder and harder to adapt to the foibles and quirks of others – particularly domestically. We've tried Chinese food, and we know we like bird's nest soup and we don't like sweet and sour shrimp. We no longer need to experiment. And the older we get the less that need.

It's no new thought that life is cyclical. Something else that binds the infant and the dotard is their yearning for the familiar. Because for both, the familiar represents safety – and the new or untried or innovative, those are threatening.

For me *happiness* is threatening. That, I'm sure, sounds odd. Bizarre, even. But I don't think I'm alone. For people like me happiness can seem very threatening. Come from some village in Southern Italy, and the underground system in Milan is threatening. The first time, though, a Milanese visits London, the underground system there, because it is several times larger, that is also threatening. But that threat is nothing against that of a Londoner for the first time presented with the smaller Athens underground system, or the Moscow one. Because for the Londoner not even the characters on the maps there are familiar. In Athens or Moscow, I mean. The place names on the tube map in either place are just for an English speaker so many squiggles.

I know my way around unhappiness. That's what I'm trying to say. It's familiar territory. I know I change at Leicester Square for the Piccadilly line and I disembark at L'Etoile for the Arc de Triomphe. But happiness? That can be really scary. Daunting, even. On a good day, it is Athens – hot, exciting, challenging even, domitable. An adventure. But on a bad day, happiness can seem like the Moscow underground in the middle of a Russian winter during the worst of the Stalinist purges: cold, hostile, dangerous, overpowering, nerve-racking. A nightmare.

And on such days I find myself scurrying back to safety – to the unhappiness I know and that I'm familiar with – with as much despatch as my creaking legs can muster.

You see, I deserve unhappiness.

Well, I don't, of course. No-one deserves it – not as staple fare. And yet for so many of us, myself included, it was that which we heard in childhood. It was that the lesson we took home with us from childhood. And we heard it time after time after time again. You'll notice I don't say that was what I was told. I have no idea. There's so much of my childhood I won't allow myself to remember – and so much more I've simply, and uncompli-catedly, forgotten. But I *am* saying that's what I *heard*. Over and over – and over again.

Yes, from my parents. But, do you know what? I'm not sure *that's* the issue. If it was from my parents that I first heard it, the over and over again which *validated* it, which made it real and keeps it real, that was from teachers, primarily, from friends, from things I saw on television, read in the papers. It was an entire culture which said if I wasn't outstanding I was worthless. And the worthless, so that culture goes on to say, they deserve *every* drop of misery which they create for themselves.

The end of 'us' saddens me for two … entities, I suppose the right word is – for me and for the 'us' that now is no more. For me it saddens me because, with you, I found myself more often on the Athens metro of happiness than the Gulag Express. I was even getting used to the idea of happiness. Thinking of getting my own copy of the tube map. Even – God bless the mark –

believing I was *entitled* to some happiness. And if that sounds whiney then I apologise. It wasn't meant to be. And I certainly do not mean that you introduced me to happiness. There have throughout my life been joyous times – enormously joyous times. And with Eva, I found that a sort of sedentary, un-wow-wooppee un-*un*happiness was possible, even desirable, as an emotional base. (Whereas, pre-Eva, I had always imagined that the only plausible base was one of discontentedness, permanently rumbling, often fractious, sometimes explosive.) With you, I was beginning to find that happiness need not be attached only to the momentary. I was beginning to discover that cohabitation was possible between sedentary contentment and a more restless, more quixotic and temperamental, positive joy. And that such joy does not compromise, but rather enhances, that contentment.

But because I continue today to have that un-unhappiness as an emotional base, it's okay too that the lesson I was receiving from you <u>was</u> truncated. You've embarked me on a journey – something for which I shall always be grateful. More than that. It's now down to me whether or not I continue with it. That is my responsibility. And mine alone.

For 'us', what saddens me about 'us', about the now deceased 'us', is that the lesson *was* truncated. Or, rather, that the scenario was not allowed to play itself out. It's a bit like leaving 'Hamlet' before the dénouement. Oh, you know how it's going to end – there is an inevitability, at that point, about its end. And yet you still need, don't you, to see the bodies strewn across the stage? You still need Ophelia to lose her marbles and for Yorick to be alased over.

I knew we wouldn't last. Maybe even knew we shouldn't. Our flame initially had burnt too brightly. It had to be spent quickly. Had to be. I just felt – feel – that I needed too to experience some kind of flickering and fizzling, not have the light just snuffed out. That bright, bright light. That incandescent flame.

I have loved you, Trove, and I always will. That won't stop me loving others. It might even enable me to love them more completely. Because the love I have for you – as the love I have for Eva – that has been absorbed by me now. It is not even a part of me, but one with me. You have been absorbed as Handel's 'Messiah' has been. Or 'Yesterday'. Or Yorkshire Pudding. And I love having you as integral to me. It is an aspect of my own personality of which I am very fond.

Please look after yourself. Always with my love – Mike xx.

Chapter 8

"I tried to go back to Al. Really. You're looking perplexed. Sure, I was back living with him. What I mean, I tried, I mean, to go back to Al *emotionally.*

"Or do I mean emotionally? Commitmently would be more accurate, I guess. I had to return – I guess this is what I'm saying – to the commitment I'd had. Or made. To the, anyway, *whatever* I had or made.

"Twenty-three years, that's a lot of years. I mean, a *lot* of years. Well, sure, I know, back home, they're handing out prison time like that for going the wrong way down a one-way street. But in most civilised countries, you'd have change – twenty-three years – from a couple of murder sentences.

"Shit, sorry, that was slightly more than unfortunate, that too. I didn't mean it. It just sort of came out, and sort of from nowhere. Don't ask me why – the similarity, I guess, between 'commitment' and 'committal'. Some kind of word play – word *association* – in my head. Not conscious. 'Commit', now I think of it, 'commitment', 'committal': what a strange trio. I mean, clearly they've got the same base, the three of them. 'Parade' and 'paradise', same deal – 'laughter' and 'slaughter'. Those eyes of yours, hon, they've glassed over again!"

+++

Maison d'arrêt de Toulouse-Seysses, 27th April 06
Dear Mom and Dad:
Thank you so much for your letter. Brief though it was, it was incredibly welcome. And let in a chunk of light that was like a fluorescent beam to me.
I do know how much you're hurting and that that hurt was caused by me. And I want you to know therefore how particularly grateful I am for your words.
There is still a chasm – I know that. I appreciate it and do not make light of it. But before any bridge can be built there has to be the agreement that it's a good idea

to build one.

I know we haven't yet arrived at that point. But I think we have arrived at a point where we agree to talk about whether or not a bridge be built. It was a milestone in the Middle East – remember? – when both sides agreed to talk about talks about talks.

I'm rambling on, forgive me. Yes, please do forgive me for that. Because if you forgive me today for that and tomorrow for rambling even more on and on and on, then (at some distant time in the future) there's just a chance you may end up forgiving me for the rest. It is the hope of one day achieving that goal that which pulls me through one bleak and dreary day to the next.

Your loving son – Al.

+++

"Emotionally, is what I'm saying, I needed to be at home. Emotionally, see, all the time now I was with Al, I was with Mike. And when I had sex with Al ... No, I wasn't actually having sex with Mike. But the comparison was constant – and the comparison*s*.

"He'd been a great lover, Al. A *great* lover. But sex in marriage, it all becomes a little bit, doesn't it, like painting by numbers? You know what I mean? Those pictures you can buy – leastways, that you used to be able to – where you paint in the numbered spaces: one is for, like, scarlet, two for olive green, three for chestnut brown ... you know the idea. Well, sex in marriage, doesn't it, becomes rather like that? Two minutes of making out. During the second minute of which, hand goes to right breast. Suck on the right breast ... two, three ... whilst the left hand ... two, three ... tweaks the left's nipple. It's all mechanical. Rote. Sexual parroting ... sexual Pavlov's dogs. *Panting*, I should say, by numbers.

"I make it sound awful. Sorry. It wasn't, and I didn't mean to. I make *him* sound awful. And that's not right either. Or fair. It wasn't and he wasn't. It was, what it was, it was routine. If a routine *had* developed, which it had, and if it *was* routine, which it was, then I was just as guilty as he was of having allowed it to develop.

"More, goddammit. Shoot, yes, more. Because, at the end of the day, the initiative was mine. And that – Jesus, did it ever! – that started to gripe. Of *course* I made all the mistakes: I was the only one *doing* anything. You know what I mean? I mean – Jesus – it's so easy never to make a mistake if you never *do* anything. Know the easiest way never to fall off a horse? Never get *on* one of the suckers.

"It was like a sledge-hammer.

"I was sitting at home one afternoon. No big deal. I wasn't travelling in the direction of Damascus, or anything. This was, what, three weeks, I guess, thereabouts after I'd, as it were, said good-bye to Mike, and I was sitting, I remember, on the couch. Stroking one of the cats. Wondering why it was I was feeling so un-at-home at home. And then it hit me: I *wasn't* at home. *'Course* I wasn't feeling at home, I wasn't there.

"I mean, does a koala feel at home in a bee-hive? Or a penguin in the rain forest?"

+++

"What did I tell you? You ever eaten a bouillabaisse as good as that? You've got a wonderful smile. I'm sure you've been told that a hundred times before. Nevertheless, you should hear it again. A wonderful smile and wonderful eyes.

"Sorry. Back to business. Sorry. No, *why* am I apologising? It *is* a lovely smile. And you *should* be told it is. Michael didn't even mention Petrova in our phone calls. That's how I knew he was still hurting. It was the most deafening aspect of those calls, the silence around Petrova. Thinking about it, that was probably the most resonant aspect of all. Michael normally didn't call unless he was okay.

"Let me make myself clear here: If there were something up with *you*, if there were some crisis in *your* life, Michael was on the phone at least daily. You almost sensed he thrived on it. He was waiting by the telephone, you sensed, waiting like a wolf for a wounded moose to happen by. And when it did, he would pounce. Very concerned, very counselly – and, fairly often, very condescending. As if problems could only be solved – problems could only be *voiced* – if he were the other end of a telephone. A sort of emotional Sherlock Holmes, if you will.

"But if there was nothing happening to *you*, even if big things were happening to *him*, months could go by without his ever making a call. A lot of months.

"At that time, I remember, he had to talk about nothing. Petrova was a taboo subject. I don't think he would have seen it in those terms. I'm sure he wouldn't, in fact. I'm sure he would indeed have vehemently denied it had it been described in those terms. But, de facto, that was what she was. And it was almost as if that had given license for taboo to be hung around the neck of any other subject likely to upset him.

"It took him three calls, for instance, to mention that his grandson had been born: Franklyn Edward. And it only emerged during the reply to 'how's the family?'. 'Fine,' he said. 'Just fine. 'Course Jane's ⋯' – Jane, that was his daughter-in-law – '⋯ Jane's getting a bit tired. Franklyn's not sleeping too well at night. 'Course I told her ⋯'

"'Whoa,' I said. 'Hold your horses there, Michael, a moment. Franklyn? I take it you're now a grandfather.'

"'Did I not tell you?' he asked.

"It was almost the more he cared the less he was able to talk about it."

+++

Maison d'arrêt de Toulouse-Seysses, 7th May 06

Dear Mom and Dad:

I'm really glad that both you (Mom) and Lassie are so much better. It's hard enough to imagine you (Dad) as Dr Kildare. As James Herriot ... no, it's too much.

The news from here isn't, I'm afraid, too great. My attorney(s) had been hoping (as you know) that the prosecution might drop the murder charge. But they won't. Bit of a blow. Still ... The rather more cheerful news is that (most of) the team remains confident they can get me acquitted – at least, of that! I'd like to be acquitted of murder, I must say. And not just because that's likely to be reflected in the sentence.

The other bit of good news is that my French is improving by leaps and bounds. I kept threatening – remember – to go to college. I suppose one way of looking at this, is that it's a rather severe English-type boarding school. Offering some sort of crash course in some sort of French. (Though the French it is, frankly, I'm not sure would be welcomed in the more prissy of the Paris salons!)

The food, as you might expect, is really pretty good. And the prison officers, as you might also expect, are Frenchly officious. The French have always found joy in being arrogant towards Americans. Imagine then their glee that they can be so (oh, and how they can be 'so'!) not only with impunity, but with official sanction!

The thing that most gets to me? That the pace is so petty which so creeps on from day to day.

I've been thinking of contacting Trove. What do you think?

Keep care of yourselves and each other. Stroke Lassie for me.

Your loving son – Al.

+++

"Mike had talked to me. That was his greatest gift to me. And also his greatest non-gift or un-gift or whatever it is the opposite of gift.

"Wham! That hit me too like a sledge-hammer. Sitting on that couch. Stroking the cat. Al and me, we hadn't talked. Wham! We didn't talk.

"Do you know? I don't think we ever talked. Not ever. And I couldn't face that. I was so open, for Christ's sake. I'd been into therapy. Shit, I told you that. *We* had been. Together. I'd poured my heart out at therapy sessions – I told you that too. Then I'd come home and poured my heart out all over again. Or another heart out. A sort of heart extension – it was that I poured out when I got home. There was nothing – *nothing* – that I hadn't told Al about me. Even when *I* was finding out about me. Even the bits of me I didn't want to tell *myself* about, I told him. Even those bits I really didn't like. No secrets. No holds barred – no holds, rather, unbarred. No part of my soul unbarred.

"If there had been that much talking going on, I told myself, we had to have been talking. We had to have been. It wasn't possible for there not to have been.

"Wham! it hit me. *WHAT*?! That was exactly what *had* been happening – or not. *I* had been talking; *we* had not.

"I was Toad delivering a monologue. Worse, I was Toad in a whole bunch of ways delivering a monologue. 'Poop, poop!' I was in fact – 'poop, poop!' – Toad delivering his monologue in a whole bunch of ways I didn't care for. Like Toad I was vain – vainglorious, even. Prompted by vanity, no, motivated, impelled by it, by vanity-glory, vaingloriousness, whatever. 'Poop, poop.' I suddenly saw, like Toad, that I wasn't really too concerned about who was listening to me, whether anyone was. I was more interested in talking than being listened to, I guess is what I mean. I had spoken, I guess I also mean, and therefore I expected that I should have been heard.

"And Al had not spoken. I would, I reasoned, have listened to him *had* he spoken. Do you know, now I'm not so sure?"

+++

My dearest Trove,
It's odd: It was you who wanted me to start this damn writing practice; you're no longer on the scene; and yet I still don't seem able to break myself of the habit. Why is that, do you suppose?

And I write to you, even knowing that it is not to you that I write. There is no realistic prospect of you ever seeing these words, let alone reacting to them – one way or another. And yet, it's this simple: If I don't write to you, then I will not write. There's no-one else I feel a need to talk to. Hold on, let me think about that. No, that's not it, not exactly. It's more like, there's no-one else I want to know about me. Not in this kind of way, nor in this kind of depth.

No, that's not true either. I've been writing also to Drew. I'd like him also to know me better – to know me at all would be okay. And I've tried to be open with him. I've probably been far too open. I really don't know any longer. I'm groping my way through a dark and slimy tunnel. I keep coming across, like, Piccadilly Circus-like underground stations and I simply flounder, not knowing which exit to take, not even knowing which exit I have taken. Not having the faintest idea which direction I'm headed in, or why. Or whether it's the right direction or not. I suppose I'm bound to make some navigational mistakes. And if it's only me who gets wounded by them, that's okay. But it rarely is. And that's less okay.

I accepted a long time ago that our abilities to shield those we love from their own pain is severely limited. There's still a vast difference between that and causing them pain.

Oh Christ, Trove, you know all of this. And I know you know all of this. What the hell am I blathering on about?

There was the time in Oslo – I wonder if you remember: We'd just returned from having that magnificent sea-food dinner on the fjord there by the town hall, and we'd just made love – or were just making love – for the gazillionth time of that trip, and I told you I wanted *you* to fuck *me*. I meant figuratively. But you thought I meant actually and you also thought therefore I was joking. And I got too scared of being pompous or talking symbollocks, so I changed the subject. With despatch. I wanted you inside me, is what I meant. I wanted you to know me as no-one else had, from the inside out.

An Eskimo must get tired of ice-blocks, don't you think? I mean, day after day, chopping up new ice-blocks, building an igloo. Day after day after day. He must yearn, wouldn't you imagine, for some clay bricks or some lengths of timber – anything to give him some respite from bloody blocks of ice? Well, I'm a bit like that these days with secrets. I've igloo'd myself in secrets for too many years. It may be a good way to ward off polar bears, but it gets very lonely inside that igloo – and as cold as hell. Which is quite enough about igloos! The analogy wasn't working very well anyway.

Because most of my secrets I have kept secret even from myself – and it is that, the thing I find most tiresome of all. Oh, mostly I've trained myself out of lying to myself. That was hard work. But that is just ridiculous. It's like cheating, isn't it, at 'Patience'? At 'Solitaire', as you would call it. What on earth's the point? I was amazed how hard it was to break myself of the habit, how engrained it had become. But I did think … Well, when I gave up smoking, I didn't want to find – I would have been really pissed off to find – that my smoking had concealed another addiction to, I don't know, chewing tobacco, let's say. But that was precisely what I did discover when I stopped myself from lying to myself: I found out then I had secrets from myself. Secrets not even I knew about – or even, for Christ's sake, *know* about. Secrets that would be revealed to me by circumstance or coincidence; secrets which I could now understand *were* secrets because now they were no longer being veiled by the lies I told myself.

One secret I had was that, fundamentally, I was a

kind person; but another secret I had was that, even more fundamentally, I was in need of being recognised as one. I was an Alan Ladd, in other words – certainly valiant, but driven less by the need of the moment or by the welfare of his colleagues, and more by the hankering after a medal. Nothing too virtuous in that.

+++

"Hi."

"Trove?"

"You sound surprised."

"I am."

"Nice surprised …?"

"Or?"

"I don't want to ask 'or?'."

"*Nicely* surprised, Trove."

"How have you been keeping?"

"Oh … you know."

"Comme ci, comme ça?

"More 'ça', than 'ci'."

"Same. I told Al about us, Mike."

"Right."

"I felt I had to."

"Yes, I thought probably you would feel that."

"You don't hate me, Mike?"

"Would you like me to?"

"No."

"How did he take it?"

"He said, he figured it had to be something like that."

"Well, it *did* have to be, didn't it?"

"It's twenty-three years, Mike."

"I know."

"Twenty-three years, and all he could say was that he figured it had to be something like that."

"What were you expecting, honey?"

"You called me 'honey', Mike."

"What were you expecting?"

"You never answered if you hated me."

"It was a silly question."

"You called me 'honey'."

"Trove, what were you expecting?"

"Oh, I don't know, after twenty something years, a reaction might've been nice."

"I'm not sure, Trove, that 'nice' was available to him."

"Excuse me?"

"Sorry."

"'Nice' wasn't available to him?"

"I'm sorry, Trove."

"Maybe you should go and fuck *Al*."

"I trod on a corn, Trove. And I apologised. I didn't break your leg."

"No."

"You're hurting. It's okay to hurt."

"And you?"

"You know I'm hurting."

"We're hurting each other, right?"

"Breaking the first condition. That *was* the first condition, right?"

"The second, hon, was that I wouldn't leave Al."

"You haven't left Al."

"For the most part, I have. The physical move, that won't be long."

"I didn't want us, Trove, to split."

"That was kind of tactless."

"Sorry."

"Not the act of an English gentleman."

"You told me to stop all that."

"I did?"

"Opening doors, helping you on with your jacket."

"Why, of all things to believe I meant, Mike, did you choose to believe in that one?"

"I also believed it when you said we were through."

"Did you?"

"No."

"Hey, that was a real long pause, Mike."

"A pregnant pause?"

"I think it miscarried."

"That'd explain the blood on the floor."

"Would it, Mike?"

"No."

"*Do* you believe that, Mike?"

"That we're through?"

"Yeah."

"No. No, I don't."

"I love you, Mike."

"I love you too, honey."

Chapter 9

"Kiss me, Mike."

"You smell of peanut butter."

"What?"

"Very pungent smell, Trove, peanut butter."

"Four months ago would that have stopped you kissing me?"

"You'd have to ask me that four months ago."

"Think about it."

"Four months ago, Trove, would you have *eaten* peanut butter?"

"I always eat peanut butter."

"Right before you were going to kiss me?"

"That's not the same point."

"Think about it."

"Do you like your Limoges Troved, Mike?"

"I can't imagine another kind of Limoges."

"It's lousy, the peanut butter, by the way. I thought you'd like to know."

"I'll write a letter of protest to 'The Times'."

"Better, no?, 'Le Monde'. I want you to want to be here, Mike."

"I do want that."

"I need you, Mike, to want to be here."

"I already said I want to be here."

"I've become needy."

"We're all needy, Trove."

"I don't like it, my neediness. I hear myself whining from time to time."

"You don't whine to me."

"I whine *about* you, Mike. That's almost as bad. Whine about missing you. Neediness, see?"

"I miss you too."

"And you whine?"

"Constantly."

"Who to?"

"Who, Trove, do *you* whine to?"

"I have an army of girlfriends, Mike. Confidantes. Men friends too. Less now than I had. Friends don't like to be whined at."

"Then they're not friends."

"Yes, they are."

"Not true friends."

"Yes, Mike. There's this strange perception ... some woman sometime in history lifted a juggernaut off her child crushed beneath its wheels. Now, anyone who can't lift juggernauts is not fit for motherhood."

"Okay."

"Not everyone, Mike, is an emotional Superman ... or -woman. Most of us, you know, we're carrying too much emotional crap, too much ballast, to be able to fly."

"They don't have to fly, Trove, true friends, they merely have to listen."

"Listening, to a lot of people, is as hard as flying."

"You're very tolerant all of a sudden."

"It's because we're talking in the abstract, hon."

"That does make things easier, yes."

"Face-to-face, they drive me crazy. Why don't they *listen*?, I want to say."

"Right."

"Why *won't* they listen?"

"Right."

"Why don't you, Mike?"

"What?"

"We don't have sex like we used to. You don't listen."

"You think?"

"The sex is a shame. I miss it. Miss the intensity and the ...

ardour, I guess. Miss even the soreness. But that was predictable. Inevitable, in fact. But the listening? No, Mike, that's not inevitable. I need that listening, Mike. I need the intensity of our first listenings together, need that ardour. I warned you about my neediness."

"You did?"

"Am I whining now?"

"Oh yes."

+++

"Digestif of some sort? A cognac, perhaps? How about an armagnac?

"Poire William? I've no idea. I can ask. You're not dashing somewhere, are you? I mean, we can take our time, can we? Enjoy a drink together, stroll back leisurely?

"Good.

"About that sort of time Petrova moved out of the house. When I say 'house', I believe the legal term is 'matrimonial home'. She rented a place. Outside, if I remember correctly, Limoges. Mike, I seem to remember, visited her there. He was still living with Drew. Still somewhere near Nottingham: that's somewhere near where Robin Hood used to live. No, what am I talking about? She didn't rent it at all. No, that's right, it was a 'gite' they'd bought, an investment. Used to rent it out for the summer, that sort of idea.

And, from what I can gather, it was also about that sort of time that Al started drinking. I never really knew him. But I recognised him. He was very recognisable. He always wore that absurd fedora which, absurdly, rather suited him. In a cup final crowd you'd spot Al – spot that red fedora. The whole of Toulouse, I'd venture to suggest, knew that fedora. It's almost as famous locally as he is.

"And, not that I've spoken to too many people about it, but I'd put money on the fact that the whole of Toulouse had never seen that fedora in an otherwise than upright position. I'm trying to say that I don't think anyone had seen Al drunk.

"Suddenly, that fedora was not strutting about town, but lurching."

+++

Maison d'arrêt de Toulouse-Seysses, 12th May o6

Dear Trove:

I would like to write to you. I would completely understand if you preferred me not to. Reply to me only if I may write back. Otherwise, may God keep and protect you.
– Al.

+++

"See, what I'm not saying, I'm not saying I'm leaving Al for you."

"I know."

"I'm leaving him, is what I'm saying. But it's not for you: Not *because* of you, I mean, and not so's I can move in with you. Well, it *is* because of you. 'Course it is. But it's not because I want to move in with you."

"I know this, Trove."

"Not that I could, right? Not even if I wanted to. Right?"

"Right."

"You've still got no place to live."

"I'm okay at Drew's."

"Living at Drew's, though, means you've still got no place to live."

"I've said this a few times, Trove: ..."

"Remind me."

"I want to try and establish a relationship. Create one, or re-discover it or something."

"And *our* relationship, Mike?"

"You're not leaving Al for me."

"But I *can't* – is what I'm saying. I'm saying, Mike, the option isn't open to me."

"Right."

"How do I know, Mike – is what I'm saying – whether or not I'm leaving Al for you when there isn't the possibility that I'm leaving him for you?"

"If I walk out again on Drew, if (as he would see it) I *desert* him again, that'll be it. There'll be no third chance, Trove."

"I know that."

"If our relationship is going to work, honey, this one has got to work too, the one with Drew. This new one also, with Franklyn."

"Christ, Mike."

"You know all this."

"And I don't need lecturing about it."

"I'm sorry."

"I feel so vulnerable here, Mike. So fragile."

"Was I being insensitive? I didn't mean to be insensitive."

"Love always hurts. Why *is* that?"

"Part of being in love is being vulnerable."

"You know what I didn't need just right now?"

"You didn't need a lecture."

"I didn't need a lecture, Mike."

"Right."

"I know I'm vulnerable. Shit, I just said that. Yes, and I do know, hon, you're vulnerable too."

+++

"I'm not quite sure what Pandora's box actually is. I know that's a hell of a confession, but that's the truth. I guess it's something like the bag you don't want to let the cat out of. Well, I'd opened it, that bag, let out not a gentle little moggy, but several prides of ... I don't know ... great goddamn pumas, or something.

"See, what doesn't happen – I thought it did but it doesn't – you don't stuff down one emotion and the rest are all fine. Emotions, see – I understand this now – they've gotten an entire ... physiognomy, is that the right word? ... I *think* that's the right word ... all of their own. They've gotten their own body, is what I'm trying to say. You know, as in sort of arms, legs, liver, big toe, that whole kind of deal. And just like the body, you can't do something to one bit of it without it encroaching on the rest. Did you know the major source of back pain was dental decay? Well, maybe not *the* major source, but certainly *a* major one. Amazing, isn't it?

"Same deal, sort of thing, here. I mean, there's an abscess in my creativity, which leads me to holding my head of love in an odd way, which starts affecting the spine of my peace-of-mind. It all impacts on each other. See, round Al – no, around Al-and-me, around that relationship – I'd stuffed down the emotions. I wouldn't allow myself to feel what it was I was feeling. If I started feeling them, Christ, that might mean I might have to *do* something about it, to change feeling shitty about something into feeling good. Don't want any of *that*, for Christ's sake. Christ, that's almost subversive. Almost un-American, for Christ's sake.

"For *years* I chose rather to ignore my feelings. Rather than deal with them, is what I mean. But I don't beat myself up for that any longer. Not only was that the way I was brought up, it was the expected way of the entire world about me. And it still is. Newspapers and tv shows deride us. Anyone trying to work through problems is seen as a figure of fun. Even Oprah, they try to laugh about. So none of this stuff gets talked about. Not really. Not in any kind of meaningful way. Know the consequence of that? It turns what would be anyway a difficult process into one which is that much harder. And for two reasons.

"Firstly, because those of us embarked on it think we're involved in something, I don't know, sinister somehow or harmful, and we therefore try to make the trip sneakily – like stowaways, kind of deal; and secondly, because if there *is* a map, which I doubt, then that map is kept hidden – and for the same reason.

"Which is why there are so many phoney maps around. I mean, *so* frigging many. Look at the 'Body, Mind and Spirit' shelves of your bookstore. They're *crammed* with phoney guides and invented atlases. There has to be more crap written about self-discovery than about almost anything else.

"See, I didn't realise, if I shoved down all the stuff there was around the 'us' of Al and me, I had to shove down very big bits too of me – the Al-less me. I had to. You can't put on a pantyhose without also covering your feet. If we suppress one chunk of our emotions, other chunks (whether we want them to or not) also get suppressed. And if I start suppressing chunks of me, it's no longer possible for me to be the me that, above all else, I'm supposed to be true to.

"And it's more accurate to say that than that I'm being *untrue* to myself. I'm being true to myself, alright. I've spent a lifetime being true to myself. Only problem was, that *wasn't* myself: It was an imitation of myself, an abridged version, a Wilde who wasn't bisexual or a Wagner who wasn't an anti-Semite.

"Lady Macbeth – She is the one, right, who killed the king? Then got her husband crowned? – Just checking. If she'd really have known herself, Lady Macbeth, would she, is what I'm asking, have had the king killed? Wouldn't someone who really knew herself say to herself, 'Who do you think you're kidding, girl? The price you'll have to pay'll be too high. *Way* too high. You'll end up cracking, not being able to wash the blood off of your hands.' If a person really knew himself, is what I'm asking, would he ... I don't know ... trample all over his rivals to make a billion dollars ... or invade a foreign country to get Pop's approval ... or ... or ... or?

"We talk about these things as if they were exclusive to us, as if they had no effect – at all – on other people's lives. We talk about them like the drunk talks of his drink. 'Even if it *is* a problem,' we say to ourselves, 'I'm not saying it is, but even if it were, the problem it is, it's no-one's but mine.' Meantime his kids are shop-lifting, his wife is demented, his parents don't know whether or not to call the Social Services.

"You been into a jail recently? Of course you have! Jeez, *of course* you frigging have. Sorry, that's just me being dumber than usual. Duh! Well, next time you're there, you take a straw poll, find out how many of the inmates there have happy memories of childhood. These are people who go on to *destroy* other people's lives. Not even Hitler was born. Somehow we created him. And it frightens the crap out of me that we don't ask ourselves how in the fuck we managed to build ourselves a Hitler.

"But that, that extreme, those kinds of extreme, they're not even the tip of the iceberg: They're the *tip* of the tip of the iceberg. Most of the problems which possess us or consume us are *completely* invisible – many of them even, for Christ's sake, to ourselves. Probably most of them.

"You know all I know opening Pandora's box? Letting some of the emotions breathe which I had suppressed? The only thing I've learnt, the only piece of knowledge I now have that I didn't is ... wait for it ... wait for this cataclysmic announcement ... all I now know is that I've got a couple of problems; that there are a couple of things about myself I don't like; a couple of things I need to change.

"No, I need something else too: I need someone else around me who knows *he's* got problems, who knows enough about himself to want to change himself. If only a little. Maybe even herself would be alright. Maybe."

+++

"Know how long the pause was?"

"What?"

"Since we spoke, know how long the pause was?"

"You can't, Trove, spend your whole life eating."

"What does that mean?"

"We need some time off eating in order for the food to digest. Talking's not dissimilar."

"Know how long it is, Mike, since we *truly* spoke?"

"I'm not holding anything back."

"You're holding *everything* back, Mike."

"No."

"I'm beginning to think ... No, forget it."

"Not *intentionally*, Trove, holding anything back."

"I don't know whether I believe you or not."

"That's a pretty painful thing to say."

"It's also painful, Mike, what I'm hearing. What I'm not hearing: this oh so eloquent fucking silence. See, I asked – this is what it feels like – I asked for champagne. Not Dom Perignon, I don't think, not even the vintage stuff, just common-or-garden, break-it-over-the-nose-of-a-launching-ship champagne. And what I get, Mike ... from Al, what I got was grape juice, and from you I get goddamn Asti. Oh, you seem like champagne. Drunk enough (as I was at the beginning – drunk, I mean, on love), it might even *taste* like champagne. But, know what, hon? Asti, that's even more phoney than grape juice. And, because there was that much more deception, there's therefore that much more disappointment involved."

"You want me to react."

"Something might be nice. Some kind of recognition that I've just said something."

"I don't know *how* to react."

"And you seriously believe, Mike, that's *not* a reaction?"

"Is it some kind of axiom that if it starts hard it has to get harder?"

"I hope that wasn't some kind of really bad dirty joke."

"I wasn't joking, Trove."

"No."

"This is painful for me too."

"Yes."

"Yes."

"It's more, Mike, it's more ... window-shopping, I guess, is so much better than shopping."

"Right."

"The bikini is sexier than the birthday suit."

"Right."

"Disneylife is so much easier, hon, than real life."

"I get the point."

"The trouble is, Mike, if we blow a bubble and the bubble bursts ..."

"Poof!"

"Poof, as you say. A splash of detergent and then ..."

"Nothing?"

"Nothing."

"That's what we've got, Trove?"

"Nothing?"

"Yes."

"That what you think?"

"I asked first."

"If the question, Mike, is not as rhetorical as the answer, shit, then we do have nothing."

"There's gold, Trove, in them there pauses."

"They do seem to be getting longer."

"But not more eloquent?"

"No, Mike."

"Is there such a thing as a rhetorical answer?"

"Look in a mirror."

"Mirror?"

"Look in it, Mike, you'll *see* a rhetorical answer."

"I think I even know that."

+++

Maison d'arrêt de Toulouse-Seysses, 21st May 06

Dear Trove:

It was generous of you to write back so quickly. You've said often enough that I'm unemotional – accused me of it, even. I wasn't 'unemotional' – that I can promise you – when I got your letter. Hosts of emotions charged through me at that point. And each one gave birth to another. And each gave birth also to a tear. There was, by the time I'd finished, a small lake in the middle of my cell.

Another thing you often accused me of was never telling you anything. About that you were righter. But, you know what?, so were my protests that I told you everything. You see, it was that 'everything' meant something different to me than it did to you. In those days, I didn't think everything meant *everything*. I thought it meant every-*big*-thing or -*important*-thing ... every-*significant*-thing. Headaches weren't significant, they weren't part of everything. The only 'everything' worth mentioning was a brain tumour.

Wealth here is a packet of 'tailor-mades' (as pre-rolled cigarettes are called); a carton of those makes you a billionaire. What I'm struggling to say is that, stripped of everything, you realize it is only – finally – the headaches that *are* significant. The extraordinary, you start to realize, is far more present in the mundane than in the fantastic, far more present in the present than in the future, far more grounded than it is celestial or supernatural.

There is so much I now need to tell you, so many headaches and pin-pricks I need to let you know about. I don't know where to start. And, Jesus, I want to do it right.

I have a need, Trove, to do it right.

I've done so many things so wrong, mismanaged the whole of my life so completely, I have a need now to do one thing right. Finally one thing right.

That one right thing, Trove, is writing to you. I've got so much time in here – *so* much. I can afford to do draft after draft. I *will* get it right. I owe you that. Oh, no question about that. But know what? I also owe myself that.

Once before I die, my voice *will* be heard.

Know something else? I'm not at all sure what I mean by that. I do know I had to write it, though. I'll try and figure out why later, and get back to you.

I don't even know that the letter will be written before the trial. It's not something which responds to time pressure.

Do you yet know whether or not you intend to come? I know that's your decision, and (for what it's worth) I'll be okay with whatever your decision is. I'm just trying to decide what I would like that decision to be. The truth is that I don't know.

And the truth is also that that is the truth.

This is all very ramshackle. Sorry. I don't want 'the' letter to be the same. I want it to be clear and cogent and ... me.

Thank you for helping me towards that. You know, I hope, this is sent with love — Al.

+++

Dear Trove,
You're lying next to me in bed. It's like there is an ocean between us. We could make love and there would still be an ocean between us. It's as though our very nearness is distancing us from each other.

I think I'm responsible for that. And that thought further heavies my heart. (Yes, I do know there is no verb 'to heavy'! There is a time for pedantry and a time for laissez-faire. And I've, of course, now realised that even to make this point is the act of a pedant. And you also know what? I don't know whether that's ironic or indicative or irrelevant or ... well, anything else.) I don't know how I'm responsible. But not knowing how does not mean that I am - or am not.

I want to lean over and shake you. And I want to say to you, "For Christ's sake, let's talk. We have to talk. This is us, Trove. We owe it to ourselves, for Christ's sake, to talk." You texted me once, I wonder whether you remember. 'Could we,' you wrote, 'be the love of each other's lives?' 'Yes, we could,' I replied. And for the love we could be of each other's lives I want to sit you bolt upright, and I want to thrash it out. Whatever the hell 'it' is.

And I want to lean over and kiss you, rouse you gently and lovingly, lots of kissing and tasting and brushing. And I want to mount you languorously and simmer you into a frenzy. I want to lean over and take you. Brutally. Bruisingly. Hurt you. Scorch you into a frenzy. I want to lean over and hold you and cry with you about the absurdity of life and the absurdity of us and to feel your skin as I cry and to lap your tears from the corners of your eyes. I want to lean over and lie with you and gaze up at stars and be overcome by the wonder of it all and revel in all its mystery and mysteries. I want to talk until the cows come home and bask in silence forever.

And I won't do any of those things. Probably because I'm a coward. The coward's punishment is not that he disappoints others but that he disappoints himself. Caliban, when he tried to rape Miranda, was punished by being nipped incessantly by crabs – 'pinched', I think the actual word is. That's how it feels, Trove. It feels like I'm nipped, by a thousand disappointments. Pinched permanently by them. And the biggest and most permanent nip of all, the kind of monster crab whose claws dwarf all of those around him, that is the disappointment that I seem to be unable to learn from my mistakes.

That's gnawing at me now as I write. Weevilling into me. Spreading, cancer-like, all over me; like a cancer, trailing a path of destruction. Emotional organs damaged beyond repair: the capacity to give.

I thought I gave. Really and sincerely. Really and sincerely, I mean, I thought I gave really and sincerely. But that's all it was. I didn't give. I just thought I did. As I thought I talked. But the action was the thinking not the talking. My hand had the fiver poised above the charity tin – but it never let loose of the money. It's

Buddhists, isn't it, who believe the intention is more important than the act? I can't help feeling I took them a little too literally.

You look so peaceful. So peaceful. The Earth too looks peaceful, seen from space. I mean, which alien flying past us wouldn't say to itself, "What a beautiful place that looks like. How tranquil and colourful and serene. What an amazing place to live!"

We're in orbit, aren't we, around our fellow human beings? We see them from afar, see the oceans and the continents, the blues and browns and yellows, the greens and whites, and we have no idea – not the foggiest bloody notion – of the turbulence that's actually going on. Our own private presidents and prime ministers, our own earthquakes and hurricanes, our own riots and revolutions and genocides and apartheids. Our own Hells. Even, I suspect, our own Heavens.

We are, each one of us, also our own universe. And maybe that's thrilling. Maybe I should find it thrilling. But I don't. I find it chilling. Not thrilling but chilling. Is that my epitaph? Is it ours?

+++

"I liked to think, see, that I was unpredictable. Mike, I thought, was attractive to me because, like me, *he* was unpredictable. I thought, in that as in so many other things, I'd found a kindred spirit.

"And then, know what? I started finding a pattern to Mike's unpredictability. Not a template, you understand. Not quite. But more of a template than I liked. And much more of one than *he* would have liked, Mike. Whose unpredictability, I realised, had an element in it of being forced. The unpredictability, is what I'm saying, was not as spontaneous as he would've liked it to be – not even as spontaneous as he imagined it to be.

"And know what then? I started finding a pattern also in *my* unpredictability. And that was *really* the pits. I started finding out there was around my unpredictability that which was forced – and that which, therefore, was predictable. Man, did that hurt!

"Ever tried taking advice? Is that hard or what? Ever tried *giving* it? Easiest thing in the whole frigging world. You don't have to be a friend to give advice, but – shit – you know your friends if they sit down and take it.

"See, being predictably now (as it were) unpredictable, I had to do something *unpredictably* predictable. I went round to see Al.

"I'd moved out by then. Did I say that? I'd moved to a little summer place we had – very rentable, very utilitarian, very hotel-décor and -feel. An anonymous kind of a place. I'm a lot of things, but an anonymous kind of a gal ain't one of them. I tried to like that holiday home, that *gite*. I tried to think it was good for my soul – to be alone and, as the place was, isolated. I tried to think it was strengthening, and that I'd be helped to some pretty crucial decisions.

"What the hell did I want to do with the rest of my life? That was one. They don't really come a lot bigger than that.

"I'd made strict rules. Al did not visit without calling first. And that, 'course, went for me too. 'Cept one day I was in town. And I, you know, just had to use the bathroom and I thought, what the hell, the house is just around the corner and Al's bound to be out – 'cause it was that time of day when Al was always out – and, like I say, what the hell, I thought.

"What the hell?

"Well, it *was* a hell. A hell of a hell, in fact. In fact, a black hole of Calcutta kind of a hell. It was hard to believe it was the same house. I mean, don't get me wrong, little Miss Houseproud I ain't, but this … this was just disgusting. If I said 'shit-hole', I'd be being unfair to shit. There were half-eaten meals all over the place, grains of rice trodden into the rugs, the shards of potato chips, pizza boxes like it was a branch or something of Pizza Express. The cats had been sick and he hadn't cleaned up the vomit. There were streaks of ketchup on the walls. Christ, it was horrible. Disgusting, like I said. But the worst of it, the absolute worst of it, was the bottles. The *cans* and the bottles, I should say. They were everywhere. I mean *everywhere*. Beer, wine, that cheap Spanish brandy, pastis ... some of it drunk, some of it still seeping into the rugs.

"Al was never Mr Smart – but he wasn't Mr Filthy. And, you know what, I'd've been okay with it if I'd called ahead and let him know I was coming. I'd have thought it was like set dressing or something. I might have told him he'd gone way over the top, but it wouldn't have alarmed me. What did alarm me was that this image, this vision of hell, this Dante's goddamn 'Inferno', this was for *no-one's* benefit. This was just Al being what Al had become.

"And I really did almost use the bathroom – 'cept not to pee in, but to throw up. My stomach was heaving just like a cat's with a fur ball. And I knew I had to get out of that place. I had to. Right then. Or I would have chucked up. No question.

"'Course it was a cry for help. 'Course it was. You didn't have to be Sigmund Freud to know that. But who the hell was he crying to? There was one of those wildlife documentaries I saw. (I'm not really very into them, so this one that I saw, I think I was round at someone's house. It might've been Al's parents now that I think of it.) An adolescent wolf had gotten separated from the pack. He was lost. The image was stark. The moon crescented silver onto a sequinned snow. And there was this wolf. This lone vulnerable and frightened wolf. And he was baying forlornly to the moon. That was Al, it occurred to me. That was who Al was crying to for help: a silver moon crescenting onto a sequinned snow.

"And I wanted to howl as well. Howl not for my loneliness but his. For his vulnerability and fear.

"Except that it wasn't. It *was* for mine."

Chapter 10

"I didn't leave Al for you."

"Right."

"I did tell you that."

"You did, yes, Trove, tell me that."

"See, what I'm not saying, Mike, I'm not saying we won't keep on seeing each other."

"Right."

"And when I say 'see each other' I mean 'sleep with each other'."

"Right."

"Though probably there won't either be a lot of sleeping done."

"No."

"Right, Mike?"

"Oh, right."

"What I *am* saying, I *guess* what I'm saying, I'm saying because, Mike, I left Al, it doesn't mean I left him for you."

"You did, Trove, tell me that."

"Did I? Did I tell it enough that you understood?"

"You did and I do."

"Do you, though?"

"Understand?"

"Yes."

"Yes, Trove."

"Really, I mean? Fundamentally? I mean, I know you understand the words. But do you understand the concept? Fully, I mean? Its implications? Have you, as I think you might say, 'taken it on board'?"

"Jesus Christ! I understand, Trove."

"Do you prefer your Nottingham Troved, honey, or Troveless?"

"You're starting a new sport, I see."

"New sport?"

"Called 'brazen' fishing."

"What's a brazen look like? I want you to want me to be there, Mike."

"I do want you here."

"I need you, Mike, to want me to be there."

"I'm experiencing some déjà-vu, here."

"Déjà-vu me to bed, then."

"You just want me for my body."

"Are you complaining?"

"Not yet."

+++

"Petrova followed him back to England. She wanted to know him, she said, in *his* environment, wanted to know him in an ambience where he was at home and she was clearly the stranger.

"Except that, of course, Mike was no longer at home in England. England had moved on, you see, from the England Mike had known. I feel when I'm in England very much the same. It's like meeting a lover again you haven't seen in twenty years: She's so different she's almost not the same person. The wrinkles are the easy bit. It's the inside wrinkles that are so difficult to cope with: the wisdom bestowed by life or the damage done by it. The stranger feels more comfortable with this new person considerably sooner than the ex-lover.

"Those of us who were used to typewriters took a great deal more time learning to work a computer than the two-fingered typists. Sometimes it is the process of *un*learning which is the hardest one of all. Thus it was with Petrova and Michael. She became familiar with England far more quickly than he did. And therefore England was clearly not the ambience in which she was clearly the stranger. Indeed, if anything, it was even more clearly he who was. "That was, I think, cause of more friction than either of them chose to acknowledge.

"Mike, now I think about it, he'd moved out of Drew's by then. He'd rented a broom cupboard somewhere close-by. He couldn't live any longer 'en famille', but he was absolutely determined, so he then insisted (and, yes, I do think he was being sincere), to have a relationship, if not with Drew himself, at least with Franklyn, his grandson. His wife had joked that his only commitment was to a lack of commitment. I think it was worrying him that he was starting to agree with her. And that hurt him, I think.

"Do you ever take a rest from work? How long have we been at this now?

"No, no, no, I have absolutely nothing else to do. Just one thing, though, if I later take you out to dinner, that dinner is a date. As in boy-meets-girl date. We're not just moving the venue of our conversation.

"Well, that begs the question, then: Will you have dinner with me?

"Good. Well, then, that *is* a date.

"The other source of friction ⋯ You are very lovely, you do know that? ⋯ The other source of friction was that Mike simply would not introduce her to Drew. He thought it an unnecessary complication. And he had a point. But she felt rejected. Maybe even cheapened. And, if she did feel that, *she* had a point as well. But also, as I said earlier, as far as Petrova's concerned, I have to do a fair amount of brain-reading, so that is only surmise.

"Another glass of wine?"

+++

"He tried not to make this big thing out of something that wasn't a big thing. I mean, Christ, why would I *want* to meet his son, or his grandson? They didn't live with him any longer. I'd meet them when I met them. There was no rush. No big deal either.

"And then, all the other so-called 'no big deal's, they started to become them. They became deals first, and then, cumulatively, that's what they became: *big* deals. All the 'no big deals' we weren't talking about, or we were glossing over, or we were putting to one side until we'd talked about the deals that *were* big deals.

"You've heard about the elephant in the kitchen – the thing that, however obvious, no-one talks about – well, they exist. Of course they exist. Mike called it 'the galley pachy', short for 'galley pachyderm', nothing to do with Pakistan. It's not a mythological creature, and certainly not an endangered species. I doubt there's a kitchen anywhere in the world which doesn't house at least one. But the elephant isn't the *only* thing in the house, is what I'm saying.

"See, even when there's a war on, is what I'm saying, the dog still needs to be fed.

"We concentrate so much on the galley pachy, we forget also there's cheetahs in the parlour, and conger eels in the bathroom. No, no, it's not that. Well, it *is* that, of course it's that. I mean, like I say, in wars people still get killed by cancer and by cars. And it's important, 'course it's important, that we recognise that.

"But it's also important that we recognise that we don't recognise everything.

"I mean, the elephant's easy. It's big and grey and got a trunk. The cheetahs and the conger eels, they're easy too. But there are so many creatures in our domestic, let's say, menagerie that we just don't see: the dust-bunnies behind the cupboards, for instance. Virtually of no significance at all, except that, by not recognising them, they assume an importance.

"And then there are the microscopic foes, the viruses and bacteria of the soul. I mean, I doubt even Mao managed to kill more people than the Black Death. There are these microscopic foes too attacking our souls, if you like, the core of our emotions. Those things that are gnawing at you, but you just ignore them – or should that be, you just 'ig-gnaw' them? Sorry. You know what I mean, though. You kind of know you're not up to speed, you're two degrees under – whatever the expression is – but because you're not actually running a fever or going through a ream of Kleenex each day, you ignore it. You tell yourself you're just imagining it.

"And none of which is to mention the intangible beasts – the sort of poltergeists, if you like, of the house's aura. The intangibles, the 'I'm-not-sure-whether-they're-there-or-not's, the imponderables, the abstracts, the sensed and the imagined. And – shit – those babies *really* need to be talked about. Christ, those mothers can wreak *so* much havoc. 'Did you just mean what you said?'; 'You know how mean it was, what you just said?'

"And suddenly, Mike and me, we weren't talking about any of those suckers any more. Because we weren't talking about the elephant, we'd stopped talking too about the mice and the lice. Know what? If you don't deal with the lice and the mice, there's no *point* talking about the elephant."

+++

Maison d'arrêt de Toulouse-Seysses, 25th May o6

Dear Mom and Dad:

It was good to see you today. I know it wasn't good for you. And for that reason I was doubly grateful. (Is it me, or these days am I always 'doubly' grateful?) No, I'm more than doubly grateful. Jetting all the way here, leaving home, all that, dealing with all the bureaucracies and the embassies, all that as well. All *that* pressure as well. Dealing with the *French*, for God's sake, and in *France* – and *in* French. Christ, Congressional Medal of Honor stuff, Mom and Dad. Thank you. Thank you so much.

I saw on your faces how unspeakable it was, the visit, how hard for you not just to cry, or despair. I'd forgotten. Prisoners become inured to prison. We're with it the whole time. You on the outside, however, you who visit the watering-hole only from time to time, you haven't the time to build your shield. And for you therefore it is both shocking and a shock.

There is always beauty. Even within grimness there is beauty. I vaguely remember Oscar Wilde saying something about there being worse places to end up than prison. I now know what he meant. As I also know you don't. And can't.

It's written, isn't it, over the gates of Hell: 'Abandon hope all ye who enter here'? It's written over the gates of any hell. And it is the secret of surviving it. If you have no hope you have no future. And the absence of any future means that you have to live in the present. You just have to. And, living in the present, you have to find succour and joy in the present. Anything else leads not to no-hope but to hopelessness. A lack of hope is not hopelessness. Hopelessness leads to lunacy. But a lack of hope leads to a certain focus, even a certain clarity. A clarity both of vision and of sight. A painter's clarity. Even an abstract painter's.

I'm alright. I suppose that's what I'm trying to say. And what I was trying to say when you were here. And couldn't. No, I'm not all alright. Not: hey! fantastic! how right I am. But alright. I am alright. And I'm alright being alright. I'd be more alright if you were alright too. But I know you aren't. And can't be. And my being less alright than I might be because you can't be alright, that too – finally – I'm alright with. I keep hoping, if you know I'm alright, that may just help you too to find some kind of all-rightness with the situation. Okay, enough.

I heard again from Trove. Not a long letter, nor a very intimate one. Full of news about the weather, mutual friends. I derive some comfort, though, from her continued correspondence. She's offered to come and visit, but I don't think I'm quite ready for that.

The thing is ... the thing I'm not alright with, is what I did. I can't come to terms with it. I can never forgive myself for it. And that puts me into a minority of one in the prison population. Which is around the 1,000 mark. Of which 999 are innocent. And I am guilty. Probably more guilty than of just those offences I've been charged with. Condemned or acquitted, I will remain guilty. And no punishment inflicted on me by the state will ever equal that handed out to me by me and my conscience. Handed out to me with vengeance and with a vengeance.

Want still to help me? Then teach me how to live with that. I'm more than anxious for your forgiveness. Even – don't laugh – for Trove's. Mostly because I *know that, from me, I will never get it – forgiveness.*

Thanks again. Take care of yourselves. With my love – Al.

+++

"You have to know one thing: I'm doing this for Al.

"I mean, if I didn't think this might help Al … sister, you wouldn't see me for dust.

"I don't want to see Al behind bars. Jesus! There's not too many people, frankly, I *would* like to see behind them. There's Bush, of course. And Jane Fonda, maybe. But that's only 'cause she gets on my tits.

"Why did I do that? Will you answer me that? Why the hell did I *do* that? Do you know how much I hate that expression, 'get on my tits'? Do you know how much I despise – and vilify – the people who use it? And then, who goes and uses the frigging thing? There are times, Trove, there are times, hon, when I simply do not believe you.

"What I was trying to say: The last person, I was trying to say, the last person in the whole goddamn world bar none who should be behind bars is Al. Al freaks out if he drops me off in the car on a Sunday where there's parking restrictions on a weekday; Al slows down if he sees a pedestrian in the same street as a pedestrian crossing. And if you don't know that, you don't know him.

"And he doesn't do those things, Al, out of fear or anything, out of not wanting to get into trouble. He begged his folks to let him go on freedom marches – aged, what?, six and a bit? He burnt his draft card, emigrated to Canada. He's not afraid of authority, nor shy of challenging it. But he sees the sense in laws. He obeys laws – to the letter – because he does see the sense in them. Like I say, the last person in the world who should be behind bars.

"And I'm sure as hell not doing anything to get him put there. I'd rather be behind bars myself.

"Tell you the truth, I have to convince myself – I *sometimes* have to convince myself – that I shouldn't be there anyway. Behind bars. I feel responsible, is what I'm saying. Responsible for so much of it. I mean, I blamed Al for not talking, but I put up with his not talking. I put up, for Christ's sake, with *our* not talking. And I forget that sometimes. Just as sometimes I forget it also takes two not to tango.

"Why do you suppose it was that 'tango' was used for that expression? I mean, you can't waltz alone either, can you? Or foxtrot or quickstep? Foxtrot's part of the international code, isn't it, for 'f'? 'Foxtrot Oscar', that's probably the most frequent combination of words heard over official airwaves, wouldn't you think? So, why isn't it that we say 'it takes two to foxtrot'? Or, in this case, not? Your eyes have glassed over again, honey.

"After that time with the drink – being confronted by all that mess at the house, all those empty cans and bottles – I was, I don't know, a bit … circumspect, let's say, about going back to the house again. And yet I was pulled to it with incredible force. I mean, *incredible* force. It was like the early days again of quitting smoking. You know, when you're revolted by it – I mean, it is a *disgusting* habit, right? – and yet drawn to that disgusting habit like it was the greatest thing that ever existed. You really hate it and you crave it at one and the same time. Same deal.

"It wasn't either the house that I craved. It was the mess. And the fact that Al was living in it. That was another element I both hated and craved. So, phoning'd have been of no use. He'd have tidied the house – he wasn't that far gone. Or if he hadn't, the message would have become more apparent. He'd have been baying not at the moon, but at me. He'd have tidied, gotten rid of the empties, depizza'd the paintwork. The acceptable face of Al living alone would again be presented. And that didn't do it for me. Not at any level.

"I found myself opting to go to shops that took me past the door. Then I found myself actually detouring to do so. And then I started detouring and checking whether he was in or out.

"I lasted three days.

"It was nine o'clock that morning. Al was always in his studio by nine o'clock. Usually before. Regular as clockwork. More regular. But still – sixth sense, I guess, something like that – I kept real quiet. I mean, burglar quiet. Made sure the latch didn't shoot back in a rasp, you know what I'm talking about. And Al was shouting from upstairs. Something like, 'The water's getting cold, honey. You coming or what?' And then, also from upstairs, from the direction of our bedroom, a woman's voice. 'J'arrive,' she said in that mock testiness of new 'amour'. 'J'arrive.' Nothing something-like about *those* words. 'J'arrive,' she said and I can hear her saying it just as clearly as if it were five minutes ago.

"'J'arrive.'"

+++

"You haven't phoned me, Mike."

"You asked me not to."

"You never used to do what I told you to do."

"Not true."

"And you're not 'honey'ing me either."

"I have always, honey, done exactly what you told me to do."

"Not in bed."

"In bed, Trove, I know better."

"I'm in bed now."

"I didn't know that."

"I'm in bed, Mike, and you didn't call me."

"I apologise."

"I like it when you apologise."

"I do a lot of it, Trove."

"You do it so well."

"I've had so much practice."

"Apologise to me again."

"There is such a thing, Trove, as too much practice. I need to see you again."

"That wasn't a pausette."

"A full-fledged pause, you're right."

"A pause, maybe, and a half."

"X-rated, you're right. An entitled-to-vote pause."

"I only left yesterday."

"It's too long. I need to see you again."

"I haven't recovered yet."

"When can we see each other again?"

"We said, remember, we needed time apart?"

"I do remember."

"You couldn't even go a measly twenty-four hours without calling."

"*You* called *me*, Trove."

"You spend your whole life, hon, splitting hairs?"

"Sorry."

"Oh!"

"What?"

"The way you say 'sorry', Mike."

"I thought you liked it."

"I love it."

"And that's why you're complaining?"

"Not complaining. Sighing in appreciation."

"Right."

"Complaining too, of course."

"Of course."

"It makes me gooey. I hate it, Mike, that it makes me gooey. I hate *being* gooey, for Christ's sake. Like I hate you."

"Hate me?"

"For making me gooey. You know how many pairs of knickers I'm getting through these days? Daily, I mean? You know how much more washing I have to do, Michael? I should be suing you for damage to my hands."

"Such beautiful hands."

"Ever been to Madrid?"

"Of course."

"I think, Mike, I could sneak a weekend to Madrid in three

weeks."

"When will you know?"

"I have this possessive lover, you see."

"Right. Any idea when he might let you know, Trove?"

"*I'll* let *you* know."

"I'll call you."

"No, Mike. What are you talking about? You mustn't call me. We had an agreement, remember?"

+++

My dearest Trove,

I do begin to see how it is people find solace in the confessional. I start to feel lighter having written these letters to you. When I finish each one (I mean), I feel a little lighter.

It's all a very new experience to me. Maybe not virginally new, but certainly adolescently. I've been trying to remember: was my up-bringing to do with not having feelings or was it to do with suppressing them? To be honest, I can't remember any longer. If truth be known, it was probably some kind of amalgam of them both. Crying wasn't actually forbidden either at home or at school. But it was ... not even discouraged ... it was just unusual. Inappropriate. Ordering sushi in an Indian restaurant, wearing jeans to Ascot. Not done. A mark of social impropriety, of unawareness or uncouthness.

In 'Brief Encounter' did they even kiss? You remember, the wartime film about a clandestine, almost illicit, romance? With Trevor Howard and Celia Johnson. I don't think they ever kissed. In order to distance himself from adulterous temptation, Trevor Howard's prepared to bury himself in the African jungle, but he's not prepared to kiss. There was still a lot of that kind of ... I don't know *what* it was ... going on in my childhood. What *was* it? Double-standards? Dishonesty? Hypocrisy? It was all of those things, of course it was, and yet it wasn't *just* those things. There was something within it, whatever it was, striving to be noble or honourable or something. There was a certain *selflessness* attached to it, I think, or some sense of obligation trying to worm its way through a miasma of less honourable intentions.

I don't think we can ever forget about our parents that they stopped Hitler. No generation needs an aim beyond that, nor an achievement. (The achievement of our generation, however, has just been to allow greed off the lead. That, though, is another story.)

In war, emotions have to be checked. If you allowed yourself in war to feel everything you needed to, you'd soon become catatonic, unable to do anything at all. And our primeval instincts for survival debar that from happening. So, we go into emotional lock-down. You and I, Trove, we were brought up in the emotional lock-down.

I first found emotions ... I was going to say, I first found emotions with Eva, but that simply isn't true. For all their suppression, I'd had emotions all my life. Even intense ones. They were like guilty secrets. I don't think I ever bedded a girl without loving her. However briefly. Even the drunk or stoned one-night stands of adolescence. I wanted intensely, certainly hated intensely, felt ... mostly intensely. But I strove lackadaisically and fought without fervour. Inside I was Lenin or Prince Hal; but outside I was Estragon or Buster Keaton. Maybe the Mona Lisa would be more accurate. I think it was obvious something was happening within. It was what that something was which was the enigma. To me, I'm talking about. I was an enigma to myself. Not to anyone else.

I'm not too sure any of us are enigmas to others. I

don't think we, as individuals, are considered by our acquaintances to be worthy of too much thought. I don't think our acquaintances think of us in those terms, as being enigmas or paradoxes or whatever. What you see, they think, is what you get. You're either a good bloke or a pain-in-the-arse.

And how many relationships does _that_ screw up? Before they've even started, I mean.

It wasn't even with Eva that I started letting emotions out. They were already, you know, seeping through the cracks. I suppose, what it was, with Eva I was encouraged to let out my emotions.

What I didn't realise - not until I met you - the only emotions I was encouraged to let out were the safe ones: Oh, being incensed by Reagan, for instance, or by some wickedness perpetrated by Thatcher. It was okay, with Eva, to rant about such things, about the evils of evil people. No, it was alright to _complain_ about such things: _Ranting_ was not encouraged!

It was alright to complain that I was tired, or to canoodle that I was feeling randy; alright to moan about work or the weather or the interest rate. It was even okay to start acknowledging things that weren't okay. I was allowed to be frustrated or feel short-changed. Not too much. But some.

What became different with you was that with you I was able also to acknowledge the _un_safe emotions. Emotions that you might find threatening or that you intuited I might find threatening. All the anger welling inside. That Mount Vesuvius of anger. Welling, did I say? Gurgling, more like, spitting, rumbling, belching. The molten lava of that anger.

And it is dangerous - _they_ are, such eruptions, such _threats_ of eruption. There is a violence and a strength in them which is intimidating and scary. Only an idiot would not be frightened of it – and in awe of it.

I can't remember who it was who said, "Courage is not an absence of fear. Courage is having the fear and triumphing over it." I think it might have been Mandela but it doesn't really matter who said it, its truth speaks for itself.

And that was your courage, Trove.

And your courage it was which led me to unmask mine. And that's what now makes it worse. Because now I know that somewhere in me there is courage and I can no longer find the bloody thing.

Know the frustration of mislaying your glasses or your car keys? It's that kind of deal. Only a hundred times worse. A thousand times bloody worse.

And that caused the problems with my sleeping.

There was a time in my adolescence – a particularly dreadful time in what was generally, and almost exclusively, an awful time – a time when I had so many nightmares I started to get frightened of going to sleep. Touch wood, I've never returned to quite such a dreadful sleep pattern. But if that was the Pacific Ocean, I have since had my Mediterranean blues. And I have had my Black Seas.

When Eva was dying, that was one Black Sea. Fractious sleep I had then. An almost cantankerous sleep. A gnarled, embittered old hag I had then of sleep. The odd nightmare now and again. Made worse by the fact I couldn't scream in my sleep for fear of waking her.

And when I first started my affair with you …

No, around you I had three different types of sleep. The first I misunderstood. The first I thought then was the sun blazing. I thought it was an awakening, almost an epiphany.

The second was waves of blue. _Radio_-wave-like, not sea-waves - but like sea-waves I was surfing them. Bronzed, even muscular, certainly fit. Young and strong. Except that I wasn't astride them but rather nestled <u>by</u> them. It was, I think, almost uterine. I think they were trying to nourish me, the waves. Those blue waves, royal blue and navy blue, light blue and lighter. Yes, those waves were the womb, I thought, and the bright light, that was birth.

And in the middle, there was the sleep of nothing. Just a blackness, just a void. Not unpleasant. Not a nightmare, not even a bad dream. If there was unpleasantness it was that of the vapid. That was all at the beginning. And at the beginning I gave not one of them any mind. If an acknowledgement, a cursory one. Mostly none at all.

Over time I started to realise one thing about these sleeps: I wasn't being refreshed by them. It would be an exaggeration to say that I was waking up as tired as I went to sleep, but I was waking up tired. And jaundiced. Tired physically, in other words, and tired emotionally. And the emotions that I could feel - and _what_ I could feel of them, which wasn't much - had a staleness about them. Teeth uncleaned for a day. Not seriously dodgy - not uncleaned for a week. The morning after a one-night stand where there's no toothbrush to be had.

And I realised that everything I'd been feeling was stale. All the emotions in my larder had passed their sell-by dates not weeks before, but years. Decades. I realised the bright light _wasn't_ birth, it wasn't even sunlight. It was a white light, rather, similar to white sound - a cacophony of sensation so extreme it destroys all subtlety or nuance.

I realised the blue of the radio-waves was not uterine

but was my engulfment by a tsunami. And the darkness I thought vapid was the blackness of despair to which I had become inured. And I wasn't sleeping well because I wasn't living well.

The famous soliloquy in 'Hamlet', it refers to 'that sleep of death'. Well, mine was the sleep of life. I was not refreshed by my sleep because my life was stagnant. 'For in that sleep of life,' I might well have written, 'what dream may come if we just shuffle on this mortal coil?'

You were my wake-up call. I started to understand that. 'Started' because I'm not nearly as bright as I like to imagine myself.

And I also started to understand - mostly because you *helped* me to understand - that with you it was safe not only to feel but to express. I started airing the emotions, started to open windows, started to let out some of the rankness and dankness.

And then I started to _feel_.

There was an onrush suddenly of emotions. An avalanche of them. I started to feel. And it was ten zillion sensations at a time - ten zillion zings. A Hallelujah Chorus of zings. But also ten zillion nips and stings.

What I tried to do, I tried to stuff that whole avalanche into the one, albeit vast, container: the love increasingly I felt for you. I thought that's what it was, in fact. I thought, these huge feelings, they were all manifestations of my love. No, wrong: off-shoots, rather, from the same trunk. Without the trunk, no off-shoots. And, thinking about it, I was probably right. Except that often the off-shoots had nothing whatever to do with the trunk. Which was, say, a Californian redwood. But the shoots? Some were orchids, others were holly; some nettles, others dock-leaves; some pine-cones and others pineapples. And some were squirrels or icebergs or the Sydney Opera House. Or Black Forest Gateau.

I should always be grateful to you for that. I should be, but I'm not. And I'm not sure why I'm not. Maybe because, mixed in with reverence for a creator, there is also resentment. Always. You don't die unless you live. The price of life *is* death, the price of admission. That which created you also, and simultaneously, created the germ that will destroy you.

You didn't create me, of course. But you unveiled to me a huge unknown part of me. And that unveiling is an act of creation. Maybe it's that that inhibits my gratitude. Please don't misunderstand, it's not something I'm proud of, the surliness of that gratitude. In fact I don't like me for it. But then, as a matter of fact, I don't like me a lot. And for a lot of different reasons.

I'm sure there must be some irony involved in that. That you have helped me to reveal myself to me, but the me that's been revealed to me is someone I don't like. Or, to be more accurate, who has more characteristics that I don't like of the person who had anyway a whole heap of characteristics I never liked.

Who was the first Chinaman who decided to keep an egg for a hundred years? And why? And what if, having kept it for a hundred years, he hadn't liked it? Would that have been irony? And if not, what would it have been? Well, whatever that would be – or would have been – the ersatz irony – that's what this is now. That's what it feels like.

I don't even like the honesty I've found which enables me to write this letter. I'm not sure, just at the moment, where this honesty is taking me. There is only one place I *want* to be taken, and that's closer to you. I've got a horrible feeling that's precisely _not_ where I'm being taken. In fact, it feels – if I'm being taken anywhere at all and am not just spiralling out of control – it feels like I'm being pulled *away* from you.

I'll close therefore before being dragged further away.

I love you – Mike xxx

Chapter 11

Maison d'arrêt de Toulouse-Seysses, 7th July o6

Dear Trove:

Thank you so much. It was – you cannot imagine – so special, looking round from the dock, seeing you there. Your sad little smile of encouragement, eyes glistening their support. The surprise was wonderful, a little magical even.

There's no point dwelling on what was said today. Facts are not the truth. And what's least truthful about them is that that is exactly what they pretend to be: the truth.

The fact of the matter – the awful, shameful fact of the matter – is that I remember so little – so almost nothing. Of the night itself, that maybe you'd expect. But I remember too so little of the build-up. And about that as well I feel really guilty. I was going to write, as guilty as I do about the death itself. But that would be patently absurd. And certainly not true.

I am struggling to get at the truth. I've started 'the' letter to you I can't remember how many times. Style isn't about whim, I've discovered. It's not about aesthetics or literacy or anything else even close to those things. It's simply a method of excavating the truth. And that's why, I suppose, it's so damn difficult. Still, nil desperandum.

Yes, how apposite: nil desperandum. 'Never despair,' I suppose you'd translate that as. It's sometimes hard. But, yes, one day I will crack it. And, yes, each day I do. Each day that I do not despair I have somehow cracked it.

Please look after yourself. Once again, thank you so very much for having come today. I suspect you have an idea of how much that meant to me. You cannot know how very much. With my love – Al x.

+++

"There are lots of things weird, right, Mike, about us?"

"Weird is our middle name."

"But, you know one thing that's *really* weird? I mean, weird even within the weirdness?"

"Do tell."

"The way, hon, I feel closer to you when I'm apart *from* you."

"I suppose that's taking phone sex to its obvious conclusion."

"I love talking like this to you on the phone."

"Beats the real thing, huh?"

"I've never talked, Mike, on the phone."

"You're 'Mike'ing me a lot."

"What does that mean?"

"I was hoping you'd tell me."

"I like the feel of it in my mouth."

"That's reasonable."

"I like the feel of you, Mike, in my mouth."

"Mike again."

"I'm trying to get you all hot and bothered."

"Oh, I'm hot, alright."

"You are?"

"And bothered, Trove."

"I'm gooey too."

"All dressed up, honey ..."

"You've got somewhere to go, Mike."

"Yes."

"You've got somewhere to come."

"How's Al?"

"Al's in a mess. I don't want to talk about Al right now. I don't want to *think* about him. I want to think and talk about us."

"I think about us all the time."

"And talk?"

"We're talking now, Trove."

"Madrid, hon, ..."

"I can't wait."

"We have to find a way, hon, in Madrid, to talk."

"Right."

"Not on the phone, face-to-face. Don't say one-to-one."

"Why not? I won't, but why not?"

"Because it's an awful phrase. It's a '24/7' phrase, an ugly phrase."

"It's an ..."

"Don't say that either, Michael."

"What?"

"An American phrase, you were going to say."

"How do you know that?"

"Weren't you?"

"I was. And I'm sorry."

"See, the thing is, Mike ..."

"Yes?"

"We have to find a way to talk also when we're together."

"I know."

"Do you?"

"Yes."

"*Do* you?"

"Yes, Trove."

"Madrid's important, honey."

"And I'm sure Madrid will be jolly grateful to hear that."

"There are times for jokes, Mike, ..."

"This is so serious, Trove, I *have* to joke about it."

"Hasta la vista, then, baby."

"Hasta la vista, honey."

+++

"He didn't ever phone me, Mike, to tell me he and Petrova were, as it were, back together again. He phoned me to tell me something about the baby. That was the pretext. During the phone call he mentioned that he was meeting Petrova in Madrid. A casual mention, meant to imply a casual meeting.

"I envied him Madrid. Have you ever been to Madrid?

"Well, of course you would have been. It was stupid of

me to ask.

"You weren't, I hope, even *thinking* of getting the train tonight. Nor, I hope, were you even thinking about checking into a hotel. There's a spare bed. It's all made up.

"Good.

"It's a city to me, Madrid, of exceptional charm. Mike mentioned the trip en passant, as it were. Even more en passant that he was meeting Trove there. Which, because it was Mike, meant that it was *really* important to him."

+++

"Hey!"

"I'm *so* sorry, Trove."

"You delay the plane?"

"Beg pardon?"

"You, I don't know, interfere with the engine? Or the pilot?"

"No."

"Then, what've you got to apologise for?"

"You like me apologising."

"Take your clothes off, then, and apologise properly."

"I need a pee."

"Always excuses with you, Mike, nowadays."

"It took forever from Baracas."

"How many forevers can there be in one day? It also took forever getting here from Toulouse. The traffic outside of San Sebastian, unreal! That took forever, you know, that stretch through the Pyrenees? And your forever from the airport, that makes three. Pee quickly. Don't pee forever. I don't think I could cope with four forevers in one day."

"Cold, isn't it?"

"Go warm yourself by the heater, dumbo."

"Not here. Madrid. Here's fine. Madrid, though, Madrid's

cold."

"Right."

"I didn't realise Madrid could get this cold."

"Highest capital, Mike, in Europe."

"I didn't know that either."

"It's November, is what I'm saying. Madrid is the highest capital in Europe ..."

"Not too surprising, then, it's cold?"

"I could think of things to warm you up."

"Still need a pee."

"Well, 'Stand not on the order, Mike, of thy peeing, then ...'"

"I wrote you this."

"Is it dirty?"

"No, but I am."

"Yeah, but you're dirty: sexy."

"No, at the moment, just dirty: grimey dirty."

"I like your letters, Mike."

"A bath might do me good."

"Just how long a letter is it?"

"You're right. I'll have a shower."

"Don't shower forever either. Leave the door open."

Dear Trove,

I wonder whether I'll be able to give you this. And if I do, when it will be.

I'm going to try and give it to you at the beginning of our ... sojourn together. There's stuff in it we need to talk about – no, I need that we talk about. I hope I will find that courage.

"Are there any dirty bits in this?"

"What?"

"Can I cut to the dirty bits?"

"Read it all, Trove."

"How much longer you going to be in there?"

"I just got in, for Christ's sake."

At my end, I know I'm scared. I'm scared that if I reveal too much of myself to you, you will no longer love me. You will no longer *like* me, for Christ's sake. And, at yours, there's, I suspect, an element of 'I'm not showing you mine until you show me yours'. I don't know. I'm not in your head. I'm not in the least qualified to judge. I shouldn't even be trying to guess. I'm sorry.

I know you want me to write some sexy stuff. And I will write you some. But I need to expose myself first to you in other ways.

"I agree with this bit, Mike."

"Which bit?"

"I want you to write sexy stuff."

"Read on."

"How many bodies are you washing in there?"

"Almost done."

This is so hard, so hard.

I've found God.

There it's out. I'm guessing that's the first thing I should say. It's so difficult to tell you that, you cannot imagine. 'Course I can't imagine why either, but that, as they say, is life. It's really hard to admit it. And the God I believe in?

Yeah, He's pretty much the old man with the long white beard, the da Vinci as an old man sort of God. I'm not too sure about concepts, as understood, of Heaven and Hell. But, yes, God, I'm afraid, for all the contradictions and uncertainties and ambiguities, for me He now does exist. I entirely understand those who don't believe He does. Indeed I understand those people considerably more than I understand people like me. There, it's out. A closet theist outed. Whatever it is, the opposite of atheist.

(Talking of closets, I should also admit that I'm also a

secret 'Carry On ...' fan. I know I shouldn't be. The urbane me is appalled by the very idea. But, there we go. I'm hooked. And there's nothing I can do about it. It really is all very closet stuff. Even at home, I'd only watch them on one of the satellite channels – where they seem to be repeated endlessly – if Eva was out.)

I'm not sure that either thing is defining about me. And maybe that's a fear too. That <u>nothing</u> defines me because, finally, there is nothing there *to* define. I'm so scared – I suppose this is what I'm trying to say – that I'm only a shell. That inside there is nothing. A chocolate éclair full of shaving soap; worse: a parcel-the-parcelly sort of multi-layered, multi *gift-wrapped* ... nothing.

And I'm scared that all that nothing can offer is himself – in other words, nothing. I'm scared that what I think I feel for you is also hollow, that what I think is love is only a simulation of love or a pretend-love, a mock-one. And that it is the *shell*, which *is* real, which is telling me I should tell you all this. But *is* even the shell real? And maybe now I'm doing exactly what I earlier accused you of: talking so I don't have to talk. Dissembling talking. Pretending to talk. ...

"Thank you, Mike."

"I'm sure you're welcome. You want to tell me what for?"

"What was in the envelope."

"The letter?"

"That too. The tickets, I meant, to the opera."

"Ah!"

"I found them."

"Yes, you did."

"Thank you, Mike. No-one's bought me tickets before for the opera."

"Then, I'm twice as desolate, Trove, to disappoint you."

"They're not for me?"

"They're for you."

"Then …?"

"They're for the ballet, Trove."

"Not the opera?"

"It's a bit like the opera, only without the singing."

"Quite a lot of dance, though, huh?"

"Quite a lot. You going to put that book down, now?"

"I haven't got to the dirty bit yet."

"We could maybe write our own dirty bit."

"Just look at that view. Madrid's so beautiful. Mike, you're not looking at the view."

"Oh, believe me, I am."

"Isn't it beautiful?"

"Oh, yes."

"Isn't Madrid a beautiful city, Mike?"

"And yours, Trove, is a beautiful body."

"And you want to go sight-seeing?"

"And flavour-tasting and bouquet-smelling and …"

"Touch-touching?"

"Especially touch-touching."

"Mike?"

"Hi."

"I love you, Mike. Now and always."

"I love you too."

"No."

"No?"

"See, you're saying it all soft, all mushy: 'I love you too', all soft and marshmallowy."

"It's a soft emotion, Trove. Famous for being one."

"No, it's not. Did you hear the way I said, 'I love you'?"

"Not soft."

"Hard, Mike. Like it's a liability. Which it is. Like it's a liability, not (as the marshmallow would have it) that it's an … unliability. Whatever the goddamn word is."

"Boon?"

"That'll do. Like it's a liability, Mike, and not a boon. 'Cause, guess what, Mike?"

"It *is* a liability and not a boon?"

"Maybe a bit of both. You know we're not going to last."

"I think the chances are against it. Us, I should say."

"We're never going to last, Mike."

"Not if you're adamant, we won't. We haven't got even the ghost of a chance."

"Adamant?"

"If you decide, before even we've really started, we're not going to last, guess what, Trove?"

"You think I'm being adamant?"

"Entrenched, then."

"You think I'm becoming entrenched, Mike?"

"You're very sexy when you pout."

"I'm trying to talk. To talk talk, Mike."

"I don't think so."

"What does *that* mean?"

"We're tired, Trove. Let's make love, go to sleep."

"We need to talk. No, joking apart, Mike. Now. Your letter, for Christ's sake, was all about the same thing. *This* goddamn letter, for Christ's sake. We need to talk. Now, Mike."

"We're not talking, honey. This isn't talking. This is squabbling. Bickering. Making a noise to avoid a silence. These are anxious times. We do have to talk. We're, neither of us, too practised at talking. But now's not the time to start trying."

"Now is never the right time."

"Well, that's true too."

"*Is* there anything, Mike? Between us?"

"We know the sex is good."

"The sex is great."

"The rest ... the *talking* ... I think that's best kept till the morning."

"But you know what happens ..."

"What?"

"We wake up ... *I* wake up, and you rouse *a*roused and ... well, tomorrow morning too the sex becomes more urgent than the talking."

"Sex is a form of communication, honey."

"You 'honey'ed me again, Mike."

"I did earlier."

"And I didn't notice?"

"I do love you, Trove."

"It is also, sex, a form, Mike, of not communicating."

"Well, come closer then, and let me not communicate with you till it hurts."

Chapter 12

"Mike called me from Madrid. Three times, in fact. And in as many days. The first time, to be honest, I thought it was to rub my nose in it, you know? I'm in Madrid and you're not, sort of nonsense.

"Now I say that, there was that edge to Mike's behaviour. Not as a constant, true. Nor even as anything overt. No, *covert*, rather. Subtle. A whiff, a taste, a hint. Something well hidden, quite deep. There was, thinking about it, a need Mike had somehow to be on a higher plane than you were. I'm not talking about *moral* high ground here. Not exactly. If the conversation were about licentiousness, say, he'd give you the impression – he didn't *say* anything, just gave the impression – that if you were, I don't know, a member of the Hell Fire Club or something, he was one of its founding fathers; if you'd broken into a house, he'd have robbed the odd bank.

"You know, you're much too attractive to be a hack. I'm amazed television hasn't gobbled you up. Got you fronting the Six o'clock News.

"Well, if they've got any sense at all, the job'll be yours. Bright *and* beautiful, that's the stuff normally only of hymns.

"Mike claimed he was anxious to start co-habiting. He may even have said 'desperate'. Trove, of course, was now homeless. Well, they both were, effectively."

+++

"See, then – in Madrid, I'm talking about – it had to do with practicalities. I mean, it just wasn't feasible, us living together. We neither of us had homes. Not 'homes' as any sensible person would understand the word. But, know what? If we didn't exactly manufacture that situation, I wonder whether we might not somehow have encouraged it. No, not quite that either. I wonder – is what I'm saying – whether we might not somehow have allowed that situation to continue, rather than resolving it. I don't know. I get kinda nervous around amateur psycho-analysis, especially *my* amateur psycho-analysis. Especially of me. I psycho-babble more than I analyse, and find myself blaming the fact that I forgot to put out the garbage last night on the fact that I wasn't, aged six, invited to Marianne Sebac's seventh birthday party.

"He couldn't see it, Mike. Couldn't see that I was not leaving Al for him. Just thought, we loved each other therefore we moved in together and therefore we lived happily-ish ever after. And I wasn't ready. I just wasn't ready. I'm not sure I would ever have been ready. But then ...?

"See, there was that about Mike which was incredibly ... what was it? ... naïve, I guess ... simple, maybe ... simplistic, even. Maybe a bit of all three. For all his apparent canniness and insight, he still liked to label all his jars. Cause and effect, type of thing. You broke eggs into a pan and swirled them round, you got scrambled eggs. I think therefore I am: cogito ergo sum. She loves me ergo she must want to live with me. She's left Al ergo she never loved him.

"I doubt there's a human being on the planet who's that simple. And I certainly wasn't. Nor was he, for Christ's sake. But that's where that kind of intellectual arrogance implodes in on itself. You know what I mean. 'Well, of course, it's not that simple in *my* case,' so such thinking says, 'but I'm me. Complicated. Superior to all you lesser beings. But you, you are *lesser* beings. Intellectual and emotional amoebas, incapable of any kind of complexity.'

"There is that about the intellectually arrogant which aspires to the god-like, which tries to see all us amoebas merely as specimens. I think there's a tendency for academics, for scientists and general smart-Alecs to do that. Maybe, you know, the thing that truly distinguishes both Einstein and Stephen Hawking is not the enormity of their brain, but the fact that that's coupled with a great deal of humanity. Newton, I understand, was a really unpleasant s-o-b. Edison, too.

"Mike wasn't *unpleasant*. It wasn't that simple. And he did have humanity. Mostly, I suspect, because deep down he knew he lacked the intellect to support his degree of arrogance. He was a bit like that scene in 'Beau Geste' where they stick rifles into the arms of corpses and line them up on the castle wall so the dastardly Arabs believe the fort is fully manned. Well, the crenallations of Fort Mike were also manned by corpses. And he knew it. Just felt that if he admitted that he'd have to surrender.

"You know the craziest thing of all that? There was no frigging enemy. There was no-one attacking Fort Mike. No-one the least bit interested in attacking it. But he simply could not see that! And, yet, somehow he did. And saw it clearly. It was ... No, how the hell do I know it '*was*'? ... It *seemed* like he thought he'd gone to all this trouble, draping all those legionnaires into battlements, in the midday Saharan sun, sweat dripping down his back like ice-cream dribbling down a cone ... he had expended all that energy for a reason. Ergo there *had* to be an enemy. Cogito ergo sum.

"I've never really understood that one, you know. 'Cogito ergo sum': 'I think therefore I am'. I mean it's not really a sequitur, is it? Not like, I don't know, it's hot therefore I sweat. I mean, it's just as rational, isn't it, the thought that 'I think therefore I *think* I am.' When you think about it, I mean."

+++

"You're crying."

"Not crying, Trove. A sniffle, no more."

"Some sniffle! You're crying."

"Something in my eye."

"Yeah, right! Like tears, maybe."

"It's a ballet, Trove."

"And ballets are like onions?"

"It was very beautiful. —-"

"I thought it was beautiful too, Mike. ..."

" —- So beautiful."

"... You don't see me crying."

"It's good to cry."

"Sure it is."

"Healthy."

"Even healthier, Mike, if you know why."

"It's the ballet."

"That's the pretext. What's the *reason*?"

"It's 'Cinderella'."

"I was there, remember? Sitting next to you? I do know, Mike, which ballet it was."

"You don't think it's redolent?"

"Redolent? Don't tell me what the word means, Mike."

"No."

"I know what 'redolent' means, 'kay? *Why* is it 'redolent'?"

"It's a love story."

"My sisters aren't ugly, hon. I was not treated like a scullery-maid. I've yet to come across my fairy-godmother. And, let me tell you, if she *is* there, she's doing a pretty crappy job."

"And I'm not Prince Charming, right?"

"No, you are. That's it, the whole problem. There in a nutshell."

"Sorry?"

"You *are* Prince Charming, hon. I see that now. That's what makes me uneasy around you."

"Trove, you're talking in riddles."

"I don't want Prince Charming, Mike. You know what, the second the fairy-tale finishes, there is no Prince Charming any more. The djinni returns to his bottle. I don't want Prince Charming, Mike. Mike, it's *Mike* I want. And all you can give me is not-Mike, is Mike-as-Prince-Charming Mike."

"It would be Mike, Trove, who would live with you."

"Yeah. But which one?"

+++

"We had a great time in Madrid. It's a great town for lovers, and we loved a lot being there. In just about every sense, now I think about it. And I was happy just going on the way we were. Just, I don't know, having this occasional-dirty-weekend sort of fling thing, whatever the hell it was.

"But Mike?

"No, Mike wanted more. Is it a law of Nature, do you suppose, that the more you want the less you get?

"I told him I couldn't cope with that, cope with the level of commitment he was expecting from me. I told him, on that last day in Madrid, we'd be better off being just the friends we'd always been.

"And I seriously thought I'd be okay with that!"

+++

Thru Security etc Qing 4 coffee. How's the drive? MxXx
   Can barely c the rd 4 tears. B gd 2 yrself. Safe flight
 - T
   Must this be the end? Can't we just say au revoir?
MxXx
   Yes. & no. I will always love u - TxXx

+++

Know something, Drew? This time it wasn't okay. I don't know whether you remember, but you kept asking me what was wrong. And I kept telling you I wasn't sleeping well or that my back was troubling me or that it was just the bloody British weather, nothing to worry about. And, because I had let you know so little of me, that satisfied you. And you suggested things to make me sleep or pills that would ease my back, or chuckled wryly in sympathy

about the weather. All very 'pub-friend'ly. Nothing dangerous or toe-threatening.

Inside I was slivered. Not eviscerated. Nothing so merciful. All my organs were sliced to wafer-thinness by an electronic cleaver, but they were still pounding, still throbbing. Still bleeding. I wanted to cry like a baby. And, like a baby, I wanted Mummy and for Mummy to make the world go away, and make the horribleness of the world go away.

I tried to find some solace in Franklyn. I told myself I was closer to you. Starting, at least and at some kind of level, to communicate.

But - I see this now and I apologise - you can't communicate when you're in that kind of pain. It's not possible. When they're tightening the thumb-screws you may ask about the neighbour's cat, but you won't be listening to the reply.

And when I woke up to that, I also woke up to the fact that I was involved in a fool's errand. How could I possibly expect to have a relationship? With you, I mean? The fact that we'd had none to date would sour any we might have in the future. And any I might have had with Franklyn would also likewise be soured. Yet again I repeat that, for all of which I hold myself completely and exclusively responsible. You are a remarkable man, Drew. And you will, I feel sure, be the father to Franklyn that I never was to you. But that is what you are: You are a man. Even remarkable men are men. And we forget that at our peril.

I know you will be angry with me at the moment. No, I don't know that, but I think it is a sensible surmise. If you are not angry with me, then you are an even more remarkable man than I took you for. A saint, as near as dammit.

I'm sorry that you're angry. More sorry, I'm sure, than you'll believe. But I did what I did from what I sincerely believed were the best of intentions – those same best of intentions that the road to Hell is paved with! Maybe your mother was right, her little 'joke'. The only thing I'm committed to is a lack of commitment – the only thing I should be committed <u>for</u>.

The pain of having lost Trove this time was indescribable. So much worse than the previous times. But rather than swamping all the other pains around it, it seemed to force them all to the surface. Just as, in fact, it was physically. My aching back was making me aware that my teeth were also aching, so was the instep of my right foot and my left shoulder-blade. Trove was my back, but my teeth were you, and the instep was for a wasted life, and my left shoulder-blade was for all the pain I had caused. Shit, that pain was a real pain too. <u>All</u> the pain, in fact, it was all real pain. All *too* real even. It was, in fact, *so* real that I can feel it again as I write. May God forgive me.

+++

"Orgasm, it's not one thing, is it? I mean, it *is* one thing – of course it's one thing – but the one thing it is, it's an agglomeration, isn't it, of all sorts of other things? Smaller things? Spasms, jerks, gushes, on-rushes – all sorts of different sensations – some of which, in fact, taken in isolation would not even be pleasurable; may even, in fact, be quite painful. Like I understand the elements which combine to make sugar are all bitter. Orgasms, they're all sorts of sensations combining together into one sort of whoosh of an emotion or a discharge or whatever the hell it is.

"Well, what I went through on the drive back from Madrid, that was, in that case, orgasmic. 'Cept it was an orgasm of absolutely no pleasure whatsoever. Oh, not too much pain either. Which was curious. Not pain, at any rate, in the accepted use of the word. Just ... turbulence. Violent and remorseless turbulence. And anger. Jesus, *was* I angry?!

"Angry with Mike. And then angry with myself for being angry with Mike. Mike hadn't done that much for me to be angry with him about. Not yet. Angry with Al. Furious with Al. And angry with myself that I hadn't been angry with Al at a time when it would have served some purpose my being angry at him. Angry at myself for a whole host of other reasons too. Opening that Pandora's box, getting involved in the first place, not having noticed what had been happening to Al and me ... happening, for Christ's sake, under my very nose. Furious with myself, spitting tacks at myself, hellfire-and-brimstoning at myself. And at the world, Fate, God, the universe ... you name it.

"Boiling, raging, searing, seething, scorching ...

"And I kept expecting some kind of peace to descend, some kind of eye of the hurricane. And none came. Like I said, it was remorseless. Just wave after wave after wave of turbulence and rage and more rage and more turbulence.

"I wasn't fit to drive like that. Fit to drive?! Shit, like that, I wasn't fit to live! And I couldn't live. Not like that. I couldn't contain life like that. It would be confiscated from me, or, in some volcanic spew, life would explode out of me.

"I got back to Toulouse in one hit. I stopped twice for the restroom and once for gas. I didn't even have a coffee. It's in these kinds of mood, I'm sure, that murders are committed. I had to get rid of it. I had to.

"I got home and got drunk. Very drunk.

"I staggered to bed and collapsed. But the turbulence didn't stop, it just reeled. And the waves kept coming – wave after wave – except that now, as an added bonus, they were also making me sea-sick!

+++

Home? M xXx

    No. Not home. Where the f's that? In this s/hole in T/lousy. V NOT @ home. I cannot stop crying. We can see each other, no? - T

    Whenever. MxXx

+++

Maison d'arrêt de Toulouse-Seysses, 25th July 06

Dear Trove – my dearest Trove – my darling:

My first night as a convicted prisoner! It doesn't feel too different, if I'm honest, to my other nights here as an unconvicted prisoner. I feel more sorry for those who have today been convicted without having been remanded. It's a considerably bigger shock to their system than it is to mine.

    I've drafted this letter endless times. *Endless* times. I've got all the drafts here. I had imagined, what'd I'd do, I'd read them all back again, steal the best bits and cobble those bits together. And you know what? There's only one way to write this, and that's from scratch. Oh, the previous drafts will be there, of course. If for no other reason than that they will have *informed* this one. But there is only one right time to write this letter and that's today. And it has to be written from me today. It's not, I don't think, that the spontaneous is necessarily more truthful, but it is more honest. I can't remember who said it – Nietzsche, probably – but whoever it was once wrote, 'Misery introduces a man to himself'. There can be few places of greater combined misery than prison. And at that level, it is therefore the building probably housing the most honesty, or at least self-awareness, in the entire of society. But that's just crap, frankly. Sentimental eyewash. There is no place on the planet where self-delusion rules more firmly than in prison. Maybe because survival in prison depends on it. And maybe that's why, finally, prison so seldom works.

    It's under a year since the whole thing started. Under a *year*, can you believe that?

    Meanwhile, as I can hear you saying, back at the point ...

+++

"And that, I think, is quite enough about Al and Trove for one day. Time, I think, to concentrate on quite another romance. I have this overwhelming urge to kiss you. I think I may have to do something about that urge before we repair to dinner.

"Isn't that better? Hasn't that urge been intruding, oh, certainly for the last hour? In my case, if I'm honest, from when you walked through the door. We could have dinner here.

"No, what am I thinking? You've seen enough of this place for a day. 'Le Bistro d'Orléans', I think. Dinner, my dear, is ours. What I mean by that is, *just* ours, ours exclusively, no third parties. Petrova and Al can rejoin us, say, at breakfast tomorrow morning? Okay? Alright?

"Just one more kiss, I think, before we leave."

Chapter 13

"Answer me something: Why is it that women in men's clothes look so sexy? Whereas men in women's clothes just look grotesque? You look so lovely in that dressing-gown of mine. Pretty, sexy, so desirable. Can I take it off for you?

"I made Eggs Benedict.

"Want to know why?

"I made Eggs Benedict because there's an old joke. Have you heard the old joke?

"The old joke goes: 'Why is Eggs Benedict like a blow-job?' No? 'Because you don't get either at home.' Well, ... let's call it my concession to the concept of quid pro quo. Bon appétit.

"You switched your tape-recorder back on.

"Already? How are the eggs?

"I don't know about Petrova. I didn't see Petrova during that time. Mike, of course, was still in England. But I did see Al. I did, rather, see the red fedora. And ducked into the nearest shadows when I did. He'd got to the really boring stage of being a drunk. Well, drunks are drunks are drunks, of course, and drunks are *always* boring, but you know what I mean. The stage, I'm talking about, when the drunk's boring even when he appears to be sober. Because, of course, he never is. Sober. Not really. Not fully. He's just, I believe the phrase is, 'topping up'. Talking of topping up, how does a buck's fizz sound? It's so naughty, isn't it, drinking champagne for breakfast? Naughty but delicious. Like last night, no?: naughty but delicious. Naughty, rather, *and* delicious. What do you say? Buck's fizz? What do you say?

"Shall we take them outside? Drink them on the

terrace? It's such a lovely day. But then, even if it were pouring with rain, it would be a lovely day. Noël Coward was once asked by a journalist whether it was true he always drank a bottle of champagne before breakfast. Coward fixed him with his enigmatic, lightly contemptuous stare, and replied blandly, 'Doesn't everyone?' Santé. Doorstepped on another occasion by another hack ⋯ – not that you're a hack, my dear. Perish indeed the thought. There is a difference, and I recognise it, between the dope-peddler and the chemist. – Doorstepped, as I said, by one such of the more tabloid variety, he was asked: 'Do you have anything to say to "The Sun"?' Again that withering half-smile. 'Shine!' the dramatist enjoined.

"Mike?

"Mike sulked. I think that would be the way to describe it. Oh, we still talked often on the phone. Sulked not in a petulant way, but in a feet-stomping way.

"'How are you?' I would ask.

"'Fine,' he would stomp in reply, slamming the door shut. Metaphorically, I mean. Very firmly. And venturing no further.

"I once saw Dustin Hoffman being interviewed by a talk-show host called Michael Parkinson. You won't have heard of him. Not here. He's a sort of professional sycophant, arse-licker to the stars. I'm sure you have an equivalent. 'You're here, Dustin, I understand,' said Mr Parkinson, 'to promote your new film.' 'Yes,' replied Hoffman. Parkinson waited for him to continue. Nothing. And he waited and he waited. Still nothing. Eventually Parkinson continued, 'In it you co-star with ⋯' whoever it was. 'Yup,' said Hoffman and said no more. 'And how was he to work with?' Parkinson floundered, his professional Yorkshire accent flattening a few more vowels than usual. 'Fine,' replied the star. And thus it continued. Between you and me, I actually quite enjoyed it. Quite enjoyed Parkinson's discomfort with it all. Those prepared to sojourn in astral recta, I smirked to myself, must expect occasionally to find themselves in shit. And the schaden-freude involved in watching him drowning in the stuff ⋯ well, it was what the young today would call 'wicked'.

"But the point is, that's how it was 'talking' to Mike in those days. You had to supply the entire dynamic of the conversation. Though even the word 'conversation' would be an exaggeration. It was very one-sided: You talked, he grunted. Talking of grunting, could we go back to bed now?"

+++

Wld it help us 2 talk? Or not? U decide - T xXx
    Sorry. If we talked Id just fall in love w/ u again. Wld that b helpful? Mxx
    I understand - T
    Hasta ⋯? Mxx

+++

... I know Mike wasn't your first fling, Trove. When I say 'fling' I'm not trying to underestimate the affair with him. But I know he wasn't your first detour off, let's call it, the matrimonial path. And that was okay. Was, and is. I had a couple of flings myself, one of which might even have developed into something serious. It didn't because, I suppose, aged around 40 I became aware that I wanted comfort more than passion. In my work as well. I remember we even talked about it. Yeah! One of the rare occasions when we did talk. We talked about the way my pieces lacked the passion of ten years previously. That they had mellowed. And I liked that they had. And you ... you, let's say, were less sure. In the same way, I became aware too, around that time, that I was comfortable with you. I became aware that all the passion inside me had mellowed: the fire was no longer roaring, embers (rather) were glowing.

Oh, I could see the passion in you – you were passion, Trove. You've always been passion. Since before I knew you. All those stories your folks told about your childhood, always the hallmark was passion. You made Carmen look like a lump of granite. I'd loved that about you, revered it. More, I was in awe of it. And then, at around that same age, 40 thereabouts, I became aware that I was no longer in awe of your passion. It wasn't sudden, the realization. It was a creeping awareness that some time in the recentish past I'd come to that realization. And know what I realized I now felt? Instead of reverence for your passion, I mean? Instead of awe for it? I pitied you your passion, Trove. I felt sorry for you that you had it, like feeling sorry for someone with diabetes – it's not usually a life-threatening condition, but it is one helluva drag.

Patronizing or what? ...

+++

"A one-edged sword – think about it, hon – is not a sword at all: It's an overgrown carving knife. So I've never been too sure why it's used so often as a metaphor, a 'two-edged sword'. I mean, a more appropriate image, wouldn't it, would be a gun-barrel with holes either end – so you don't know whether the bullet's going to kill its target or you. Kind of cumbersome, though – I take the point –, for a metaphor. I guess we're going to be stuck with a 'two-edged sword' – like 'not having your cake and eat it': another phrase I could never quite grasp how to use. Me and Marian Keyes both! You know Marian Keyes, right?

"Take my advice, you *should* know Marian Keyes. Now, what the hell was it, now I've got that out of my hair, that *was* a two-edged goddamn sword? What got me started on all that? Right: Love! Love, is what I was going to say. Love is a two-edged sword. No, it's not. What am I talking about? No, love, it's rather more like owning, I don't know, a Rottweiler or something. All sweet and lolloping and doting all over you ... right up till the day he turns round and takes a hunk out of your right thigh. Until the goddamn thing, it *savages* you.

"That savaging was the turbulence. The turbulence which went on and on. And which was churning up all the milk of human kindness inside of me into some kind of cheese – some really niffy cheese, at that – not nifty, hon, niffy: bad smell cheese, gorgonzola, kind of deal, past its gone-rancid-by date.

"I was *so* mad. So *completely* mad. I had to do something about it. I had to.

"I tried being pissed at Mike. Really I did. But I couldn't hack it. Oh, I could get sore at him, irked by him, 'miffed' (as the Brits would have it) by him. – Great word, isn't it, 'miffed'? – Jesus, there were enough miffed-making things about him, for Christ's sake. But 'miffed' didn't do it. 'Miffed' wasn't enough. 'Miffed' was not up to the job. 'Miffed' was the tortoise and I wasn't the hare, I was the goddamn cheetah.

"So mild was my miffedness with Mike, in fact, that I wrote him. I wrote him unmiffedly. I wrote him that I loved him and that I always would. And that I was real sorry things hadn't worked out for us. And that I hoped they would for him. And that there were heaps more women out there for him, and heaps more heaps more attractive than I was. I tried to tell myself that the letter was a waste of time, that he wouldn't reply, that even if he did it'd only be to whine like a baby. But not even that worked as a device for me to get mad at him.

"So then I tried getting mad at myself. And that worked better. I had more things to be mad with myself about than I had with Mike. But know what? I may have gotten beyond 'miffed', may even have gotten as far as 'mad', but 'mad as hell'? No, I couldn't get there with me. I kept find extenuating … *mitigating* circumstances for me. And, just as I was travelling nice-and-smoothly towards 'mad as hell', the train of thought would stop. Or go backwards or something. Drop me off at 'mad as purgatory' or 'mad as limbo' or some place.

"Al! Tailor-made. Al: designer-label vent-my-wrath-onner Al! I *could* get 'mad as hell' at Al. 'Course, Al hadn't really done anything either which would justify me getting 'mad as hell' at him, but – know what? – I could somehow justify to myself that I didn't need any justi-fication to get mad at him. He was one helluva getting-mad-as-hell-at-him maker.

+++

... 'Course, as we didn't talk, I never said anything about this. And, to be frank, I'm not sure I would have said anything even if we had been talking. Because it's not easy trying to say that kind of thing to someone else. And what good does it do? I mean, if I'd suddenly become aware that I felt sorry for you because you had chestnut hair and not blond, maybe that's worth the saying: You can always choose to have your hair dyed. But if I become aware that I feel sorry for you because you have to breathe, what is the point? I mean, my feeling sorry about it is not going to affect — not by one millimetre — your compulsion to breathe. Your passion, Trove, that was as innate to you as your need to breathe. It's what defined you. And, as so many things which define us, it was also probably going to destroy you.

Which was not why I felt sorry for you. No. It wasn't the destruction. It was the conflagration — the energy, if you like. I realized I was tired just watching your passion. It's exhausting. I didn't know where you got your energy from, to be so passionate. I'm not talking sexual passion here. (Well, I am, but only partially. And that part of it I'll get onto in a little while. This section is about non-sexual passion.) I know you know what I'm talking about. I'm talking about eruptions over some presidential misjudgement or over the plans for a new flyover or over your niece's refusal even to try snails. You could not not be passionate. You ate a boiled egg passionately, brushed your teeth, filled the car with gas, changed the sheets on the bed, all with passion. Not always positive passion, of course. You tutted with passion, sighed, remonstrated, even whined, again always with passion.

And, of course, (although I'm still not talking about sexual passion) that passion too had to be involved with sex. Except that most sex is a cocktail. It's a combination of the two people involved. If one's 100º and the other's 0º, the climate of their sex together will be 50º. And that was one of the problems. That was one of the bigger elephants of the entire herd which was stoically taking up residence in our kitchen. See, sex between us, I'd have been happy to have at a steady, oh, 25º, say. With the occasional splurge to 35º and the annual volcano of 50º. Your staple sexual fare, on the other hand, you expected to be 75º, with occasional slumps to 65º and an annual trough of 50º. (This, Trove, is all with the benefit of analytical hindsight. None of this was clear to my consciousness then, and I suspect not to my sub-consciousness either.)

Christ, you know I'm no kind of meteorologist, but I'm sure something fairly dramatic happens when a tornado meets a sort of indolent, malleable, vapid front. And, of course, tornadoes want dramatic things to happen. Why else *be* a tornado? And they therefore get fairly pissed if indolent, malleable, vapid fronts just cede to them. They become King Lear, ranting without an audience. Sometimes without even the Fool for company.

Passion needs passion. Maybe for its own survival. And it was inevitable you would have lovers. You had to have them. If your passion could not be reciprocated or echoed in other ways, at least it could be with sex. *Now* I completely understand that. Then? ...

You know, I really don't know. I think I must have *intuited* something. Even if the something I intuited was only not to enquire too deeply. I think there were moments (looking back on it) when I suspected – there must have been an atmosphere, the unexplained grin or two. But ... well, you have no idea how seductive comfort is. Only the passionate swim. Those of us who lack that dynamicism (or dynamo!), we need to be in a boat. And when surrounded by sharks you know what you don't do to that boat? You don't rock it.

I was so comfortable with you. I mean, <u>so</u> comfortable. I've never thought of you as a possession – You must excuse me, Trove, if I tell you things you already know. I'm taking the stance in this letter that you don't know anything. The danger otherwise is, if I assume knowledge, I may assume that there is greater knowledge than there is; or I may make the same mistake I have so many times in the past: of assuming that because *I* know something you will also know that something, or that something I surmised (or guessed or deduced or felt or reckoned) is something I have learned. How many of the world's horrors, I wonder, have occurred because people have mistaken learning something for surmising it, or guessing, deducing, feeling it? – I have never thought your attention or time was exclusive to me. Indeed, not even that I had first call on either. If I thought about it, then I'd have to realize that that amount of passion simply *had* to find an outlet. And then I'd have had to ask myself all sorts of difficult questions. About whether I felt jealous, for instance. And if I did, whether I had any right to. About whether I was adequate as a lover. Whether the comfort of our sex together was enough. (God, that's a really uncomfortable subject for me to touch on. I don't want to but I'll come back to this also in a while.) ...

+++

My dearest Trove,

Thank you for your letter. It was a sweet letter. Well, of course it was, it was from you. I'm very sad. Deeply sad. I have loved you in a special way. The special way in which I shall continue to love you will, yes, be different – but it will still be special.

It's hard, and probably fruitless, to describe the pain. It's not even that it is one. It's a series, rather, of pains. A chain. And not just of pains. Oh, there certainly are some pains, but there are also aches, stings, sores, jolts – a whole gamut, probably. And some are concurrent and others coincidental. At its best, it is extremely uncomfortable; at its worst, excruciating.

But not for a moment (and this is the point of what I'm saying), not for a second – even knowing that there was this welter of pain awaiting me at its end – would I have taken another path. With you I touched something sublime, ate some kind of spiritual ambrosia. You were both the answer to so many of my prayers and the personification of prayer. But, as the axiom has it, when the gods want to punish us, they answer our prayers.

And this is precisely how they do punish us.

You may remember that at the start of our 'amour' I was worried that it might compromise our friendship. Today I have no such worry. Indeed, to the contrary. I have, as well as falling in love with you, fallen deeper in 'like' with you.

If ever either that lover or that friend can tender you any help at all you need do no more than ask. In return for which, you can do me the favour of looking after yourself. With my love – Mike xx

+++

"I was going to go round and kill Al: Al, the s-o-b, the little shit, the total bastard. Al, the target of my wrath. I was going to boil him in oil, flay him alive. I'd give the cock-sucker a major piece of my mind. "The mad that I was? Well, all the way over to his, I was whipping it up into an ever steamier lather. And then, just before I knocked at the door, I gave it another whoosh or two – you know, like Brits making tea adding an extra teaspoon 'for the pot' – just to make sure it was all good and real whirry. Going to explode just as soon as the cap was taken off the bottle.

"He blinked when he opened the door. Made me feel real welcome – about as welcome as Colonel Sanders at a convention of Yankee vegans.

"'I thought,' he said, 'we were going to let each other know. If we were coming visiting, I mean.'

"'Yeah, right!' I said and simply pushed past him.

"'Now's not convenient, Trove,' he said.

"'Well, it's convenient for me,' I said. I was halfway to the kitchen by then. 'I'm making some coffee. Want some?' I asked him, being very hospitable in a glaring-daggers sort of way. The house wasn't the total shambles it had been previously. That much was true. But it wasn't going to be the cover picture either for 'House Cleaner Monthly' or anything. I, on the other hand, would have made the perfect cover for … I don't know … 'Fury Unrestrained', say, or 'My life as a man-eating Amazon'.

"'I've got someone …' he started to blurt.

"'Oh, shit, Al,' I spat back. 'You think I don't know about your sleazy little affair?' *Wrong*, Trove! Not going to win the Nobel Peace Prize with that one.

"'How dare you!' he hissed. 'How *dare* you!' And, know what?, for a moment there, I was frightened. Real frightened, I mean. Rabbit-caught-in-headlights time. I mean, this was emotion. Genuine emotion. Feeling. Gut feeling. And that was more scary than the fact that the emotion was anger. You know, it you're at a temperance meeting, you're more surprised that there's booze there at all, than at what that booze is.

"'We need to talk, honey,' I said. Suddenly Miss Reasonableness, Miss Sanity and Relationship Counsellor and Magical, Mysterious Miss Mystic!

"'No, we don't,' he replied, his eyes still covered in a sheen of anger. '*We* don't need to talk at all, Trove. I don't need to talk. And Monique – Monique, she's the girl upstairs, my "sleazy affair", as you so eloquently put it –, she doesn't need to talk. Know what? I doubt even Mike needs to talk. You're the one who needs to talk, Trove. You. And guess what? I'm not in the mood right now. So, I'd like you to leave.'

"'And the coffee?' I asked, tail between legs which had shrunk from being a wolfhound's to a dachshund's.

"'I'm sure,' he said, 'you'll remember there's a café on the corner.'

"I wanted to apologise. Really I did. But I just couldn't. I just couldn't. The words, literally, shrivelled inside my mouth. Shrunk to nothing. It wasn't that they got stuck in my wind-pipe. When I opened my mouth, there was nothing there. You know how much today I regret that lack of apology? You have any idea the shit I've put myself through for not having made that apology? No, you can't have any idea!"

+++

... Please don't mistake any of this for the fact I didn't care. Because I did. Care. I was going to write 'passionately', but that (clearly) would have been a mistake. It would also be wrong to say 'dispassionately'. I would have killed anyone who had harmed a hair on your head. And I think you both knew that and know that. And now I think about it, there was passion. Of course there was. For Christ's sake, that is passion. Oh, maybe not passion to the same degree or intensity as yours. At least not on the surface. But there was passion nevertheless. It's just that ... Well, it wasn't a family trait, not a, as it were, 'Tregunter' thing, passion.

When I shook hands with my father at our wedding, that was the first physical contact I'd had with the man since I was a child. (Yes, I do know you know that, Trove.) Was he a man without passion? Was my bookworm mother? She whose care was far more manifest stroking the dog than hugging one of us?

Do you know what? Since my incarceration, I'm finding the passion in them too. The passion, I mean, in my parents. I'm finding a closeness, even an intimacy with them not only that I didn't believe I could have but which (had I have been asked) I would have thought unhaveable. Not just between my parents and me. Universally I thought such intimacy did not exist.

And do you know what else? The discomfort I used to tell you I always felt between them? Well, it isn't. They may be cacti, but cacti have their place. And, to a cactus, another cactus is far more attractive than, say, a tulip or a pansy. And one thing more: Who am I to judge? Can a eucalyptus tree judge a cactus? Or a koala bear? Or a tube of toothpaste? Because me the tulip, I find it inconceivable to have a prickly partner does not mean that *another* tulip might not. And certainly doesn't mean that another cactus might not.

My parents – I can see this now – are really comfortable within what I perceive to be their prickly shell. And it is one shell – this I also see now – which they both inhabit. It's not, I mean, that they both have separate shells, they cohabit within the same one. It's not even the ascetic getting inured to the dankness of his cave and therefore feeling at home there. There is warmth between them, real warmth, between Mom and Dad, which is very Axminster carpet and Dunhill pipe and fur-lined slippers. I suppose what I'm trying to say is that they're both, and together, considerably less cactus-like than I had imagined. Because their warmth rarely showed itself in tactile expression I imagined the warmth to be a coldness. And I got used to that coldness, as a child.

The trouble with our childhood is that we're so young when we go through it. Shaw said that youth is wasted on the young. And of course it is. But that's only half the story. The young, more fully, don't have the wherewithal to deal with youth.

It's a fundamental problem. And this is only now becoming apparent to me.

I'm sure I read somewhere that, by far, the most intense learning curve of our lives is that which occurs between birth and six months. Which means our most intense bout of education is sifted through a sieve of perception that we are the center of the universe. By five, we have learned more than we're ever going to learn again. *Aged five our self-importance is still enormous. Is it any wonder, then, that humankind is so unbelievably selfish? To shed such selfishness would require us to return to our infancy and to unlearn everything we had then learned and then relearn similar information this time using the sieve of perception that we are not the center of the universe. How many of us would be prepared to do that?*

Unless, of course, you have – like a convicted prisoner – got plenty of idle time on your hands. ...

+++

Know what day it is? – T xx
　　Yup. M xx
　　Can I phone u? – T xx
　　Please. M xx

+++

"Hi."

"Hi."

"Happy Valentine's."

"To you too, Trove."

"This is really awkward. Don't you feel awkward?"

"No."

"*No?*"

"I'm sure I should, honey, but I don't."

"You 'honey'ed me."

"I did."

"Was that deliberate?"

"Of course."

"I've missed you, Mike."

"I've missed you too."

"Dumb. This is so dumb. It's Valentine's and we're apart. That's so dumb. Doesn't that sound dumb to you?"

"It's the dumbest thing I ever heard of, Trove."

"That was almost American."

"I do try."

"Will you come to me?"

"Trove ..."

"No, no excuses, no reasons. No nothings, Mike. Will you come to me?"

"I've got things planned here. I have to unplan them."

"I need you to unplan them, Mike. Come to me."

"I'll call you later."

"Call me later. I'll be waiting."

"You know I love you, Trove?"

"Call me later."

+++

"They decided to meet on neutral ground. Paris was considered neutral ground.

"And three days later, that's where they were. And the day after that, of course, was the night of the ⋯ 'incident', I suppose you're going to call it, are you? The night of the murder, the manslaughter, whatever. And Al was in jail. And life would never be the same again.

"How on earth did you get that scar on your breast? And how come I didn't notice it before?"

Chapter 14

"Honey ..."

"I'm alright, Mike."

"You're not alright. You're crying."

"Crying's alright. It's okay, Mike."

"Not, you told me, at the ballet. And not, Trove, after you've just made love."

"It was beautiful, making love to you. As beautiful as it's always been. You make my body sing, Mike – make it sing and make it zing."

"I know tears of happiness, honey. These aren't tears of happiness."

"*Sprinkled* with happiness, though. And *joy*, Mike. Yeah, there's both those things in 'them there' tears. Feeling zingy from the sex, all kind of mushy with joy at this view – look at the view, hon. Have you ever seen anything more lovely? The Louvre there? The Seine slithering its way before it? Wouldn't you *kill* to have a view like this? And we don't need to kill. You know why? Because we already have it. And each other. And we just made love. It's beautiful. Life's beautiful, Mike. Magnificent. How could those tears, Mike, *not* have sprinkles in them of joy? Of rapture, even? But, no, you're right: That's not the full story. Not even, maybe, the major part of the story. There *is* sadness there. The biggest part of the tears, Mike – you're right – is one of sadness. It's one, Mike, of regret. Me? Miss je-ne-regrette-rien, Edith-Piaf-take-two me – I'm crying from regret.

"Mike, and I say this with regret, I'm leaving Al for you."

+++

... And a charge went through me, Drew, as she said that. An electronic charge. Packed. Not a buzz, even. Not in

any sense a buzz. A jolt rather of elation followed by a thunderclap of despair.

Despair and disappointment. When the gods want to punish us, they answer our prayers. When the gods, Drew, want to punish us ...

+++

"He looked startled, stunned. That's okay. Shock is shock. Looking at them, I don't suppose there'd be a lot of difference in the expressions of a lottery winner or the mother of a plane crash victim.

"I pulled him to me, like a mother pulls her baby to her – as an act of comfort and reassurance, and I'll-always-be-there-for-you clinch. 'You're safe, baby' kind of thing. Except that I soon figured – even me – it was me seeking the comfort and reassurance.

"See, me, I'm pretty convinced that a major reason for marriage bust-ups is marriage itself. People have somehow 'gotten' each other. They stop trying. Well, same deal here. Sameish. I mean, I'd, as it were, given myself to him. He'd netted me – like a fish – and, like a fish, I was sort of flapping around over the marble slab and I didn't know, you know, whether I'd have the same appeal to him. The fun of the chase, after all, *is* the chase. It's not the capture.

"I managed to get him aroused again. Not through passion, not through stratagem or technique, but just by being very languid, very laid back and kind of unhurriedly sensuous. And we made a kind of lazy love, a meander-through-bluebells kind of love. Almost a chaste love.

"Almost holy. Completely peaceful.

"Which was just before the most unholy row broke out, and peace was shattered into a zillion pieces."

+++

... You've heard, I'm sure, of Donne's famous line: '... ask

not for whom the bell tolls. It tolls for thee.' Well sometimes that bell is not just a metaphor. There are some bells, I mean, which seem to be imbued with doom. They do toll. They even knell. And such a ring, Drew, was that of the telephone that evening. That bitterly cold February evening in Paris.

It's weird. It had rung at other times that day. And all the ring had been on those other occasions was an indication that someone wanted to talk to one of us. But that ring, that was something different. There was a resonance in that ring, an ominousness, a menace. ...

+++

"I didn't know anything about it then. I read about it first in the papers, as a matter of fact. That Al had been arrested. I thought at first it had been Mike he'd killed. Or Petrova.

"I don't want to come to the end of this story. I have a feeling that its end will also be ours. Can I see you again?"

+++

"Trove ..."

"I'll be alright, Mike."

"Alright? You're as white as a sheet."

"I'll be alright."

"Sit down, for God's sake."

"Sit? Are you crazy? I've got to go, Mike. Got to pack."

"Whoa there. Hold your horses a minute."

"I've got to go."

"What happened?"

"It's Al."

"Al?"

"Yeah."

"He's alright?"

"He's alive, Mike."

"What was it? Accident?"

"Accident, sure. Fucking great big accident. Not in the way you might be thinking, though. He's been arrested, Mike."

"Al?"

"No, the Prince of frigging Wales."

"It's got to be a mistake."

"You *think*? Know what he's been arrested for?"

"Al?"

"For murder, Mike."

"Well, now I know you're kidding."

"For fucking murder, hon."

"It's a mistake, Trove. It's a grotesque mistake. There's absolutely no way Al could murder *anyone*. Do we know who is he supposed to have murdered?"

"His girlfriend."

"Monique?"

"He have a harem? You want to stand even more in the way, Mike? I've got a suitcase to pack, for Christ's sake."

"No way. There is no way, Trove. Someone's got their facts wrong. Or muddled anyway. It's a Chinese whisper, just taken to the nth degree of absurdity – beyond the nth degree: a Chinese whisper painted by Dali."

"I have to go, Mike. And I have to pack."

"Phone someone. Check it's true. You don't want to get all the way back to Toulouse, find out it's a hoax."

"It's not a hoax."

"You need to know more details."

"*What* more details, for Christ's sake? A woman who was hale-and-hearty yesterday today is dead. And my husband – he is still my husband, Mike – has been arrested for killing her. Just how much more detail does it require, Mike, for this to be serious?"

"I'll come with you."

"No."

"You can't be alone, Trove."

"I *have* to be alone. I *want* to be alone."

"I'll come with you to Toulouse. I won't say a word in the train ... plane ... whatever. I should be with you, Trove. If you go back without me, I'll have lost you."

"I am leaving Al for you, Mike."

"Not if you go back alone."

"Excuse me?"

"Look at yourself, Trove. Look at the state you're in."

"He's been arrested, dear one, for murder. He hasn't been given a ticket, Mike, for speeding."

"He needs you. You need to be needed, Trove."

"Don't *you* need me?"

"I didn't commit murder."

"Al didn't commit murder either, Mike. Jeez! You not heard about due process? A man's innocent until blah-di-blah. He's been *arrested*, Mike, for murder. That's different. There's a *world* of difference between those two things."

"I, however, am not in jail."

"I love you. Well, leastwise, I did till you stopped me packing. It's a cute butt, hon, but move it, huh?"

"I love you too, Trove. But I'm not sure that love is the issue here."

"Don't get profound on me, sweetie. Not right now, huh?"

"I'll expect you to keep your options open."

"What the hell does that mean?"

"It means, when you get to Toulouse, things might get clearer. I'm saying, whatever commitment you made to me I'll put on ice. I won't hold you to it, Trove, is what I'm saying. If you get to Toulouse, feel that your rightful place is with Al ..."

"You won't hold me to it?"

"Right."

"The commitment I made?"

"Right."

"You know what a commitment is, right?"

"Yes, Trove, I know what it is."

"Then how can you say that to me? You know how long it took for me to make that commitment? You know how much heart-searching, how much heart-*ache* that involved? You think, all that can just be dismissed with a click of the fingers? Whoops! Situation's changed. I don't any longer want to live with him. Like a train or something. This is Grand Central Station, all change. It's more, Mike, commitment's more like being on board an airplane. You go where the hell *it's* going. You think you're going to Kennedy. But, shit, you develop engine trouble, you get hijacked, you could be diverted to Shannon, end up on the runway at Entebbe. I told you, Mike, I'm leaving Al for you.

"This ... whatever it is ... this incident, this scenario, this is a complication, sure, this is a *gigantic* complication, but it doesn't affect the commitment. It impacts on the realisation, not on its reality."

"Okay."

"That's all you've got to say?"

"What would you like me to say, Trove?"

"That was a pretty long speech, honey. A pretty *pretty* speech too, not without eloquence. Don't you think, I don't know, a standing ovation or something might not be called for?"

"Bravo."

"That, I presume, was British phlegm. Know the best thing to do with phlegm, Mike? I got to go pack. You want to do me a favour, hon? Find the quickest way to get me home?"

+++

... I saw my parents though a child's eyes. My perception of them was one formed in childhood. All I sought in my adult years was confirmation that my childhood perception had been correct. I never really examined that perception or questioned it. I probably ignored the evidence that would otherwise have contradicted it. That confirmation process manifested itself in so many ways. I thought (for instance) I was being so wise, so adult, so charitable when I eventually forgave them. A forgiveness which was incredibly fragile. The most insignificant of slights would witness the return, and with a vengeance, of all the carefully nurtured resentments.

And they were nurtured, those resentments – visited often, watered and fertilized, taken out often for exercise. What it's taken this experience to make me realize is that my forgiveness was misdirected. I didn't need to forgive them. They'd done nothing which warranted forgiveness – no, correction: They'd done very little which warranted forgiveness. The person who did need such forgiveness was the idiot me, Worsdsworth's 'Idiot Child', the infant me who so clearly misread the instruction book, who so lamentably misinterpreted the signals being sent him.

And, of course, I must forgive him – the baby Al, the infant Al. How could I not? He's far too young to be accountable for his actions, nor to understand the consequences of his mistakes. But, Jesus, did he screw up my life, the little bastard. Even that anger has changed direction – no, is changing direction. I'm involved in a process here. One which is a long way from being completed. But I've started, at any rate, being less angry with the baby and being more angry with the adult for having taken so long to realize (a) that it was the baby's mistake; and (b) that it was a baby and therefore almost bound to make a mistake. 'Course the next stop will be to forgive the grown-up me. Because, without that, the baby will start suffering because the grown-up's suffering ... It's – sure, it is – it's a process.

I don't think I'm alone in any of this. Not even exceptional. I suspect that the vast majority of humankind suffers from exactly the same syndrome – a version of the world perceived with the eyes of an infant. It's a huge design fault, when you think about it. (Please tell God!) It might be, when you think about it, the seed that renders humankind's eventual suicide inevitable. Unless, of course, we start to recognize that fault and address it.

And I can't see us doing that. We work hard – most of us ludicrously hard. But we work hard for the wrong reasons and towards the wrong ends. We, most of us, work hard so that a handful of ... well, 'not-us'es ... can get ever richer. But we also work hard so that we lack the time to work on our relationships. Because working at our relationships, that too would require us to look at ourselves. And it seems to be the thing of all the rest which frightens us, which most cows and appals us.

There was, I remember, this documentary on television. One of those intrepid types, you know the ones I mean, all rucksacks and granite chins and worthy eyes. He went to live for six weeks or so with a tribe in some African rain-forest. The rite of passage involved eating some kind of hallucinogenic plant which would return you to the misdemeanours of your past. Well, this guy had been spat at by cobras and growled at by crocodiles, he'd been attacked by killer-bees and ravaged by mosquitoes. All of which he'd taken in his intrepid stride. But the drug 'trip' frightened the crap out of him. Not because it was drugs, I don't think , but because of where that 'trip' was going to take him. Back inside himself to areas he'd wanted to close the door on. It really _really_ frightened him.

The sloth which is a deadly sin is conveniently interpreted to mean sloth at your place of work. That kind of sloth, though, is unlikely to cause fatalities. (Well, except, let's say, if you're a member of the emergency services or an aircraft maintenance engineer.) What is far more deadly, and with far more lethal consequences (directly and indirectly), is the sloth of a lack of self-care. That's not just eating enough roughage or doing enough exercise, that's also about keeping yourself in emotional balance. It is not possible, I don't think, to keep yourself in emotional balance without working on yourself. It would be like a juggler expecting the balls to throw themselves.

Far from being discouraged, such sloth is actively encouraged. Second only to our fear of being forced to confront ourselves, our greatest fear, humankind's, seems to be derision. There is more derision heaped on people working on themselves than, probably, on any other section of society, maybe barring politicians. Of course, the deriders are frightened themselves. It is a derision which wafts the stench of fear wherever it occurs. The last thing those deriders want to do is to visit areas inside themselves where doors are sealed. And derision always presumes of the derider that he has the moral high ground. So the act of derision endows the derider with a sort of narcissistic arrogance. And it is that arrogance which makes it such an effective tool. The derided seem to buy into that arrogance, seem to allow the derider the moral high ground.

But it is also an inhibiting tool. It stops the derider from looking at himself. Worse, it enables him not to. He believes his own arrogance as well. Believes it and believes in it.

I know you know all of this. I know you told me most of it. But knowledge does vary depending on context. I'm just trying to let you know the context in which I'm presently trying to apply and develop such knowledge. And I'm also not casting too many stones. I recognize that my own glasshouse has got far too many panes for me to be able safely to do that.

I wanted comfort, you see. And the result of my wanting comfort – no, coveting it – was that I ended up in one of the world's most uncomfortable places: prison.

If I'd been prepared to work on myself, we would have talked. And if we'd talked you wouldn't have had that thing with Mike – or, if you had, it would have been a fling and not a thing. And if you hadn't have fallen for Mike, you wouldn't have left. Which would have meant that I wouldn't have started drinking. Sober, I may have had sex with Monique, I might even have had a fling of my own, but I'd never have brought her to the house. And if I hadn't have brought her to the house ... well, I would never have killed her.

She wouldn't have been in the house, is what I'm saying, for me to kill.

The verdict was actually the best possible I could have hoped for. I was glad to have been acquitted of murder. I didn't want Monique's parents, her friends, to think that there was ill-will between us, that I concocted some kind of plan to kill her. But I also needed them to know that I knew a crime had been committed. A human being who should be alive isn't. And isn't because of me. If a crime has been committed, its perpetrator has to be punished. Monique's kith and kin, they needed me to be punished. I think if I'd walked out of court today a free man, that would have been a heavy blow indeed. A devastating blow, in fact. Certainly to me. Probably too to them. ...

Chapter 15

"Christ, the flight! You know, I don't even want to talk about the flight. It was quicker, was all, than taking the train. Quicker? It felt like I was flying backwards. And in time. It felt like forever. And it was.

"I started feeling sick – not a bit off-colour, but violently ill – then giddy, almost light-headed. And then soporific, as if I were going to sleep for a week. And then out of my mind with rage. And then out of my mind with worry. And then determined I would never speak to Al for the rest of my life. And then sure I would rush into him and give him a blow-job through the bars. And then I'd feel sick again. And this cycle, sometimes, would be repeated several times per second, and at other times, every three Ice Ages or so.

"It was first thing in the morning when I got to Toulouse. I went straight from the airport to your office. Were you even working here then?

"Away, what? On vacation? Right. So, anyway, then it was just Philippe who was involved. It wasn't till later that all you other guys got on board. Well, why am I telling *you* that? If anyone knew the state of play, I figured it would be his lawyer – *our* lawyer, for Christ's sake. If anyone knew what the deal was, how *big* the deal was, what the next move might be … all that stuff. Most of all, where Al was now.

"Not that I knew whether or not I wanted to see him. But I did want to know where he was.

"I don't know whether Philippe even knew at that stage, tell you the truth. He told me, at that stage, I wasn't allowed to see him. After that, of course, when the authorities said I *could* see him, Al didn't want me to. So much for rushing back!

"Did I tell you he wrote me again before the trial? I told you about the first letter, the angry one. I tried to understand it. I said I under-stood it more than I did. I thought that was what was expected of me. I thought I owed Al at least that: that I would understand why he wrote me such a mean – and I do mean 'mean' – letter. Well, the other day I got this other one, asking whether he might carry on writing me? He said, if not, he'd understand. He said, if not, he sent me his love. I thought it was very sweet. Jesus H! Could anything sound more patronising than that? And that's not what I meant. Absolutely not what I meant.

"It stirred stuff up inside me again. Oh, all the coming-back-from-Paris-on-the-plane stuff, sure, all those whooshing emotions, those whirring emotions, all of them creating other whooshing, whirring physical reactions. But his letter too, that caused ... well, the stuff to gloop around within me which he used to make gloop around with me, but which I'd forgotten he could. Mushy stuff mostly, but ... well, yeah, sexy stuff too. And not just sexy stuff, quite raunchy sexy stuff. Squidgy stuff, know what I mean? I was surprised. No, I wasn't. I wasn't *surprised*, I was frigging *amazed*.

"I was in two minds whether or not to go to the trial. I mean, to see someone you've loved – whom you love, for Christ's sake – so demeaned, that's hard. It wasn't that I didn't sympathise with his plight. Jesus, I did. And that's not to say either that I didn't recognise that a relatively young woman had completely unnecessarily lost her life. And, sure I know, no-one was standing next to him with a pistol to his head threatening to blow it off unless he drank. Still and all ...

"'Course in the midst of all this, Mike took off.

"But that's another story."

+++

"Are you going to let me see the article before you publish it? Before it's published, perhaps I should say.

"Of course not to change anything. Just out of academic interest. Well, probably more out of sexual interest, if I'm scrupulously honest. Maybe we could meet for dinner, discuss the more purple of the prose ⋯

"Promise?

"Great.

"Well, she heard nothing, Petrova. From Mike, that is. Nor did I. She phoned me two, three times a week. Had I heard from him? She didn't need to make contact, she just wanted to be sure he was alright. She'd even tried Drew. But the number he'd given her, strictly 'for emergencies', turned out to be a false one.

"She was in a bit of state, one way and another. Mike had disappeared, Al refused to see her ⋯ Suddenly, the two most important people in her life were confiscated from her.

"What time's your train?

"Don't be ridiculous. I'll drive you."

+++

"Zilch. I heard nothing from Mike literally for weeks. I tried everything, even tried phoning Drew – but Mike'd given me a duff number – even phoned Sheridan. I ever talk to you about Sheridan? He's something of a roué, Sheridan. Likes to think of himself as a rake, but roué is a better word for him. He's giving an interview to one of the French Sundays. Some journalist, she contacted me too. I thought it might compromise Al's trial. I wasn't that interested. The only reason Sheridan was? The reporter was a woman.

"I think he was a good friend to Mike. And he wasn't unfriendly to me. It's just that … well, he didn't know anything. Long story short, no-one knew anything about him. Mike, I mean.

"I was inconsolable. I felt duped. Cheated. I felt like I had offered my soul to Mephistopheles and Mephistopheles had laughed in my face and told me my soul wasn't worth the buying. I felt betrayed and I felt about three inches tall.

"And then I started to think. No, I didn't. I didn't start to think for weeks after that. First of all I had to go on this roller-coaster of a ride for every waking minute, and many sleeping ones. Up and down, side to side, rocking, reeling, whooshing, receding, in … out, round and frigging round, like a pitched ball, spinning wheels within wheels, on and on, a kaleidoscope of time, a vortex of energy and emotions and Christ only knows what else. And only when I had gotten so sick and tired – I mean *so* sick and tired – of being so giddy all the time, so disorientated, so screwed, only then did I start thinking. No, not even that: Only then did I *force* myself to start thinking. To start thinking it through – and 'us' through ... and 'Al and me' through.

"Thank God.

"Because by the time the postcard arrived I was through thinking it through – if you see what I mean. The shock was copable with. If it had gotten there even a week earlier, even a couple of days, who knows? I'm not sure I *could* have coped with it. It was from Bangkok – which was pretty much a shock to begin with. Know what it said? 'Sorry,' it said. That was it. 'Sorry.' He didn't even sign it. He didn't even say what it was he was sorry about. 'Sorry', can you believe that? If I ever see him again, the sorry little asshole, I'd 'sorry' his sorry little ass. I mean to frigging say: 'Sorry'?! I still cannot believe it."

+++

... So, the right verdict.

Sentence? I don't think there could have been a right sentence. I suspect in most cases the most you can hope for in any sentence is a least wrong one. Anyone in jail – anyone at all – is also partially a victim. Oh, I'm not banging my do-gooder tambourine here. Merely stating a fact. And that is a fact. How many of the 'zero tolerance' brigade have driven a car over the alcohol limit? Or over the *speed* limit? How many have been economical with the truth when filing their tax returns or filling up their expense accounts? How many have not resorted to blackmail, if only of the emotional variety, or who have not pushed the grounds of appropriacy in their sexual conduct? There are very few, is all I'm saying, who haven't committed in miniature what those behind bars have committed full-scale. And if (and when) we fail to recognize that, we do a disservice not only to ourselves, not only to penology, but also (because it fails to address something central to the cause of law and order) to society as a whole.

Very few of the real criminals are in prison. For every Jeffrey Archer or John Dean there are a thousand Blairs or Nixons – or Amins!; for every pusher there are scores on the streets (even scores of scores on the streets!), and literally hundreds working in medical practices or pharmaceutical companies – or breweries. You know the litany. The chief cause of incarceration is bad luck. Well, it's probably usually stupidity, actually, mixed with bad luck.

It was in my case.

The stupidity lay in getting stupefied. That was compounded with luck which, yes, was bad. Not as bad as Monique's. Of course not. Not, as you would say, by ten zillion miles. But lying in a hospital bed next to someone with two broken arms and two broken legs does not mean that your broken finger does not hurt. In other words, your recognition that there are those worse off than you should help you to a degree of humility. But it becomes a false humility if it starts to tell you that therefore your problems aren't real ones. The death of a parent is not the devastating blow of that of a child. But it is still a blow. The pain it exacts is real. I know you know that. It wasn't a cheap shot.

How do you quantify pain? Or blame? It's not possible. And therefore there can be no such thing as a right sentence. Or a just one. Only a least wrong, a least unjust one. To think otherwise is again to do a disservice to society as a whole.

Similarly, there is due process but there is no just process. To call themselves the Courts of Justice is already to strive for a remit which is simply not available. They can be Courts of Law ... but of Justice?

People are dissatisfied with the courts for precisely that reason. They believe the name. They therefore expect the courts to do something which the courts simply *cannot* do. Justice is entirely too subjective in its interpretation, in (that is) one's understanding of it – the personal understanding each one of us has of it.

There would have been no punishment meted out to me which Monique's parents would think 'just'. Most of those back home who witness the execution of their loved one's murderer leave the execution chamber still dissatisfied. They could hang, draw and quarter me, castrate me and boil me in oil, Monique's parents would not consider the punishment 'just'. How could they? I have been the cause of so much pain to them. So much unbelievable pain. Pain is so blinding it has become a cliché: We say we are 'blinded by pain'.

Talking of blindness, we blindfold justice. Brilliant!

So even the imagery is confused. And confusing.

For justice to be justice it doesn't need to be blinded, it needs to be Janus – Janus multiplied a hundredfold – with eyes in the back of her head, in her ass, her elbows, ankles. For justice to be justice, justice needs the eyes of God. We blindfold Justice precisely because we cannot endow her with the eyes of God. But as soon as we do blindfold her we actually not only disable her, but we annihilate her. A blindfolded justice is no justice at all. At the moment of blindfolding her, justice becomes only the law. And the law, ironically, has no need to be blindfolded. The law is born blind. The law has only one interest, finally, and that is to protect itself. Any entity with only one interest is blind.

It could only be something self-obsessed and blind that would bestow on a blind-folded figure a lethal weapon. The concept is mind-blowing. I mean, who better to give a tool of destruction to than someone who cannot see whom she is slashing with it?! Even slaying with it?! But it is, again ironically, entirely appropriate – maybe not 'le mot juste', but sure as hell the image 'juste'. Because it's not that there are miscar-riages of justice, it is that justice, as practised by the law, can do nothing but miscarry.

By calling the law 'justice' we hype it. And, like a book that a friend has overly raved about, hype inevitably leads to disappointment. Once we start to realize that not only vengeance but justice too is not within the purview of us humans, then we can start dealing in different ways with our pain. It is only in that way that we can stop the tragedy propagating itself, continuing into some disgruntled eternity.

When I found out I'd killed Monique I wanted to kill myself. Desperately I wanted to. But it would have been too easy. I couldn't let myself off the hook that easily.

It doesn't matter that I was drunk. Nor that she was. It doesn't matter a damn. It doesn't matter that the row was about nothing, that I didn't mean to push her that hard, nor that she tripped over the cat. None of that matters. It doesn't matter that I tried to revive her. God, how I tried to revive her! It matters only that, way before her appointed hour, she was robbed of life. That I got nothing from the robbery – nothing, at least, positive – does not stop me from having been the robber. ...

+++

"Another week went by. And I got this from Drew, that's Mike's son. Listen to this: *'Dear Petrova Tregunter, I received this missive from my father. For reasons which are probably obvious I chose not to read it. However, from a quick skim of some of its pages, it would seem that this is much more your business than mine. If you are/ were able to have a relationship with my father, well done. You would, I suspect, have been unique in that regard. Yours sincerely ...'* et cetera'.

"And I realized, then – Jesus, I am so frigging stupid – I realised, when I'd finished reading the letter, that the whole thing with Mike ... no, Mike's whole thing, this had nothing to do with me, Mike's whole I'm-going-to-let-you-know-who-I-am thing, that wasn't a portrait but a trompe-l'oeil, you know one of those pictures which make you believe it's a door, say, and it's just a painting. Mike never truly revealed *anything* to me. That whole big deal about God, for instance. It meant nothing. Not a frigging thing. His life wasn't dictated to by his belief in God. It wasn't, as far as I could see, even *affected* by it. It was just emotional sleight-of-hand, as so much of his so-called striptease was sleight-of-hand, pulling the attention away from where it needs to be to where it needs not to be. And that makes it actually more crushing than simply not revealing anything.

+++

... Just after 'lights out' here, that's my nightmare time of day. That's the time, block it though I try to, I'm back looking down the stairs, back – that inert figure catapulting towards me –, back in that moment of realization that Monique was no more. Back – and I say this to my eternal shame – in that moment of panic when I started wondering how best I could conceal my crime. God, the things that I thought of! I was sober in that moment. In under that moment. In a stretch of time which would make a nanosecond seem like an eternity. So sober, so scared.

I did try to revive her. God, did I try! I thought she stirred, you see. That's when I called the ambulance. May God forgive me. Oh, it was delusion. She was dead before she'd gotten to the bottom of the stairs – well, you heard the medical evidence. Broken neck. Whatever she did, she didn't stir. But, such as I am, it saved me. Because, God help me, had she not 'stirred', I have no idea what I might have done. I had visions of going to the forest round Clairac, burying the body somewhere there, pretending she'd walked out on me. God help me. I had all sorts of crazy, desperate visions. They don't punish you, though, for visions. And yet still we allow them their talk of justice?

It is a Buddhist prayer, you know, to seek forgiveness for any evil you may have done – or *thought*. I'm not even sure that in the Catholic Church too, sinful *thoughts* are not quite as blame-worthy as sinful actions. I don't think you have to believe in a standard god to acknowledge that justice does not belong amongst mortal concerns.

Poor Monique. Poor, poor Monique. I never loved her. I could never love her. Oh, I tried. But the love I felt for her, I realized, was the inversion, the flipside, of what I thought then was my hatred for you. She was fair and fairly tall and pretty quiet. She liked watching television and listening to Country and Western. And if she *had* been the flip side of my hatred for you I *might* have been able to love her.

But she wasn't.

Of course she wasn't.

She was the flip side of the love I continued to feel for you. A love whose passion was burning through the crust of comfort I realized I'd created for myself. Not because I wanted the comfort but because I was appallingly afraid of what I knew was indeed passion bubbling away God knows where within me.

"L'état c'est moi." Who was it said that? Louis XIV, was it? Yes, Louis XIV, I'm pretty sure. Know what Al says? Al the First-as-far-as-I-know? Al, he say, "La normalité, c'est nous."

Yeah, I know I said that before. Well, not that exactly, but something pretty like it. And I also know it's not exactly an original thought. But it is, in my book, so important, so central, that it can stand repetition. No, it cries out to be repeated. 'La normalité, c'est nous.' We believe that what makes us tick makes everyone else tick. As (now I think about it) embodied by that very sentence. What makes me think that 'we believe what makes us tick is...'? Because, fundamentally, *I* believe that, of course. I assume because *I* do, so does everyone else.

We are the theme and those around us are the variations. Always.

How much misery has been caused by that assumption? Untold wars, of course.

I mean, untold wars. All the misery attached to that. All the Bush's of history, and all the Kaisers, all the Genghis Khans and Julius Caesars. But that's only a part of it. How much strife in relationships, in marriages, has that as its root cause? How many times do we stand totally bemused by our partner's stance? Astounded by it? A bemusement which, of course, turns to anger. Because the feeling of being bemused is one which is very painful. And pain almost inevitably leads to anger. And anger (particularly unacknowledged or misdiagnosed anger) leads to misery. Always.

Always. ...

+++

"He emailed me from Bangkok. Petrova – well, he said 'Trove', of course – Petrova had broken his heart, he said. Henceforward, he said, he'd fall in love strictly on a cash-only basis. That was the last time I heard from him.

"Will you break *my* heart, my dear?"

+++

... There was an episode – remember? – of 'West Wing', the tv show, in which President Bartlett was handed a note by his Chief of Staff outlining the proposed policy stance of the Executive's future. All that was written on the note was 'Let Bartlett be Bartlett'.

How much misery would we save the world if we extended that policy commitment to one which said 'let everyone be themselves'? If we gloried in our differences, therefore. If we stopped judging books by their covers, and people's insides by their shells. And if we started to recognize that each reader handed an identical text will still be reading an entirely different book. The 'Mona Lisa' that I see, the 'Ave Maria' that I hear, the crispy duck I taste, the lavender I smell, the leather that I touch – these are all different to those that anyone else sees, hears, tastes. Those sensations are as unique to us as our DNA. How much more individually, then, do we read!

'Othello', for instance, will be read vastly differently by a man possessed of jealousy than by a woman who is a victim of it. It'll be read differently by someone who has been the victim of racial abuse than by one who has meted out such abuse. It'll be read differently by a man and by a woman, for God's sake. By someone with a drink problem, and by one with none. By connivers and by those connived against. By those who like Shakespeare and by those that loathe him. By actors and by directors. By musicians and by painters. Oh, some readings will be so similar as to be nigh-on identical. And others will be so different you could wonder whether the reader had been presented with the same play.

We all like to think, though, that our individual interpretation is the interpretation — which, of course, it is. Provided that we restrict its interpretation to ourselves. The problem begins when we try to convince others to our side. How many hundreds of books have been written about 'Hamlet', say? Or 'Tartuffe'? All of them defining the work for us.

And this is an *uncontroversial* book! Beautiful, yes. Important, certainly. But not planet-shaking or -shaping. Will we ever be able to quantify the misery which has been inflicted on the world because the same principles are applied to reading, let's say, 'The Qur'an'? Or 'Das Kapital'? Or our Constitution?

The world has simply become a macrocosm of the conflicts that exist domestically. And those, probably, are only a macrocosm of the conflicts that exist internally within each of us. And those conflicts arise almost exclusively because we won't let 'Bartlett be Bartlett'. Or our partner be him-/herself. Or our neighbour. We most certainly don't let our parents be themselves. But, then — such is our inherent insanity — neither do we allow our children to be *them*selves.

Even our own children we judge through our own eyes. I know of no-one who tries to see themselves — to judge themselves — through the eyes of their children. And, thinking about it, that too would be a forlorn attempt. Because those eyes would *not* be the children's eyes, they would be eyes imposed on a child by a parent. However altruistically and apparently objectively. ...

Chapter 16

The look, Drew, in her eyes when she was packing … Well, it said it all. Said it more than all. It wasn't that she loved Al: I'd always known she still loved him. I'd always known she'd never leave him for me. The only time in our entire time together that I doubted something Trove said to me was when she told me she was leaving him for me.

And she'd no sooner said it, before even I'd had time register my disbelief in what she'd said, than the telephone rang. And there was that look in her eyes. That look which told me – and so eloquently – that not only had I lost her, but that I had never won her. Not in any complete sense.

And that was alright. That was painful, but acceptable. *Less* acceptable, though, was what it trawled.

It was a realisation that not only had I never had a relationship – probably not even with myself – but that I never deserved to. And that was excruciating. And still is.

I really hope you never have to know what that pain is. It is one which consumes all of you. If I am not able to have a relationship, I think it behoves me to remove myself, so that the sham need no longer be perpetrated.

You won't be able to forgive me, so I don't even ask you to. As much as I have loved anyone, I have loved you. I know that's not enough.

Franklyn is lucky to have had such a special man as a father. He pulled the long straw quite as much as, I'm afraid, you pulled the short one.

"He signed it 'Dad'. When I read it I didn't know whether to laugh or cry. At it, at him … at me. It did so completely vindicate my impression of him: the trompe-l'oeil-thing, I mean. How *could* I have been so stupid? So *unbelievably* stupid?

+++

... For all the wickedness that is latent within us, what surfaces far more often is Man's good. It is incredible, the amount of good in mankind. Simply incredible. After the Boxing Day tsunami the British public raised over a million pounds sterling per hour – considerably more than came from the coffers of the world's richest country, or from the coffers (that we know) of any of the world's richest people. This fact prompted Mr Blair (how could anyone ever forget it?) to declare – his body shaking with the emotion of his magnanimity – that the British government would at least match the generosity of the British public. As if, for God's sake, the money was coming from his own bank account. It could only be a politician of Blair's arrogance who would not recognize that the government's money was *already* that of the "generous" British public. No wonder he's such great chums with George W.

For every such cynical act by government, though, for every one act committed by the wicked of unkindness or even cruelty, I see ten – maybe a hundred – acts of kindness and generosity. Enormous kindness, I'm talking about, and generosity that brings tears to my eyes: those who volunteer for 'front-line' charities like Save The Children; the Erin Brokovich's of this world: moral Davids taking on venal Goliaths; firefighters rushing not only into the Two Towers, but onto airplanes to tender their services in earthquakes abroad. Simpler acts of kindness. Of great kindness. Even in prison you see acts of kindness. Daily. It's often covert. Prison exacts a penalty for kindness. But, despite that penalty, it's there. Even in abundance.

And it exacts a penalty too in the non-prison world. Even if that penalty is only derision. No, I'm not going down that path again.

+++

"I was right, you know. Sheridan *is* knocking her up. The journalist. She going to write about herself, do you think? 'Tabloid reporter involved with murderer's wife's lover's best friend shock, horror'!? I'm not often vindictive but, you know, I really hope she gets hurt by him. The amount of hurt *they* cause, tabloids, that whole cesspit of journalism.

"You okay for time? You don't have to get back to the office or anything, prepare stuff for tomorrow? I've been watching too many movies, I guess. Well, it's good of you to see me. I wanted to see you. I really don't now have anyone left I can talk to.

"It was so strange, the whole thing: the atmosphere in the Court room, all that pomp and mundanity at one at the same time, the smell of paper and (it seemed to me) stale cooking fat, the starch of officialdom, the smell of floor polish, the silent screams all around you – *all* around you. Al as I've never seen Al before. Wan, contrite … a felon. With that prison paleness – that famous prison paleness. Not in ten zillion years would I ever have imagined Al a felon.

"Not paleness, pallor. That's the phrase, isn't it?: 'prison pallor'.

"If he hadn't have noticed me, you know (and if I hadn't noticed him noticing me), I would've gone. Sidled out the back. Disappeared from the court. I found it so difficult to see him like that. In the dock like that. I mean, so fucking difficult.

"*And* to see his folks like that. That too was hard. Harder than I'd imagined it would be. Them not knowing whether to acknowledge me. And if so, how. What to say to one another? Do we kiss? Do we smile? If we did smile at one another, would that somehow impact on Al?

"His folks don't matter. Well, they do – of course they do – but they're not going to influence anything, is what I'm saying. Most times I like them a lot, sometimes they drive me crazy, but they're not going to feature, is what I'm saying, in my thoughts, in my considerations and deliberations – neither mine nor the Court's.

"I couldn't keep my eyes off of Al, is the thing. He knows he's going to be found guilty, he knows he's going to jail – and he's okay with both of those things. Know what? Because he is, so am I.

"What I'm not okay with is how I was able to know that just by the looking at him. I'm not okay with not knowing how fantastically expressive his face is. I had no idea. I mean, no frigging idea. And it suddenly clicked: It wasn't that Al didn't express himself. That wasn't it at all. It was a moment, that, almost of epiphany. It isn't that he doesn't express himself, it's that he doesn't use words to do so. He doesn't, as the phrase is, 'do' words, Al. Watch him, though, look at him and his whole face is a neon sign of what he's feeling.

"I felt two inches goddamm tall. I mean, that was my entire bitch with the marriage, this whole Al-not-talking number, his entire lack of communication. I mean, shit, that's what the thing with Mike had been all about: Al's not talking, and my *knowing* he wasn't talking. And God knows how many years before that, I'd *felt* there was something wrong, without being able, you know, to give it a name. I knew then, in that moment of epiphany, it *wasn't* that he wasn't speaking, Al. It was just that I wasn't listening.

"Watching him today in Court I realised that.

"I also realised it was me who had betrayed him. Oh, not by screwing Mike, not even by leaving him for Mike (as I had every intention of doing), but by not taking the trouble to know him better. To know him at all, in fact. To know, for instance, that Al communicated through his face and not through his words.

"I guess the whole fun of the future is that we don't know what it holds. That is both its hope and its menace. And both together kind of deal. I know only this about my future. I owe it to Al to get to know him better.

"Someone said, I can't remember who, that adversity introduces a man to himself. Well, maybe it also introduces man to those who love him.

"Know what? I think it'll be good to find out."

+++

... Growing old, Trove – it's shameful to admit this, but I don't really understand why – is to me a frightening experience.

Even more frightening is that morning when you wake up and realize you have grown old. That life has passed you by. That, in the world of wannabe, you're in that of wanted-to-have-been. In my case, that was the realization of a moment. And (again talking only for myself) from that moment, the experience of further aging became frightening.

Firstly, I suppose, because it suddenly was only a matter of moments for the future to become the past. Secondly, because the slow physical erosion is uncomfortable and worrying – it begs questions about how much pain you will die in, about how decrepit you're going to be at the end of your life.

And, thirdly (and for me most importantly), because the world around you is at that very second bequeathed to the next generation. And it is a world which makes increasingly less sense to you, and that becomes, both consequently and not, increasingly more confusing to you. 'Come mothers and fathers throughout the land/ And don't criticize what you can't understand ...' – Dylan, in case you'd forgotten! Well, those lines, shit, they take on an entirely different meaning when it is you the 'mothers and fathers'. Even if, like us, Trove, you're only 'mothers and fathers' by proxy. Or by dint of being fifty.

What I've been wondering, though, the fear that I'm talking about? Is that fear for what the young might do? Or fear of the consequence of what you have done? Is it fear of the future, in other words? Or fear that you may have to regret the past?

I guess in my case it's both. The regret (and regrets) I have is/ are enormous. Just enormous. But I also loathe the ethos of the generation which has now taken over control.

More than it, though, I loathe myself. And I loathe those of my generation who, with me, left this ethos as our bequest. Which is why I simply cannot watch the news. I have to get back to my own eyes and to my own experience. See with my own eyes, hear with my own ears, experience for myself the reality of the world – and the reality is that daily across my path come a hundred acts of kindness. Even in here. That mankind still is – despite what you hear on the news –, by and large, as humane as it is human, and by and large is kind as well as it is human.

It's amazing: Stripped of all dignity, it's amazing just how much dignity those stripped can muster. Just how much dignity is innate, not just to humankind, but to life. Even skunks have the most enormous dignity. Even mosquitoes and poison ivy.

God's indulgence to Himself, of course, is the enjoyment He takes in irony. He must have His irony. God is probably an irony-junkie. And there is, of course, an enormous irony involved in the fact that the time I have best been able to talk to you is that time when I have been wrenched from you. Not, I hasten to add, by anyone but me. I do understand that. If I am complaining (which I am not) it is only against myself.

I'll be a jail-bird when I get out. A murderer. (I doubt too many will bother with the distinction between that and man-slaughterer – if the word even exists!) For all the increase in value of my work which my infamy has trawled, not exactly the catch of the century. But what I need you to know ...

I know you won't come back to me. For a host of reasons. I know you *can't*. For an even *bigger* host of different reasons. But I also need to tell you that, if the Red Sea suddenly divided or a camel was drawn through the eye of a needle or George W. told the truth, I would welcome your return not just with a fatted calf but with an entire herd, an entire *breed* of them.

Not for a nanosecond do I pretend that I have, overnight (as it were), become a stripey leopard. Not a bit of it. But I am working on it. And I do think, finally, it will happen.

No.

No, no, no.

What am I talking about? It's that I've *been* a stripey leopard. All through my life. I think that's a trait I share with most of my fellow human-leopards. And it's not that I/we/they cannot change our spots or their spots. It's more that I/we/they are discouraged – severely discouraged – from seeing them, our natural spots. It's like we've all been told, you leopards should all be stripey. And we – poor leopards that we are – believe them!

So, what I'm talking about, Trove, is about finding my spots, and scraping away at the stripes to reveal them. I know I could do that so much better with you at my side. But, of course, I also know that can never be. As I know as well that your absence does not free me from having to do the job alone.

To have met you already marks me as a lucky man. To have shared a life with you indicates my luck must be enormous. That I squandered such fortune only goes to prove how very stupid and ungrateful I was. Not any more.

I don't think any longer I'm stupid. Certainly I'm considerably less befuddled. And I am grateful. Hugely, colossally grateful. Not *only* to you – but, yes, *especially* to you.

I have no right to ask this, but ... Is there a future for us?

It is not idly that I sign this – 'Love' – Al xxx

+++

Dear Al,
Can you woo me from jail? Can you from your cell take me to the places I need to go? Can *I* take *you* where *you* need to go?

I think we could try. Shit, I think, Al, we *should* try.

What I'm saying, I'm saying, if – naked and with a broken ankle – you're prepared to piggy-back me to the top of Mount Everest, I'm prepared to sit on your shoulders.

Which is kind of a neat trick as, me, I'll also be piggy-backing you.

Deal?

Yeah, we could maybe love again – Trove xx

+++

Maison d'arrêt de Toulouse-Seysses, 1st August 06
My darling Trove,
Al's Well! – xxx

OTHER BOOKS BY GREGORY DARK

The Millennium Trilogy:

The Prophet of the New Millennium

A search for principles in an unprincipled age

Kahil Gibran's *The Prophet* is an acknowledged classic. *Millions* have read it. But it is now of a different age. *The Prophet of the New Millennium* is offered as a complement to the original – a complement not a sequel. The style is redolent, but it is a book which stands by itself as:

A political and moral atlas of, and for, today.

That "today" is one where the line becomes ever hazier between ethics and expedience.
The Prophet of the New Millennium seeks to bring principles into the 21st century. Not by defining them. But by helping us frame our questions. It aims to help us separate for ourselves truth from fantasy, and sanity from delusion – to find our own sense in a world of ever more dangerous nonsense.

The God of the New Millennium

A search for balance in an age of spin

Only the mad or bad – or politicians! – would seek to deny that mankind is currently facing the greatest crisis (and crises) in its history.

Philosophy's first adage was that you cannot plan for a future without understanding the past.

In this, his new book, Gregory Dark takes a new look at our yesterday ... in the hope that such will lead to a less cataclysmic tomorrow.

For too long man has ceded spiritual power to priests and temporal power to politicians and generals. It's one of the principle reasons why we're in the parlous and perilous position today. If our tomorrow is going to be any better, it is not our right but our duty to reclaim that power – each and every one of us.

The God of the New Millennium, though, is no dreary dialectic. The discussion evolves within a narrative of tenderness and poetry, of sacrifice and death – most of all of life.

The God of the New Millennium leaves us asking of ourselves the biggest, and most vital, question of today – one that decides whether or not there is even a tomorrow:

Do we have what it takes to do what it takes?

Man of the New Millennium

A search for us in an age of me

Man of the New Millennium is a book for us: the millions and millions of people who want to see the end of mancruel and the start of mankind. The probably billion or so of us in this world, exasperated and disenchanted by worn-out templates, trying to find new ones.

Wrapped in the most gentle of narratives, *Man of the New Millennium* leads us through the maze of history's travesties and today's duplicities to a future with a future, to a future whose potential is our potential, our potential as a species, and that potential special to all of us individually.

Man of the New Millennium is a search for us in an age of me; it is a text for humanity in fictional dress; it is a book which changes hope from an ill-defined aspiration to a realisable ambition. It is a book of today which guarantees a quality tomorrow.

Titus and Roni

Two parents who, in facing death, face life. Perhaps for the first time.

As well as being a parent Titus is a grandparent: He is kidnapped with his grandson by guerillas in Colombia. Roni is a Scots woman whose son, in 24 hours, will be executed in the United States by lethal injection.

Written with Dark's customary polish, *Titus and Roni* is as elegant in its telling as it is electric in its tale.

For younger readers:

Charming!

Or

If the glass slipper fits

It's the story they didn't want you to hear!
Finally Prince Charming talks!
The man was a cross between James Bond and Martin Luther King. Yet what is it we know about him? That he fits a mean glass slipper! And that's it.

For generations, Prince Charming has been the Watson to the Holmes of Cinderella – maybe even Charles to Diana. Far from being the nothing character of legend, however, the prince had the spirit of an unbroken horse. He was a loose cannon, one whose every move seemed dogged with intrigue and adventure.

And love? Yes, there were (shock, horror!) other girlfriends before Cinderella. But his romantic adventures are only part of his story. It's not for nothing his story's never been told.

Until now, that is.

Charming's times were a lot less fairy-taley than fairy-tales would have us believe. Is there something familiar about those times? Something even contemporary?

Well, if the glass slipper fits …

Susie and the Snow-it-alls

Who is your friend? The person who
Helps you to be your youest you.

Susie is facing expulsion from her new school. For a theft she didn't commit. Why, she despairs, is life so unfair?

To clear her name she resolves to find the real thief. She sneaks out of the house. For which offence she faces further severe punishment, this time at the hands of her parents. Why, she despairs to Mr E, is life so unfair?

If Susie really wants to know, he suggests, maybe she should get a bit of distance between herself and the question. The Sufrogs have magi powers – not magic, the 'magi' inside i-magi-nation. Using which they can whoosh Susie anywhere. The clouds are some way away. Maybe far enough to give Susie the perspective she needs.

Accompanied by six of her Sufrogs – and a large dollop of

scepticism – Susie incants the magi words. ... And whooshes
through her window.

The journey this starts is one which introduces her to a wealth
of eccentric characters – and to the wealth and eccentricity of
her own; one on which she confronts injustice on a grand scale:
death and desolation, loneliness and persecution, betrayal ...
and rescue.

It is a voyage, an odyssey, where she faces such awesome
challenges that her problems on Earth seem pedestrian and safe.
Or do they?

www.gregorydark.net

BOOKS

O is a symbol of the world, of oneness and unity. In different cultures it also means the "eye," symbolizing knowledge and insight. We aim to publish books that are accessible, constructive and that challenge accepted opinion, both that of academia and the "moral majority."

Our books are available in all good English language bookstores worldwide. If you don't see the book on the shelves ask the bookstore to order it for you, quoting the ISBN number and title. Alternatively you can order online (all major online retail sites carry our titles) or contact the distributor in the relevant country, listed on the copyright page.

See our website www.o-books.net for a full list of over 500 titles, growing by 100 a year.

And tune in to myspiritradio.com for our book review radio show, hosted by June-Elleni Laine, where you can listen to the authors discussing their books.

mySpiritRadio